# THE SIM RU PROPHECY

## BOOK TWO OF THE JAGUAR OF THE BACKWARD GLANCE SERIES

ANDREW J. PETERS

# THE JAGUAR OF THE BACKWARD GLANCE
## SERIES

*The Awakening*

*The Sim Ru Prophecy*

This second edition is a reworked and reformatted version of the acclaimed *Werecat* saga.

# ONE

JACKS SLID OPEN the glass door, stepped out to the balcony of his twelfth-floor hotel room, and carefully closed the door behind him. Caracas yawned far and wide in his vision like a constellation of stars. It was bordered by the darkened palisade of Ávila National Park, and to the north, the vast Caribbean Sea. The city's tropical swelter felt like it was drenching him, though he had come out of his air-conditioned room in just a pair of white briefs from an economy pack he had purchased at a street market.

He sat down on one of the balcony's twin plastic chairs and unfolded the weathered codex. The ancient book needed to be handled delicately. It was a miracle it had held up so well. Its creator had crafted its sheepskin pages and stitched them together possibly two millennia ago. The book's wood covers were upholstered in animal intestine that had petrified with age. They were barely secured to its frayed binding.

The room behind Jacks was dark, but he could read by a trace of light from the LED circuit that ran up the side of the hotel. His feline vision could penetrate the night. The book's arcane glyphs and bar-and-dot characters had been a hopeless mystery so far. He had studied the first page many times and scanned through the entire twenty-five pages during his sea voyage from Barbados. He thought the bar-and-dot characters represented numbers, and he had distinguished a dozen glyphs which looked like faces and animals. But he couldn't see a message or pattern. Decoding the ancient relic he had recovered from Benoit's safety deposit box was going to take an expert in archeology or ancient world linguistics.

As far as he knew, he was one of a tiny handful of people who had seen the book. It was called the Báalam-Tet, and it was a grimoire of sorts for werecat magic. Jacks felt he should be able to make sense of it. When Benoit had reared his feline soul, he awoke with a knowledge of transformation that felt as innate as any capacity of his body, so he ought to understand the language of his kind. The barbaric glyphs held his fascination with an uncanny familiarity. But they were like memories from a dream just out of grasp.

He looked over the first line of glyphs and numbers again. He had to decipher something from it, whether the combination of images formed a greater picture or they merely called up an instinct or a mood from his gut. So much depended on unriddling the codex. As Annika told him before she was killed trying to protect it, the Báalam-Tet held the secrets of the rearing ritual. If those secrets were lost, Jacks's generation of werecats would be the last of their kind. If those secrets were discovered by the Glaring, a radical werecat faction, they would use them to wipe out humankind.

His boyfriend, Farzan, opened the balcony door, and Jacks could hear snoring from Kwame, a six-foot-five, 230 pound West African. He smelled Farzan's shower-fresh scent and then the dander of his tiger-striped tabby, Bella. He grinned as he heard her scamper out the door before Farzan shut it behind him.

Bella jumped up on the ledge to look out at the city. Farzan drew up beside Jacks. His thin frame swam in an oversized T-shirt and boxer shorts, and his thick, black mop of hair was bed-tossed, putting an exclamation mark on his indignation.

"Don't you think you could give that a rest for the night?"

He laid the codex on his lap. "I couldn't sleep."

"It's three o'clock in the morning."

Jacks licked his lips. He would have gladly stayed in bed with Farzan and slept through the night. But his mind couldn't rest. "I have to make something out of this thing."

"What are you going to do? Stay up night and day looking at it? We just got into town this morning."

He knew it had been a horrible journey for Farzan. Jacks had made an enemy of the yacht's owner, Maarten, after leading him and his friends into an ambush by the Glaring when they went to retrieve the codex from Benoit's safety deposit box in Bridgetown. Two of Maarten's friends had died in the fight along with Maarten's sister, Annika. Maarten hadn't wanted to get involved with the Báalam-Tet in the first place. Annika pushed Jacks to get it, and now Jacks felt responsible for her death. Maarten had treated Jacks, Farzan, and Bella like stowaways to dispense of at the nearest port, and his arrogant attitude toward humans had pounded on Farzan's buttons.

That made for plenty of tension while they were confined on the boat, and there had also been the awkward matter of Jacks having disappeared on Farzan for weeks before Farzan came down to Barbados, fearing Jacks was dead. He had been living a carefree life with Maarten and his pride of friends. He had even joined them one night in a cuddle pile that turned into a group sex kind of thing.

He had admitted everything to Farzan, and they had reconciled since then, though it had been hard to feel good about it while stuck on Maarten's party boat—the scene of his disloyalty. They had both been relieved by the sight of the harbor of Caracas after the two and a half day sail.

Jacks tried out a wry grin. "You think we should be checking out the nightlife?"

Farzan dragged over the other chair and flopped down on it. "We'd be safer hitchhiking through Somalia. Have you seen the U.S. Department of State's travel warning for Venezuela?"

"There's supposed to be some great clubs in the Sabana Grande. That's like four or five blocks from here."

Farzan glanced from the book to Jacks. "When did you have time to work out a gay itinerary? I thought you were trying to decode that thing."

"Kwame told me about it. He's been here before."

"He could have suggested a better hotel. There's cockroaches in the bathroom."

The Continental Towers was a dingy place, well past its heyday by two or three decades. For the first time in his twenty-three-year-old life, Jacks could say the room was under budget. He had fifteen thousand U.S. dollars in cash from a withdrawal of Benoit's unclaimed assets at the bank in Barbados, and there was over fifteen million in Benoit's account, which he had access to with a debit card. The Báalam-Tet was what he had really been after. Benoit's fortune was an unexpected boon.

But Jacks was wary of drawing attention to their arrival in Caracas. They certainly didn't look like billionaires who stayed at luxury hotels. He knew Farzan understood, even if he reserved the right to gripe. They were on the run from the Glaring, and he was a fugitive from the New York City police department and the F.B.I. He had left the country in the midst of two murder investigations: Benoit's and the thief Bernard's.

Jacks had killed both shifters in self-defense, but he couldn't risk giving himself up to the authorities. They would lock him up as a freak of nature.

Kwame's snoring racket cut through the noisy air conditioner. Jacks reached over and squeezed Farzan's hand. "Maybe I should have booked two rooms."

"It's all right. I suppose it's safer this way."

Jacks studied him curiously. "You don't mind sharing the room with Kwame?" Besides his snoring, the big guy had no qualms about strutting around in the buff in the boxy room.

Farzan's expressive face darkened. "He adds to the scenery."

Jacks looked away and smirked. He supposed Farzan had a right to a wandering eye, though a touch of jealousy bit at him. Kwame was built like an Olympic water polo player. He hadn't considered what effect that would have on Farzan. Kwame had been the only one of Maarten's friends to offer to accompany them on their mission, and he was a huge asset. Besides being able to take on any werejaguars that came after them, Kwame had traveled through South America. He also knew French and could translate Benoit's notes about the codex.

Jacks clasped Farzan's slim hand and kneaded it in his. "I wish we had time to enjoy this. Like a real vacation."

"I would've preferred Aruba."

He ran his hand farther up Farzan's arm, feeling the soft hairs of his forearm, gliding up to the smooth skin of his triceps, and slipping beneath the sleeve of his T-shirt to grasp the dome of his shoulder. "When it's all over, we'll take a really good trip. Just the two of us, okay?"

"When will it be over?"

"When I figure out what's in this book. And we find Tepe."

Tepe was the Glaring's capitán. He had a secret compound

in the Amazon. He had to locate Tepe and negotiate with him. Maybe offer him Benoit's money.

Goose pimples bumped up from the skin of Farzan's arm. "You still think it's a good idea to find Tepe? What could you possibly say to a fanatic whose sole ambition is to exterminate humankind? It's like trying to negotiate with I.S.I.L."

Tepe had orchestrated a night of terror across the East Coast of the U.S., just one month ago. Three hundred people were killed, and many more were mauled by werecats. At the bank in Barbados, the Glaring must have killed a dozen bank employees and policemen.

Jacks used his free hand to push back his dirty blond hair. "What else can I do? They won't stop until they find me." He looked back to the room. "You ought to bring your phone out here in case Sammy calls." Sammy was Farzan's older brother. It was risky for them to contact anyone back in New York, but they had purchased a burner phone when they arrived in Caracas. In order to not alarm his parents, Farzan told them he was doing a three-month internship at a hospital in Puerto Rico for medical school, but he had entrusted Sammy with the truth.

"The phone needs to charge." Farzan rustled up from his chair. "We should both go back in. We can salvage a few hours of sleep before the morning."

Jacks didn't move. Farzan stared at him in exasperation.

"Just give me a little more time with the book."

"I don't understand you. It's ancient hieroglyphs, Jacks."

"I feel like I can get somewhere with it."

"Kwame has Benoit's journal with all of his notes. He'll translate them for us in the morning."

Jacks didn't know what to say. He just needed to try with the book. Otherwise, he would be staring at the ceiling all night thinking about it. Farzan turned his back to him and went back into the room without another word.

Alone on the balcony, Jacks stared unfocused into the night. He felt like such a shit. Why couldn't he be a good boyfriend and lay down with Farzan for that one night? Farzan put on a tough front, and he truly was tough when he needed to be, but he had to be going out of his mind with worries about his family. He had dropped out of medical school and left his family's home for the first time in his life to be on the run with Jacks, in constant danger.

Farzan had given up so much, and if Jacks couldn't glean some information from the codes, some way to protect Farzan's family, his sacrifices would be for nothing.

The night air was suddenly cold against his skin. Both Maarten and now Farzan said it was futile to negotiate with Tepe. Jacks couldn't let his doubts show in front of Farzan or Kwame, but he had big ones. Tepe had amassed an army of werejaguars and allied wereleopards and wereocelots from all over the world.

Bella wove around his legs, and then jumped up on his lap. He absent-mindedly raked his hand down the cat's back. She sniffed the codex, and he caught her firmly by the scruff of her neck. The book was fragile, and she could damage it, however innocently.

Bella looked up at him. Something was stirring in her head. A bizarre thought occurred to him, and what did he have to lose? He opened up the codex and laid it flat on his lap so the tabby could see the first page.

A burst of light ate up his vision, and then it was like he was peering through binoculars with fisheye lenses. The first page of the codex appeared as two planes sliding over each other, like a double-exposed photo, only fluid. He waited out the unpleasant sensation of adjusting to his vision melding with Bella's. He had always done it with his eyes shut. Otherwise, it felt like someone had hooked his eyeballs on a fishing line. But to test out his instinct, his vision had to be focused on the same thing Bella was looking at.

He strained to fix their two planes of vision on top of each other. They slid back and forth, and then they locked into position. The codex was sharp. Every detail and imperfection of the abstract symbols stood out crisply. He could even make out the minute brush strokes of the ancient stylus that had drawn them.

He looked to the first line of glyphs, and nudging Bella mentally, he brought her plane of vision squarely on top of his. The first character was a bearded man with a tall, elaborate headdress, and the ones below it were a series of dot-and-line characters interspersed with glyphs. As he looked down the column, like reading a totem, the words of a story formed inside his head.

In the year 166, the month of our lord Cit Chac, the jaguar god, the day of Ki, was born Po Nge Be, son of U Kix Chan, king of kings, ruler of the seven tribes. The boy was blessed with health and strength and beauty above all others, and the people loved him. For the prince's name day when he was to wear the sacred pagne of manhood, his subjects brought tribute to please the gods: twenty and three bushels of maize for the corn goddess, three-twenty urns of water for the god of rain, three herds of sheep for the god of gods Hunab, and a weaned jaguar cub for Cit Chac. Of these, Po Nge Be proclaimed the cat shall not be sacrificed for he was to take him as his companion, and he named him Pu Neb.

The people were afraid. As Cit Chac had blessed their warriors with fearlessness and might to overpower their enemies, so would He take vengeance on the kingdom and bring upon it bloody war.

But Po Nge Be was wise. He understood that Cit Chac plays tricks on men and that the cub Pu Neb was sent to him to test his loyalty. So did Po Nge Be take Pu Neb to our lord's temple where on the night of the jaguar's tail, when the eye of the god of death looks down upon the world beseeching those who desire to travel between the worlds, Po Nge Be stood before Cit Chac's totem and took the knife to the jaguar's throat then took it to his own.

This pleased Cit Chac, and he permitted Po Nge Be to visit his throne. When our lord returned him to our earthly realm, he was no longer Po Nge Be, and Pu Neb was no longer Pu Neb. For they were both man and cat and king of men and king of jaguars. This is how the werejaguar kings were born, on the night when Cit Chac blesses human sacrifice with the magic of the spirit world. May they protect us until the end of days.

Jacks shook off the ethereal tethers that connected his mind with Bella's. He looked around the balcony and the city below. It felt like the writing in the codex had swallowed him into another world, and he half-expected to have been transported to an ancient time and place. He was disappointed in his ordinary surroundings at first, but as he settled in with what had happened, he had to hold down a cry of victory.

Bella chewed at one of her paws, grooming. He scooped her into his arms and kissed her on the forehead. With Bella as a conduit, he could read the Báalam-Tet. He could decode the secrets of werecat magic. He felt as tall as a skyscraper.

Jacks tucked the book under one arm and carried Bella with the other, and he rushed to wake up Farzan and Kwame and tell them the news.

IT TOOK A moment for the other guys to catch on to Jacks's excitement, but they spent the rest of the night working on what he had read. Both Farzan and Kwame had been groggy and cranky when he had woken them up, but gradually they took up their respective métiers of expertise. Farzan logged on to the hotel's Wi-Fi with his phone to research Olmec culture. Kwame pulled out Benoit's writings in French from his travel bag.

"Benoit told me this story," Jacks said. "About an Olmec king who was reborn as a werejaguar. He said it was the start of the tradition that passed down to the Maya and the Aztecs."

The cell phone screen cast faint blue light on Farzan's studious face. He read from a Wikipedia article. "The Olmecs were the first Mesoamerican civilization, developed on the present-day southern Mexican Gulf Coast, and lasted from approximately 1200 B.C.E. to 400 B.C.E. They are considered to be a protoculture of Mesoamerica, and they introduced the first form of writing to the Western world, although little is understood of their language, religion, and daily life." He read a bit more to himself and looked up at Jacks in admiration. "There's only been one find of Olmec writing by archeologists. You decoded glyphs linguists say are unlikely to ever be understood."

"It was like my native language once I got Bella on the job." He strode over to her lounging on top of the dresser and gave her an enthusiastic rub beneath her chin. "But the dates and the conditions for the rearing ritual—I don't know what they mean. Whoever wrote that book was writing about the world as it was known to people tens of centuries ago."

Kwame looked up from his journal. "Benoit was working on that. He made some calculations here. It could be he was trying to translate the Olmec dates to a modern calendar, but it is a little bit tricky to follow."

Jacks took short paces through the room. He was remembering some things from an anthropology class. "The 'eye of the god of death' sounds like the moon. Many ancient cultures associated the moon with death. Suppose it's as simple as a full moon? And the 'jaguar's tail' could be a pattern of the stars, don't you think?"

"I'll look it up," Farzan said.

His head filled to bursting with many thoughts. He recalled the night when Benoit trapped him and performed an occult ritual that involved the coupling of their blood. The werejaguar kings Po Nge Be and Pu Neb were the ancestral fathers of every werecat in the Americas. Their blood had been passed down for dozens of generations. It was part of him as well. He wished he could remember more about that night in Montréal when Benoit had reared his feline soul. It had been violent and coercive, and he hadn't been paying attention to things like the position of the moon and the stars in the sky.

He turned to Kwame. The rearing was a sacred, very personal experience, but Jacks ventured a question. "Do you remember your rearing?"

Kwame hesitated. Though they had skipped around the Caribbean together for four weeks on Maarten's yacht, he knew little about Kwame's past. He had asked him how old he was since that was always a curiosity. Werecats didn't age like humans. They could live to be three hundred, even four hundred years old. Kwame had said he was ninety-four and grew up in West Africa.

"In Africa, there are two ancestral lines to the feline gods," Kwame said. "The Zulu, like Maarten and Annika, who possess the white lion spirit, and the Ashanti, who can be wereleopards or werelions like me. My family emigrated from the old kingdom to Cote D'Ivoire many years before I was born.

"What you call 'the rearing,' my people called le revenir. This happened when I was a young man. I did not know the one who gave the gift to me. I cannot say what moon or stars were in the sky that night. I can only say it was a blessing."

Jacks sat down on Kwame's bed, facing him. He very much

wanted to hear more. Farzan looked at Kwame from behind his cell phone. Kwame laid Benoit's journal beside him on the bed.

"I grew up on a coffee plantation outside of Grand Bassam. My parents, brothers and sisters, and I were farm workers, but the maître took a special interest in me." A blush burnished his swarthy face. "He was a bachelor, and I took a special interest in him as well. He made me his partner in business and in his bed. This was very much a scandalous feat for a dark-skinned country boy. Our affair began when I was fifteen years old, and he invited me to live with him in his grand chateau when I turned eighteen. My parents objected. The workers gossiped about it. I did not care. I dressed as a proper French gentleman, and if anyone regarded me with ridicule, I repaid him with a look twice as ferocious. Even then, I was stronger and taller than most men. And more, I was naïve and in love.

"In 1929, this was not a time for such an untraditional arrangement in Cote d'Ivoire. There was discontent over French colonial rule. The shipping business and most other industries were moving from Grand Bassam to the new capital of Abidjan. There were Christian missionaries 'enlightening' the country folk about their backward ways and teaching them about sexual sin."

His voice, which had rose up bitterly, dwindled, and he looked away from his companions with a hard stare. "One night, a band of rebels and the newly righteous joined together to plunder our home and burn our fields. There were too many to fight. They held me down and slaughtered my husband in front of me. They beat me so badly I could not raise my hand to protect my face, and then they dragged me through the fields to bring me to the cabanes where my family and all of the workers could witness my execution."

Farzan gaped in disbelief. For Jacks, who had heard before

stories of injustice against dual soul people, Kwame's tale struck a familiar chord. Still, it was chilling.

Kwame spoke as though haunted by the memory. "My comprehension of the world around me was bleary and delicate. I remember only a roar that seemed to eviscerate the night and then the cries of people scattering. I knew no more. It was as though I was drunk and blacked out, and I was grateful for it.

"I woke early the next morning, remembering nothing. My wounds had healed, the mob was gone, and I discovered that the raid on the plantation had not been a dream. I found my husband dead in our home, which had burned down to its scaffolding."

He shifted a bit, reawakening to his companions. "Some months later, when I was living in Marseille, I found an Ashanti witch doctor who explained what came to pass that night. A wereshaman had taken pity on me. From time to time, we had seen lions in the forest beyond our fields. It could be the shaman was one of them, watching over me. Le revenir was the only thing he could give me to save my life. But you see, my story does not help us to understand what is written in the Báalam-Tet."

"What did you do after the plantation was destroyed?" Farzan asked.

A wry grin bewitched Kwame's downcast face. "Henri, my lover, had a sizable estate in a bank in Marseille. There were papers making me his sole successor. The French governor of Grand Bassam interceded on my behalf in order to be done with the ugly affair. Through interpretation of the law, the governor even granted me French citizenship. I sailed to Marseille, collected my inheritance, and began a new life." He looked at Jacks, eager to lighten the moment. "Some sixty years later, I met Maarten at a nightclub in Nice, and he invited me for a sail on his yacht. He brought me into his pride. We were two-spirit creatures living as we wanted to, only bothering with the human world when we needed to anchor overnight at a port. That brings us to our recent trip to Barbados where I met you good people."

Farzan looked like he was bursting with questions. Jacks beat him to it. "Did you ever look for the wereshaman who saved your life?"

Kwame folded his big arms behind his neck. "There is an unspoken vow in Maarten's pride to leave the past in the past."

Jacks remembered Maarten's indifferent attitude well. He said the only thing that mattered was the present, and of that, his concern consisted of getting high on Valerian snuff and moving from one thrill to another. "What about before you joined up with him?"

"Some among us had tried to find our makers. But the twentieth century was not kind to lion priests in Africa. Between tribal feuds and lion poachers, the wereshamans were all but exterminated. In the 1940s, I traveled to Ghana and tracked down one of my half-sisters from my werelion father. She told me our father had been killed by trappers, and no one knew if any of the old masters lived."

Farzan broke in. "If your husband had lived, would you have wanted him to become a werecat like you?"

Jacks studied Farzan. He thought Farzan understood it was not that simple. Only people with an ancestral connection to feline mysticism could be transformed.

"Henri could have had that potential." Kwame looked at Farzan kindly. "There was a time when I thought about such things. But as far as I know, he was a Frenchman through and through."

Farzan looked askance. He spoke quietly. "If we figure out how and when the ritual can be performed, you two could create an army to fight back the Glaring."

Jacks twisted up his face. "Are you serious? Like we go round kidnapping people and turning them against their will?"

"It's just an idea," Farzan said with some heat. "There were nine of you at the bank in Barbados when we got ambushed by the Glaring, and six survived, barely." He modulated his tone. "I don't mean to be crass, but it wouldn't hurt to have some backup, don't you think?"

Kwame chuckled merrily. "My friend, you have a point."

Jacks stared at Farzan in disbelief.

"Maybe we get volunteers. With all the money you have, you could pay them."

Jacks rubbed his face. He'd never seen this mercenary side of Farzan. Maybe it was from the trauma he'd been through along with sleep deprivation.

"I'm just brainstorming," Farzan went on.

"Babe, creating more werecats won't solve the problem. It's not like conjuring up a zombie army. The ones we turn could just as soon run off. They could even choose to join the Glaring."

Farzan looked away in exasperation. Meanwhile, a different thought occurred to Jacks. He said to Kwame, "You think the Ashanti lion priests are extinct, and Annika told me she thought the Zulu wereshamans were gone as well. But what about weremasters from other parts of the world? They would make good allies against Tepe." He gestured to the Báalam-Tet. "Like the werejaguar kings the book talks about, the wereshamans believe in peaceful coexistence between men and cats. They're supposed to protect humankind."

"What about Egypt?" Farzan said.

Kwame gave him a woeful scowl. "We are not descendants of the Sphinx. The Egyptians worshiped feline gods, but if they knew werecat magic, it would have made front page news.

Their civilization has been studied more than any ancient culture in the world."

Farzan sat down on the bed and said quietly but thickly, "I'm sorry. I must have missed class the day my social studies teacher went over werecat history."

"There are five centers of the werecat diaspora," Jacks said. "Africa, North America, Mesoamerica—"

Kwame finished his list. "India, with its Waghia tiger cult and the Suea Saming skin-walkers of Indochine." He glanced at Jacks, gravely. "But as far as we know, their weremasters have all succumbed to age or assassination. Their progeny live in hiding or they have been corrupted into joining the Glaring."

A troubling thought occurred to Jacks. "What if Tepe is a weremaster? That would explain the respect he's earned from other werecats. Maybe he wants the book so no one else will have his power."

"A weremaster is sworn to maintain harmony between the human and spirit world," Kwame said.

Jacks thought about his maker, Benoit. One horrible night, he had watched him stalk a pair of homeless men in Central Park, bury one of them with his heft and rip open his throat. That urge to dominate was inside every werecat. Maarten, Kwame, and their party boat of friends had blunted themselves on Valerian to stave off the hunger to kill. Jacks fought against it himself, and he understood it wasn't necessarily evil.

Living in the wild, a werecat could hunt to satisfy his feline nature without hurting humans. But contact with humans was nearly unavoidable such as the world was now. That had driven Benoit to strike out ruthlessly in the end. He had lived for two hundred years containing his wild cat impulses and trying to understand the ancient histories when men and werecats shared the world in a natural balance. But his jaguar soul had overtaken him. Could the same thing have happened to Tepe?

As Jacks thought about it more, there was another plausible possibility. Tepe could have been overcome by the distinctly human characteristic of greed.

"Maybe Tepe is the reason the other masters are dead," he said.

Kwame raised his dark eyebrows.

Farzan stood. "What we do know about Tepe is that he's on a mission to wipe out humankind. It's going to take more than the three of us to stop him. We should be sharing what we know with people who deal with terrorists."

Kwame sat up on the bed, squaring his broad shoulders. "The Glaring killed three of my friends."

Jacks glanced at Farzan strangely. "What people? Like Homeland Security?"

"And the C.I.A., the British Secret Service, Interpol, and whoever else handles terrorists."

"They'll slaughter every one of them or have them locked up for study," Jacks said. "And they'll lock the two of us up for interrogation." He turned to Farzan. "You realize I'm a wanted criminal."

Farzan's face turned dark burgundy. "So, I'll make the call. Neither one of you has to be involved. We just need to give them a general idea of the location of Tepe's headquarters."

Jacks eased off for a moment. "Let's take things step-by-step. We've got the book. We need to crack it open more. We also came down here to find Tepe's location, but we'll cross that bridge when we come to it."

Kwame nodded. "Tomorrow, we will look up an old friend of mine, Javier. He spent some time with us on Maarten's yacht, and he runs tours of the rainforest out of Puerto Ayacucho. If there have been any werecats headed into the Amazon, Javier will know about it."

# TWO

LATE THE NEXT morning, they showered and dressed, packed up day bags, put Bella in her carrier, and headed down to the hotel's dining room for breakfast. Jacks didn't like keeping Bella confined in a cage, but he needed to spend more time reading the Báalam-Tet, and he needed Bella with him to do that.

He had awoken feeling spooked about being on the mainland. Domestic and feral cats would be watching them, and very possibly hunters from the Glaring were on lookout. It was best that they stayed together at all times. Bella was as much an enemy to the Glaring as any of them. The strays and the hunters knew about her connection to Jacks, and back in New York City, she helped Farzan fight off a hunter who had broken into his family's house. Jacks couldn't risk leaving her alone in the hotel.

In the dining room, he and Kwame heaped their plates with ham and liverwurst from the breakfast buffet and several glasses of milk apiece to wash the food down. They joked about the menu they had gotten used to on Maarten's yacht, prepared by a private chef who spoiled them with sushi grade fish and the best cuts of raw lamb and veal.

Farzan came back from the buffet with a stack of pancakes and a plate of scrambled eggs. Jacks fed Bella scraps of ham through her carrier door. The table was silent while they ate. They each had prodigious appetites from overtiredness and the anxiety of what lay ahead. At the most, they had managed four hours of sleep.

On his cell phone, Farzan found a bus to Puerto Ayacucho. The trip took fifteen hours, and left once a day at five o'clock by a well-rated, private bus company from La Bandera Terminal. A bus was the best way for them to travel. Besides the fact that Jacks and Kwame had dubious passports, they could encounter hunters on watch at an airport. Renting a car meant having to navigate the Venezuelan back country, and Farzan was quick to point out the prevalence of car-jacking, murder, and kidnapping in country towns. Venezuela had become the "homicide capital of the world" since the period of political instability following President Hugo Chavez' death.

The late afternoon departure gave them time to walk through the Sabana Grande district, though they found it disappointing. Kwame said it had been filled with gay bars and coffee shops when he visited in the 1990s, but now it lacked any indication of a gay community. The wide pedestrian boulevards were vestiges of a once-thriving commercial district, and the eclectic urban buildings suggested an upscale tourist area. But the shops that remained were dingy and inscrutable. Cheap street markets had overtaken the sidewalks. Behind those stalls, the low-rise buildings looked depleted, if not abandoned. Torpid clouds hung low in the sky, washing a gray mood of desolation over everything.

Through Farzan's navigation, they found their way to El Recreo, an indoor mall of a familiar American scale and with the familiar retail trappings. There, they decided to browse a sportswear store for shorts and shirts suitable for the tropical weather. None of them had more than two or three changes of clothes packed up from when they had disembarked from Maarten's yacht. Jacks and Kwame had cargo shorts and cotton tees, while Farzan favored track pants because he was self-conscious about his body. While Kwame and Jacks stripped off their shirts in the middle of a store to try on new tees, Farzan wandered away through the racks. Jacks passed a glance to Kwame to keep an eye on Bella's carrier, and he went after Farzan.

He spotted a short-sleeve World Cup soccer shirt along the way and grabbed it. He stepped over to Farzan and showed it to him.

"You'd look great in this." He wriggled his eyebrows. "And you'd fit in with the locals."

Farzan skirted his gaze. "This is my worst nightmare. Shopping for clothes with two guys who look like cover models from *Men's Fitness*."

Jacks scoffed. Kwame certainly had a ridiculous body, but Jacks still thought of himself as lanky and awkward, though he had bulked up and gained definition since his transformation. His protein diet accounted for some of that, but it seemed to be happening automatically as his human body adjusted to his hybrid physiology. He was still surprised when he caught a reflection of himself in the mirror.

"I thought you liked the 'scenery.'"

Farzan frowned. "I'll be over in the young men's collection for assless, anemic medical school dropouts while you two get suited up in Lycra."

"I was thinking of trying on one of the Speedos."

His attempt at humor didn't catch on with Farzan. He caught him lightly by the arm. "Hey, I love medical school dropouts. And you're not assless or anemic." He leaned into Farzan's ear and spoke quietly. "I think you're really hot."

Farzan blushed as Jacks pressed up closer. "How about coming with me to the changing room?"

His boyfriend smiled for the first time in days, but then he shook his head. "Thanks, but we're in enough trouble without getting locked up for public indecency in a foreign country."

Jacks glanced around the store. No customers except for Kwame, who was checking out the sneakers on a far wall of shelves. A pair of salesgirls at the cashier counter were busy chatting with each other. Jacks pulled Farzan close and kissed him.

Farzan was wooden. He told Jacks in a low voice, "Cool your heels, Romeo. Public opinion of homosexuality here is comparable to Alabama."

Their quick smooch had gotten Jacks noticeably eager. He turned modestly away from the front of the store. Luckily, the clothing rack covered him from the waist down. "It's been a while since...you know. We should find a way to have some privacy, don't you think?" He eyed Farzan playfully. "Maybe in the bathroom of the bus."

Farzan sighed and pulled away from him. "Honestly, it's not the first thing on my mind right now."

Jacks was wounded. He just wanted to show Farzan how much he cared for him and appreciated that he was risking so much. "Do you regret coming with me?"

"You're asking me that because I'm not comfortable having sex with you in a changing stall?"

Jacks bowed his head. He was much better at showing Farzan how he felt than talking about it, and Farzan had turned that around and made him feel like a creep.

Farzan stepped nearer. "I'm not trying to hurt your feelings, Jacks. Maybe when we get settled in Puerto Ayacucho, we'll have our own bedroom or something."

Jacks felt like he could break into pieces. He knew it wasn't rational, but he was suddenly a child needing Farzan to confirm his feelings for him then and there. "Did I kill things between us?"

Farzan went back to looking through shirts on hangers. "Yes. I only came along on this suicide mission for the thrill of it." He added, sharply, "Why are you bringing this up again?"

The corners of Jacks's eyes burned. "You could go home, y'know? Get a flight back to New York to be with your family. I wouldn't hold it against you."

"We already talked about this."

"I'm trying to say...I love you. And I don't want you to get hurt. And I know you're scared, Farzan." He wiped his face. "That's my fault. It's not fair to put you through this, especially after what I did."

"I'm putting myself through this. Because I want to be here, with you." He frowned, musingly. "Could it be a huge mistake? Maybe. But FOMO, y'know?"

They studied each other for a moment.

"I love you so much for doing this," Jacks said.

Farzan smiled a little. "You should."

Jacks encircled him in his arms. "I do. So, you don't have any regrets?"

"No. For the hundredth time, I don't have any regrets."

"Thanks." Jacks quickly kissed him on the cheek. "I just need to hear it again sometimes."


AFTER THE MALL, they picked up bottled water and headed to La Bandera station in a taxi well ahead of their departure time. Inside the gritty terminal, they found the cashier stand for the bus company Farzan located online, and they purchased tickets to Puerto Ayacucho. With plenty of time to kill, Jacks went to a nearby currency exchange and changed more of his US dollars for bolivars.

The fleet of luxury liners for Carina Travel Express inspired some confidence, but their five o'clock bus was nowhere to be found at five o'clock. Kwame said buses were notoriously unreliable in South America. The trip would take much longer than the posted schedule.

So, they sat on the terminal curbside eating arepas, which they bought from a street cart. Jacks and Kwame picked the shredded chicken and beef from the corn patties and threw out the rest to pigeons scavenging around the place. Only pigeons were dumb and stubborn enough to not scurry away from a werecougar and a werelion. Though their wildcat natures were invisible in their human form, they were detectable to most of the animal world. When a young woman passed by with a Rottweiler, the big dog took one look at them, drew back with his tail curled behind him, and bolted in the other direction, dragging his owner by the leash.

The bus finally arrived at quarter past six. It had comfortable seats and air conditioning, and it was only half full with South American and a few European tourists. Puerto Ayacucho was on the northernmost end of the Amazon, on the Orinoco River, which constituted Venezuela's western border with Colombia.

Beyond the concrete mire and traffic of Caracas, the landscape gave way to tree-filled highlands. Farzan sat at a window seat, and Jacks sat next to him. Kwame sat across the narrow aisle with Bella in her carrier in the empty seat beside him. The bus wove along a mountainous two-lane highway, and after a while, the only civilization was little enclaves of miniature homes with aluminum roofs.

Night crept up, and the lulling movement of the bus worked its enchantment on Kwame. His eyes sagged shut, and his breathing grew steady. Jacks and Farzan looked at each other in amusement. He could see that Farzan's eyes were getting heavy as well.

He kissed Farzan on the side of the face. "Get some sleep. We've got like fourteen hours to kill."

"You should get some sleep, too."

"I will. I'm just going to take another look at the book first."

Farzan didn't argue with him. He took his ear buds out of his bag, plugged them into his phone, and shut his eyes.

Carefully, Jacks reached over Kwame's sleeping body to retrieve Bella from her carrier. She wasn't crazy about coming out. The cabin was filled with too many bothersome scents and sounds for her liking. But she let Jacks pull her into his arms and then sat on his lap. Jacks brought out the Báalam-Tet from his backpack. Peeking around the cabin, he satisfied himself that the other passengers had settled in for the night.

He opened the codex to the page where he had left off the night before. He spoke to Bella in a language of mental images. Communicating with domestics was more about telepathizing imagery than words, and first and foremost harnessing their attention with stern eye contact. They were like toddlers in that sense. He got Bella to focus on the page. Their visions merged, and the arcane glyphs revealed themselves to him again.

The pages were filled with histories of werejaguar kings, who were said to have the power to command wild cats to battle, though Jacks could find no instructions on how to perform that kind of magic. He wondered who had recorded the stories and for what purpose. A werejaguar king himself? An Olmec priest who served the god Cit Chac? There was no mention of the author.

Annika said Benoit got the book from a Zapotec mystic he

met in the Yucatán. According to Farzan's research, Olmec civilization had disappeared mysteriously around 400 A.D. The region was subsequently dominated by Mayan and Aztec empires, and then the Spanish conquistadors killed the natives or forced them into slavery, seizing Mexico and Central America and most of South America.

Jacks had so many questions. Why hadn't the werejaguars resisted? Or had they tried and been overpowered?

He supposed their history should be no different than the countless native peoples who had been annihilated or subjugated by European imperialism. When Jacks discovered his Cherokee ancestry just four months ago, he had researched how they had been swindled by treaties with the British and later forced to a reservation in Oklahoma by the "new Americans" in the Trail of Tears. Feelings warred inside him. Though he was sickened by the Glaring's wanton killing of humans, he had always understood the basis of their position. Anger bled from him anew like scratching open a scabbed wound. Why hadn't the Cherokee werecougars fought to protect their people?

He mentally nudged Bella to return to the book, and they paged through the werejaguar king histories until Jacks came to something different. It was the jaguar-king symbol followed by a long dot-and-slash date that seemed to jump far ahead of the previous passages. The words below it read like a prophecy.

There is above our lord Cit Chac and above the great Hanub a mightier and more ancient god, Sim Ru, who reigned over gods and kings and cats in the days when the earth was young. As the circle ends whence it began, so shall he awaken on the night of nights when the eye of the god of death is in union with Sim Ru's six sons. And the one king who makes sacrifice shall be brought before Sim Ru's throne and joined in soul and body with the lord of all cats who once tramped the earth, laying claim to everything beneath his foot. He shall be the king of kings, and he shall unleash an army to raze the world, and so begins the new age of one God and one King as the age of gods and kings ends.

Jacks blinked to break his visual connection with Bella. He was anxious to dispel the cold feeling that had sunk into his bones.

Awakening to the dark and still bus cabin did not help much. He had been looking for ancient wisdom in the codex, but having found it, he wasn't so sure that had been a good idea The precise meaning of the passage floated beyond his comprehension, but it was undoubtedly a doomsday riddle a terror-mongering werecat capitán like Tepe would be salivating to figure out.

# THREE

EARLY THE NEXT morning, Farzan woke in a glare of sunlight from the window. He squinted at Jacks, and then he squinted at the sight of Bella curled into a ball and napping on Jacks's lap. His drowsy face brightened, and he gently stroked Bella's back. Then he took account of Jacks's oily, ashen face.

"Don't tell me you were up all night with the book."

He figured that he must look a fright after two nights of not sleeping. "I got a few hours sleep," he lied. He had tried closing his eyes a dozen times, but what he read in the codex kept making his chest tighten up. Just once, when his thoughts had scattered, and his mind loosened into what could have been a hypnagogic phase, he saw an otherworldly vision of a giant cat with tusked fangs watching him. The amber eyes of the magnificent creature flickered with a human intelligence.

Farzan glanced out the window. The landscape had changed dramatically overnight. The green mountains had given way to a lush river plain with many silty inland shoals. It was early September, late in the region's wet season. Nothing was to be seen in terms of civilization, but the bus passed by a billboard sign advertising a bait and tackle store for fishing on the Orinoco River.

"What time is it?"

Jacks shrugged. He had no watch. Their only clock was on Farzan's cell phone. Farzan looked at its display and showed it to Jacks. Nine thirty.

"Think we're getting close?" Farzan didn't wait for Jacks to answer. "I'm starving." He pulled up his backpack from the floor and laid it on his lap. "I've got bananas in here from the hotel and those protein bars we picked up. You should eat."

Jacks said nothing.

Farzan looked at him sharply. "What's wrong?"

"I read something in the Báalam-Tet last night."

"Why didn't you wake me up?"

"You were sleeping so well."

"What was it?"

He took a dry swallow. He explained the basics of the passage about the aboriginal god Sim Ru. He didn't mention his vision of a giant, prehistoric cat, however. It was probably a dream inspired by the story and neither here nor there.

Farzan was quiet for a moment. "You think that's why Tepe wants the book. To summon the power of some ancient feline god."

He nodded.

"Every religion has a legend about the end of the world. Like Revelations in the Bible. Or the Qiyamah Judgment Day in the Qu'ran. You're reading stories written by people who believed everything in their world was controlled by gods and fate. The Olmec calendar was a prototype for the Mayan's. You remember the Mayan Prophecy? The world was supposed to end in 2012."

"Farzan, you know this isn't bullshit."

He looked away from Jacks. He was an atheist and a

medical student, but he had to face the fact that not everything in the world could be explained by science. Farzan had seen men transform into big cats for Christ's sake.

"All right," Farzan said quietly. "What do you propose we do?"

"We decode the date and figure out what the moon in union with the six sons means. That's got to be what Tepe is looking for—how to unlock a Judgement Day for humankind."

Farzan looked at his cell phone. "It needs to charge." He retrieved the charger from his bag and plugged the phone into an outlet by his window-side armrest. He tapped at the screen. "I'm not getting a signal. Maybe we'll pick up something when we get into town."

Across the aisle, Kwame sat up from his slump and rubbed his eyes. Jacks filled him in on his finding. Kwame dug into his bag to bring out Benoit's leather-bound traveling journal. He paged through some entries while Farzan ate one of his bananas and pushed a bottled water on Jacks.

"Sim Ru," Kwame read. "This is Smilodon according to Benoit. The father of all cats."

Smilodon was generally regarded as a prehistoric link to the panther line which included lions, tigers, leopards, and jaguars. That branch was the older "big boys" of the feline world. Jacks's cougar ancestry went back a mere 100,000 years ago, whereas lions like Kwame had been around for one million years.

A theory had occurred to Jacks. "The prophecy talks about six sons. There are five geographical centers of werecat generation. But one of those centers produced two werecat lines: Africa. So it's really six. The six werecat tribes could represent the six sons."

"What's Smilodon?" Farzan asked.

"The sabretooth," Kwame said. Inside the journal, Benoit

had clipped a faded, yellowed newspaper article written in French. Kwame showed it to Farzan and Jacks. It was from *Le Figaro*, dated April 3, 1843, just two paragraphs, but it came with a much larger photograph that needed no elaboration: the fossilized skeleton of a sabretooth cat. Kwame explained it had been discovered in Brazil by a Danish paleontologist named Peter Wilhelm Lund. Jacks recalled that in 1843, Benoit had been living in Québec City managing his father's fur trading business and secretly trying to understand his transformation.

While Farzan stared at the clipping, Kwame returned to reading Benoit's journal. He looked up at Jacks. "Benoit had the same idea as you. He wrote about it here." Kwame pointed out a page with a series of pencil sketches with fine details and shading. "The werejaguar of the Olmecs in Mesoamerica. The Waghia tiger cult of India. The Suea Saming skin-walkers of Indochina. The White Lion priests of the Zulu in South Africa. The Ashanti werelion and wereleopard in West Africa. And the Wildcat Clan of the Cherokee."

Jacks gazed at the last drawing with pride. He was part of one of the oldest and most noble native traditions in the world.

"But if this codex was written by the Olmecs, how could they have known about the other werecat tribes?" Farzan said. "They lived continents and centuries apart."

It was a very reasonable question. The first Cherokee settlements dated no further back than the eleventh century, some six hundred years after the Olmecs had disappeared. Besides the possibility that the author of the book had the power to see into the future, Jacks had no explanation.

"You said there's only been one discovery of Olmec writing by archeologists, and no one knows what it means. So, how could someone beyond that era have written the book?" Jacks said.

"I don't know. They proved the Leif Ericson map of America was a forgery."

Jacks raised the delicate, foul-smelling codex from his lap. "Does this look like a forgery?"

"I'm not saying it's a sham," Farzan said. "Not exactly. Annika told you Benoit got it from a Zapotec mystic. Sometime when? The past one hundred years? Maybe that person wrote it."

"Seriously? You think this book is less than one hundred years old?"

"We have no way to prove one way or the other without an expert studying it."

"And how would you do that? Just call up the Smithsonian Institute and ask them to take a look at it?"

"No. That would be stupid. But you can pay to have things carbon dated in a lab."

Jacks minded his temper. There was no point in getting snappish with each other, though Farzan's always-right attitude grated at him. He was trying to school Jacks on werecat history?

Kwame broke in to bring their attention to something else in Benoit's journal. "He was researching stars and their position in the sky: *When the six sons are in union with the moon, the Sim Ru prophecy will be revealed.* Each of the werecat cults believed certain stars represented their feline god. Benoit recorded them here."

"Like the jaguar tail the book talks about," Jacks said.

Kwame scanned through a page of tidy cursive and diagrams. "Here," he pointed out. "It is the same as the tail of the Leo constellation."

"Could it be that simple—the formation of the lion on the night of the full moon?" Jacks asked.

Farzan pressed against his side, eager to improve his view of the book.

Kwame gave a thoughtful frown. "From what I read in Benoit's journal, that is the coordinates for the rearing rite. It happens every year: a full moon when Leo is dominant in the sky. This was something once in a lifetime he was tracking down." He turned the page in the journal and read on. "Here, he has a list of celestial bodies of significance."

Jacks and Farzan stared at the page as though the passages in French and orbital drawing would leap out with some meaning.

"Les Rois," Kwame read. "The Kings." He fastened on a pair of journal entries. "The Olmecs assigned Venus as the sovereign star. Ancient peoples from the Indian subcontinent associated kingship with Jupiter, like the Warli tribe who are believed to have founded the Waghia tiger cult."

"I thought the prophecy referred to feline stars," Farzan said.

Jacks was following Benoit's research as though he had majored in ancient world astrology. Somehow reading the Báalam-Tet had given him a newfound intuition. He told Farzan, "To people who worshiped feline gods, kings and cats were one in the same. And the six sons of Sim Ru were kings of their respective domains."

Kwame showed them a third drawing. "This is Rigel in the Orion constellation. The Blue Star. Benoit has a theory it was an emblem for the Cherokee Wildcat clan since they were also known as the Blue clan."

"What else?" Jacks said. "That leaves the three more werecat tribes—the Ashanti, the Zulu, and the Suea Saming."

Kwame flipped through the last few pages to the end of the journal. "I see nothing else here. Only numbers and calculations. It could be they relate to that date you found in the Báalam-Tet."

"If we figure out the date, we can look up an astronomical

chart online," Farzan said. "I can also do a search of unusual astronomical phenomena. For all we know, though, the date already passed. When was Benoit trying to work this out?"

Kwame shook his head. "There are no dates for any of his entries. You can see the journal looks like an antique. But that doesn't mean one thing or the other. Many of us hold on to items from the era when we were born."

A recollection and an idea formed in Jacks's head. It made the blood drain from his hands and his face.

"It will take me a while to follow Benoit's calculations," Kwame went on. "This is much more complex mathematics than I can follow." He passed the book over Jacks to Farzan. "The Olmec calendar has twenty months and thirteen days. Benoit was trying to translate their 260-day year into our 365-day year."

Farzan took the book. "That's actually pretty simple if you can isolate the date when the Olmec calendar started."

"Benoit knew the date was coming," Jacks said.

Farzan glanced at him briefly, and then he went back to studying the calculations in the journal.

Kwame kept his gaze trained on Jacks.

"It makes perfect sense," Jacks said. "Why else would he have hidden the book in an offshore bank? Why else would he have chosen me?"

That garnered Farzan's attention. "What do you mean?"

"Werecats are solitary. Benoit always told me that. But for the first time in his life, he was looking to settle down with a mate. Because he was afraid. He knew there was a chance that other werecats would discover the Sim Ru prophecy, and he didn't want to be alone when the world was shredded apart."

THE BUS ROLLED into the little city of Puerto Ayacucho an hour later. Throughout the cabin, voices piped up in Spanish, English, and German as the passengers took in the view of their destination. It was an austere town of prefabricated, sandwich-panel homes with eaved porches and a handful of grander Spanish Colonial-style houses and churches. The character of the city was hard to place. Colorful billboards advertising Amazon excursions stood alongside storefront evangelical churches. Men in military fatigues patrolled the four-lane main road carrying rifles. There didn't appear to be much in the way of tourist shops, and the few hotels they passed along the way were plain, even industrial in style.

Jacks's inner world was as confused as the changeable clouds hovering over the city. Jacks had thought he'd come to terms with killing Benoit in self-defense. Was it wrong for him to have regrets? If Benoit had told him what he discovered about the Sim Ru prophecy, Jacks might have been able to help him deal with it instead of going berserk. He should have asked more questions or picked up on deeper reasons why Benoit was so overprotective. Instead, Jacks had taken his life.

He awakened to the bus coming to a stop at a roadside depot in the center of the town. As Farzan had told him, Puerto Ayacucho was the last outpost north of the vast Amazon jungle. That meant it was dangerous territory. Tepe had a stronghold in the jungle. Jacks mentally nudged Bella back into her carrier, and they disembarked with Farzan and Kwame.

Most of the bus passengers boarded chauffeured minivans to head to points of interest outside the city. A few stood around waiting for their connections to arrive.

Kwame spotted a mercado. "I'm going to speak to a clerk," he told them. "I need to sort out some directions." He walked off, and Farzan took Jacks aside while their bus idled on the road.

"I'm sorry," Farzan said.

"For what?"

"I didn't mean to imply that what you found in the book was unimportant. I guess a part of me didn't want to believe it."

"It's okay. I think we're all a little tense." Jacks squeezed his arm in lieu of giving him a kiss. "I got a bit heated myself. I'm sorry, too."

Farzan glanced around the dusty town and shivered though it had to be at least eighty degrees and 100 percent humidity. "I thought Kwame called ahead to let his friend know we were coming."

Jacks shrugged.

"He hasn't seen Javier in years. He might not even live here anymore."

Jacks said nothing. Farzan's anxiety was winding him up again, already.

"This doesn't look like the best place to hang out. And buses probably don't come by very often. If this Javier guy isn't around, I think we better hop back in before the bus returns to Caracas."

Just then, the engine of the bus coughed and revved, and it wheeled down the road, leaving Jacks and Farzan starkly exposed on the sidewalk.

Farzan pulled out his cell phone. "At least I'm finally getting a signal." He tapped the screen. "The next bus is at five. That's Spanish for six o'clock at the earliest." He looked to Jacks. "This town looks like the set for one of those movies where American teenagers get kidnapped for their organs. What do you think it's like after dark?"

A venomous hiss rose up from Bella's carrier. Farzan startled a foot away from it. Jacks tuned into Bella's mind and quickly located the cause of her aggression. A runty, ginger stray was frozen in a watchful pose beneath the shade of an aluminum eave across the street. Jacks's stare sent the little peeping tom scuttling down a narrow alley beside its house.

Farzan missed the exchange completely, but he must've read the emotions on Jacks's face. "What was it?"

"A domestic."

Farzan looked around. "Working for the Glaring?"

"We'll find out soon enough."

"I'd prefer not to stick around to find out," Farzan said. "I'd prefer if we had never come down here in the first place."

"We'll be fine." Jacks picked up the scent of another stray in the vicinity but no trace of a werejaguar. He would be able to smell them from one hundred yards away, which wasn't a particularly big head start on a Glaring hunter, but Jacks wanted to reassure Farzan. A pair of local girls in brightly colored camisoles and hip-hugging jeans wandered past them. As soon as they had traveled a safe distance down the road, Farzan turned to Jacks with an urgent look on his face.

"You can't seriously be thinking about finding Tepe after what you read in the book."

Jacks raked a hand through his hair.

"You'd be handing him exactly what he wants. As soon as we get an idea of his location, we should call the authorities. They could take you and the book into protective custody until that Sim Ru date passes."

Jacks did agree the idea of seeking out Tepe had been naïve. The fact that they were standing on the outskirts of the jungle, Tepe's turf, had him as tight as a wire. There could be dozens of werejaguars thirsting to make a kill and bring the Báalam-Tet to Tepe. But Farzan's plan was just as dangerous.

"The Báalam-Tet doesn't belong with the authorities."

"What choice do we have?"

"It's a sacred book, Farzan. Benoit spent years decoding it."

"Benoit also locked it up in an offshore bank so no one would find it."

"He did it so the two of us would be safe. But if the rearing ritual is lost, it will be the end of werecats forever."

"If Tepe gets it, it could be the end of mankind forever."

"It would help if we knew how much time we had."

"What difference does that make?"

"If the date in the book is months or years away, we could find people to help us. There have to be other werecats out there who don't want Tepe determining our future."

"I know you don't like hearing this, Jacks, but this isn't just about werecats. The Glaring is murdering humans. Do I need to remind you they tried to murder me and my family? They're roaming free, probably plotting another attack. We have a fucking responsibility to tell the police what we know about them."

Jacks didn't disagree with Farzan's concern, but he wished he could appreciate that bringing human authorities into the situation posed a huge danger for him and Kwame, and all werecats potentially, whether they were affiliated with the Glaring or not. He still didn't know how to talk about these things with Farzan. He didn't want to sound like he was sympathetic to the werecats who had murdered humans.

Kwame came out of the mercado chewing on a hunk of beef jerky from the bag he was carrying. Jacks and Farzan looked at him expectantly. Kwame swallowed a mouthful of his breakfast.

"A nice lady in the store looked up Javier's phone number and let me borrow her phone. He will be here soon to pick us up."

ABOUT A HALF hour later, a shiny, red Chevy pickup truck rumbled down the road and halted at the bus stop where Jacks, Farzan, and Kwame stood. The driver's door swung open, and a tall, bronze-skinned man with a mop of ringlet curls and a goatee came around the front of the truck. He wore an unbuttoned, short-sleeve shirt, faded, low-rise jeans, and six-inch work boots. He greeted Kwame with a gleaming smile, and they grasped each other in a bear hug, uttering words in Portuguese. Kwame had mentioned Javier was Brazilian. He had chased some Venezuelan contractor up to Puerto Ayacucho, and though their relationship didn't work out, he ended up starting a business taking tourists on private trips into the Amazon.

Kwame made introductions in English, in which Javier was fluent as well. Javier gave Jacks and Farzan a friendly smile and warm handshakes. He had the looks and the charisma to make most people putty in his hands, and Jacks felt himself veering toward the guy instantly in a companionable way. He could smell that Javier was a werejaguar. That didn't make him a good guy or a bad guy as far as Jacks figured. Most members of the Glaring he had met had been werejaguars, but some must lead independent lives. Kwame had vouched for Javier being the latter, but they had agreed not to tell Javier about the Báalam-Tet.

Kwame told Javier they were on a quick excursion while Maarten's yacht was docked in Caracas.

"You guys are lucky I have the day free," Javier said. "Come on. I'll take you back to the house." He grinned at Kwame's grocery bag. "Maybe you'll get something better for breakfast than beef jerky."

They piled into the pickup with Bella's carrier and their bags, and Javier drove them north through town to a dirt road nearly overtaken by tropical vegetation. They disappeared into that wild hollow. Not a home was to be seen for about a mile.

The back country route ended at a fenced property with a sign announcing in English: Orinoco Tours by Javier. They pulled into a gravel yard, which faced a ranch style, cornflower blue aluminum house with barred windows. Beyond, Jacks spotted the bank of Rio Orinoco.

As soon as they climbed out of the cab, everyone wandered around the side of the house to take a look at the river scenery. Nearby, the river shoals were reefed by shrubby islands and fingers of sand bars. Farther offshore, on the main channel, the slate blue water was clipped with little peaks beneath the changeable morning sky. The Colombian bank in the distance was an untouched palisade of forested hills.

"Que bonito," Jacks told Javier, exhuming the little bit of the language he had retained from bussing tables at a Portuguese diner in college.

"I'll take you out there after breakfast." Javier drew Jacks's attention to a forty-five foot power boat with a Brazilian flag posted on its stern deck. The boat was moored at a rocky jetty. The stern hull was emblazoned with the name *A Pata de Pantera*. The panther's paw.

"We can take a trip downriver to the Atures rapids and the Curripaco Indian Village," Javier said.

That sounded great to Jacks, but when he glanced at Farzan, he could see he was worried. Javier appeared to pick up on that.

"I'll throw some steak and sausages on the grill, and we can work things out after you guys get some breakfast." Javier looked at Farzan. "I've got eggs, and I might have some farina in the cabinet."

"You don't have to go to any trouble. Whatever you have is fine," Farzan said.

Kwame offered to give Javier a hand in the kitchen, and the two men went up to the house.

Once they had traveled a safe distance away, Farzan spoke quietly to Jacks. "If we don't make that five o'clock bus, we're stuck here for another day."

Jacks moved behind him and kneaded his tense shoulders. "You get me horny when you're uptight."

"Don't tell me you're feeling inspired again."

"I could be." Jacks rested his chin on Farzan's shoulder. "But mainly I'm just glad you're here."

He encircled Farzan's waist, and they stood together looking out to the water for a while. A rusty, metal barge crawled down the river, disturbing the pristine panorama.

"Javier's a werejaguar, isn't he?" Farzan said.

"Uh-huh."

"You think he can be trusted?"

"Kwame thinks so. We'll play it cool. See what he knows."

"You could tell if the Glaring passed through here?"

Jacks took account of his sense of smell. If another werejaguar was in the house, he was certain he would notice. He was reasonably sure he would pick up the lingering scent of visitors, at least within the past few hours, and nothing but traces of Javier's musk was circulating the air.

"It's safe. I'll keep the Báalam-Tet with me when we go out on the boat just in case." He kissed him on the cheek. "C'mon. Let's be good guests and see if Javier needs some help."

# FOUR

JAVIER AND KWAME served up a hearty breakfast of shell steaks, blood sausages, and fried eggs, which they ate at a picnic table on the back deck of the house. Javier had brewed some sweet and potent café con leche to wash the meal down.

A glint of sunlight penetrated the dull canvas of clouds overhead. Javier promised that the morning clouds would pass. Such was the season. The day started gray and ended gray, but there was sun in between. When he suggested taking a cruise downriver again, everyone was game.

Jacks stood up to retrieve Bella and his backpack from the truck. Besides the Báalam-Tet, all his cash was in the backpack. When they boarded the boat, Bella scurried into its deep cabin, while Javier untied its moorings from the jetty and the others grabbed spots on the benches of the fore deck. Javier took the captain's chair behind a console platform. He ferried the boat out to the main channel and revved up the engine.

Jacks stretched his arm around Farzan's shoulder. They passed through the area around Puerto Ayacucho where fishermen trawled in long canoes thatched with browned

coconut tree branches, and then they had the river to themselves. He had never felt so apart from the modern world.
Even skipping around the Caribbean with Maarten's pride,
there had always been cruise ships or freight liners in the
distance or jets high up streaking the sky. Traveling on the
Orinoco was truly like being transported to another realm.
On either side of the river, an evergreen landscape looked
like it stretched into eternity. He half expected to see creatures from a primordial era rustling through the forested
canopy. Earthy scents filled his nostrils, pulling at Jacks to
explore.

A sort of sparrow with orange wings was abundant in the
trees that furrowed either side of the river. Scarlet ibises waded
in the shallows. Javier pointed out crocodiles camouflaged on a
rocky shore. Later, they spotted dolphins as pink as cotton
candy swimming alongside the boat.

Javier let the boat's engine sputter down to a trawl as they
approached a mucky yard of squat and pyramid-shaped grass
huts. He explained it was a camping ground.

"Who stays there?" Jacks asked.

"Americans. Brits. Scandinavians. Sometimes Australian
tourists."

"Hippies," Farzan declared.

Javier laughed. "We get some of those. Young backpackers
looking to 'find themselves' in the Amazon."

"What about anacondas?" Farzan said.

"Sure. The Orinoco basin is one of the best places to find
them. We're not likely to see any today. They're mainly
nocturnal."

"That's fine with me." Farzan looked overboard dubiously.
"What about piranhas?"

"Keep your arms and legs inside the boat," Javier told him
with a grin. Seeing Farzan's tension, he tried being more reas-

suring. "They rarely attack humans. People swim in these waters all the time."

Jacks knew that would be cold comfort to Farzan. He was a New York City boy. Any trip beyond the five boroughs was a wilderness adventure for him.

"Can you find jaguars around here?" he asked, hoping to get a lead on Tepe.

"For sure. The population thrives here in the Venezuelan Amazon where the law protects them. Sadly, we still get illegal safari hunters up this way from time to time. Mostly from Brazil."

That irked Jacks. He regained focus. They needed to ease into the topic of the Glaring. He glanced at Kwame, who didn't seem to pick up the cue.

"How are Maarten and Annika?" Javier asked Kwame.

"Good."

"I'm glad to hear that. I heard what happened in Barbados."

No one spoke for a stretch. Jacks didn't know exactly what Javier was driving at, but he must've heard about the big cat attack at a Bridgetown bank. It probably made international news. Since Javier had spent time with Maarten, he also must've known Maarten berthed his boat at a yacht club on Barbados. Did Javier know they'd been involved in the incident, and that Annika had been killed?

"We heard about it too," Kwame said. "While we were staying in Margarita." He let some silence pass after that lie. "The rumor is the Glaring's little squad of troublemakers made their way down to South America."

"It wouldn't surprise me," Javier said. "The Amazon is the perfect place to hide." He revved up the engine, and the boat took off down the river at a fast clip again.

Kwame raised his voice over the engine. "How extensive has the organization become, do you think?"

Javier drew up his face equivocally. "No one knows for sure. Tepe's gang used to be just a group of street thugs. Their main crimes were fighting for territory in Amazonas border towns and revenge murders on poachers from Bolivia. A few years back, Tepe had a faction in Mexico that killed a crew of illegal loggers. There was also an incident with a drug cartel in Guatemala. The mareros burn the forests to make landing strips for airplanes.

"The attacks in the States, and now this one in Bridgetown is something new. It looks like the Glaring is out to make a name for themselves far beyond Central and South America."

"What do you know about Tepe?" Jacks asked.

Javier shrugged. "I never met him. I never met anyone who did. But every weregato in the Amazonas has a story about him. I heard he grew up in the slums of Macapá, Brazil, near the mouth of the Amazon, and he became a freedom fighter, like a weregato Che Guevara. An old acquaintance of mine claimed Tepe is the bastard son of Pablo Escobar and funds his operations by trafficking cocaine. I once heard he was a nineteenth-century maharaja, and he's known in his inner circle as Tiger Lord." Javier shot a glance at Kwame. "Bet you can guess where the guy was from who told me that."

Kwame smirked. "Guyana."

Jacks smiled as well. Regional werecats maintained their own regional pride. Guyanese werecats with their British and Indian ancestry would naturally favor a tiger legend about Tepe.

"Maybe he doesn't exist at all," Farzan broke in. "Like Keyser Söze in *The Usual Suspects*."

Javier laughed. "Could be."

Kwame stepped up beside Javier and got a spiral bound navigational atlas from a shelf beneath the console. He flipped through its pages of maps casually. "A lot of places for the Glaring to hole up."

"The Amazon rainforest covers 5.5 million kilometers and extends into nine countries," Javier said. "That's bigger than India. Only one quarter smaller than Australia. And it's one of the most sparsely populated areas in the world. There's no effective system of military surveillance. Most of the region is only navigable by rivers."

"You must have come across some of Tepe's freedom fighters from time to time," Kwame said.

"Not my sort of people. I'm sure the feeling is mutual. I bring white imperialistas into their turf for pleasure trips." He looked at Kwame. "But my clients are decent people. I get a lot of guys from Norway. People into eco-tourism. They're a lot more environmentally conscious than the locals."

Kwame gave him a sly grin. "Norwegians? Tall, blond, and handsome?"

"I try to separate business from pleasure."

"And the Glaring leaves you alone?" Jacks asked.

"I never had a problem. Since the attacks in the U.S., I don't take tour groups any farther than Parima Tapirapecó." Javier pointed the spot out on the map, a green expanse on the border of Venezuela and Brazil.

"You think Tepe's base of operations is farther south?" Kwame said.

"It would stand to reason. He would need a base secluded from the tourist routes." Javier took the atlas from Kwame with his free hand and flipped to a middle section. "Here, north of Boca de Anjo in Brazil, it's practically uncharted territory. But there are routes Tepe could use to send his operatives to other parts of the world. The Rio Purus will take you west into Peru and east all the way to access roads leading to the Atlantic coast. With off-road vehicles, it's not too far of a trek to an interstate to Bolivia. It's also a good location for a private airfield. The airplane tours out of Manaus and Iquitos don't pass anywhere near that region."

Jacks stood up and joined Kwame while Javier pointed things out on the map. To his eyes, most of the Amazon was a huge green gap representing a jungle no-man's land. He peeked at Javier. He was a generous host and naturally proud to educate them about his part of the world. He seemed entirely genuine.

"Why do you suspect that area in particular?" Jacks said.

"Boca de Anjo has always been notoriously ungovernable, like a Dodge City of the Amazonas. For a long time, it was the center for a Christian-Animist cult that used Ayahuasca for religious ceremonies. That brought in European and American drug tourists. I booked trips down there for clients who were interested in that kind of vacation. A few months back, I phoned my contact at a hotel in town, and he told me a distressing story. A group of German tourists was found mauled at their campsite. The hotels were closing up, and traffic in and out of the city was being controlled by some native militia that had deposed the mayor."

"You think the town's been taken over by the Glaring?"

Javier hesitated for a moment. "One has to wonder. I never reached my contact again, and now it's like the phones for every business I used to know down there have been disconnected. Along with the websites. It could be the work of guerillas or a drug lord, but that area around Boca de Anjo has no political value and it's far afield of any cocaine trafficking route that I'm aware of."

Jacks returned to his place beside Farzan. They had their answer to Tepe's location, and he was feeling as jumpy as when they had first set foot in Puerto Ayacucho.

THEY BOATED AS far as Rio Tomo, which was an inlet snaking through the Colombian countryside. Then Javier turned them around to head back to his house.

Javier and Kwame got to reminiscing about old times cruising around the Caribbean with Maarten. Exhaustion bore down on Jacks, and he drifted out of the conversation. He had been running on fumes for days. He laid down on the bench with his head on Farzan's lap, not quite catching up on sleep but at least resting his mind and body. Farzan kept a close eye on the clock on his phone. He had reminded Javier twice that they needed to catch the bus back to Caracas at five o'clock.

They arrived back at Javier's at 3:45. That gave them plenty of time for the short drive back to the bus stop, but Farzan said there was no harm in being early, especially since the charter bus service minded its own whims. While they stood around the back deck of the house, swigging bottled water, Javier invited them to stay over.

"You really want to spend another night cramped on a bus? I've got plenty of room here." He glanced at Jacks and Farzan. "You two can take the guest bedroom." He looked to Kwame. "You can bed with me. As long as you've overcome that snoring problem of yours."

"He hasn't," Farzan said.

Kwame caught Javier around his neck with his big arm in a playful gesture. Javier gave him a pinch in the ribs. It was clear there was a mutual attraction and maybe a history between the two guys.

"If you serve breakfast every morning like the one today, you might never get rid of me," Kwame said. He slid his hand inside Javier's unbuttoned shirt and tweaked his brown nipple.

Javier laughed and squirmed out of his grasp. He told Jacks and Farzan, "What do you say? We can make a run into town to get some beers and catch fresh fish for dinner. I don't have clients until the weekend. It will give me a chance to take you on a more extensive tour of the river."

"That's very generous, but we've got Maarten waiting for us in Caracas," Farzan said.

They needed to get back to work decoding the Báalam-Tet, but Jacks felt bad being so deceptive with Javier.

"Give him a call," Javier said. "I'm sure he wouldn't mind making port in Caracas for a couple more days. What's he got to worry about? He's got all the time in the world on his hands."

That was a tough point to argue. Maarten, a trust funder, didn't have a single obligation, and he would hardly begrudge Kwame spending more time to visit an old friend. Now they would have to come up with a lie on top of a lie? Farzan and Kwame were momentarily stymied too.

Javier's face brightened. "How about this? I'll call Maarten and invite him. He owes me. He's never even come down here to see my place."

Jacks glanced at Kwame. If Javier called Maarten, it would be truly disastrous.

Kwame captured Javier beneath his arms and walked him toward the house. "You owe me a tour of this famous house. Then we will see about settling up terms." He winked at Jacks, and then they disappeared inside.

"What are we going to do if Kwame wants to stay?" Farzan asked.

"They're just off for a quickie to say goodbye."

"How quick of a quickie?"

"Kwame's smooth. He knows we've got to make that bus. Too bad. They make a cute couple, don't you think?"

Farzan looked over at Javier's boat moored at the jetty. He brushed past Jacks in that direction. "C'mon."

Jacks followed him down to the shore. "What are we doing?"

"The map. You think you can fit it into your bag?"

"What? We can't just steal it from Javier."

Farzan pushed forward and stepped down the jetty to the screen door of the boat. Javier had covered up the deck in a collapsible tenting. Farzan unzipped the door and passed through. Jacks glanced back at the house. Everything seemed to be still while Kwame and Javier were presumably getting reacquainted. He followed Farzan on board.

Farzan found the console and pulled out his phone. "I'm getting reception. We're going to place a call to the U.S. to tell them where to find Tepe."

"Honey, this is kind of rude."

"You heard what Javier said. We've got a good location on the bastard. With the map, we can give coordinates. They could be slaughtering people in Boca de Anjo. The U.S. could send Green Berets or try to flush Tepe out with bad rock music like they did with Noriega in Panama."

The sheltered cabin was dark. Farzan fumbled around at the console to retrieve Javier's atlas.

"We can make the call when we're back on the road."

"Not if it's a dead zone. And the sooner we do it, the better." Farzan started tapping his phone.

Jacks raked his hand through his hair and clasped Farzan's hand. "All right. But let me make the call."

"I thought you were worried about the authorities coming after you."

"You've got family back there. They don't need to be put through an interrogation by some intelligence agency. You're supposed to be in Puerto Rico."

Farzan hesitated, then he handed him the phone. "There's a number in there for the N.S.A. See if you can get through the tips hotline to speak to someone high up."

Jacks tapped the call button and brought the phone up to

his ear. His heartbeat thudded in his chest. He understood the urgency, but he felt ridiculous calling the hotline.

A woman answered the phone. He took a dry swallow. "Hi. I've got information about the attack in New York last month."

The N.S.A. representative asked for his name. He hedged for a moment. He could hear keystrokes on a computer. It was risky, but he decided to tell the rep the truth. Being a fugitive from two murder investigations ought to get the government's attention. The woman took his name down and asked him what information he had.

"The big cat attack in New York...the terrorist group that's responsible...the same ones who attacked that bank in Barbados...they're called the Glaring, and they operate out of South America." Routinely, the N.S.A. rep told Jacks international matters were handled by another department. She told him to stay on the line while she switched him over. Farzan's eyes were glued to Jacks.

"She's putting me through to the international department." Jacks listened for stirrings back at the house. How long was the call going to take?

No more than a half minute later, a man picked up identifying himself as Agent Dickerson. He repeated the same questions, and Jacks answered accordingly.

"Their ringleader goes by the name Tepe. He has a base of operations in the Amazon, near Boca de Anjo in Brazil. I think they've taken over the town."

"Taken over the town?" Dickerson said. "What do you mean by that?"

"They shut down traffic in and out. Some German tourists were killed. Business owners have disappeared."

There was a long silence on the other end of the line. Then Dickerson's even, masculine voice came back. "Where are you, Mr. Cherokee?"

Jacks shifted around his weight. "Where am I?" he repeated, glancing at Farzan. Farzan shrugged helplessly. "I'm in Venezuela."

"When will you be returning to the country?"

"I, um, don't have any immediate plans to return."

"I'd like you to come to one of our offices," Dickerson said. "Can you get to the U.S. consulate in Bogotá?"

"Bogotá?"

Farzan gave Jacks the knife across the throat sign.

"No."

"What about Aruba?"

"No. Can't we handle this over the phone?"

"Mr. Cherokee, you're alleging to have information of vital importance to national security. Are you saying that's not worth your time to meet with the proper authorities?"

"No. That's not what I'm saying." Jacks took the atlas from Farzan and zoned in on Boca de Anjo. "Look, I gave you the name of the town. I've got it on a map here with latitude and longitude coordinates." Jacks wedged the phone between his ear and his shoulder so he could examine the map closely. "It says it's about 8 ½ degrees south and 67 ¼ degrees west. The Glaring is operating out of that vicinity. Can't you send people down there to check it out?"

Another long silence followed. Jacks didn't like that. It made him imagine a team of men standing around Dickerson with phone tracing equipment.

"This isn't like calling the sheriff to check out some old lady's house with a stack of newspapers piled up on her stoop," Dickerson said. "You're asking me to deploy an anti-terrorism unit to a foreign country in the southern hemisphere based on a hunch."

"You said it's of vital importance to national security."

"Mr. Cherokee, you're the one who's telling me it's of vital importance to national security."

Jacks didn't know what to say. He got that it sounded like a sketchy tip. But he wasn't about to walk into a U.S. embassy to be ambushed by government agents and extradited. Farzan stood off to the side chewing a fingernail.

"Listen," Dickerson said. "Take down my direct line and give it some thought. We'll make some calls to our contacts in the region in the meantime to see what's going on."

Jacks found a pen on the console. He didn't have anything to write on so he tore off a scrap of paper from a sightseeing brochure. After he had scribbled down Dickerson's number, he ended the call and put Farzan's phone in the pocket of his cargo shorts.

"I gave it a try," he told Farzan. "What else can we do?"

JAVIER SURRENDERED TO their plan to return to Caracas and drove them to the bus stop in town, looking a bit downcast about it. He barely spoke along the way.

He and Kwame had managed to fit in a quick shower and a change of clothes after their tryst, and maybe that brief encounter had left Javier feeling lonely. His cabin on the river was awfully remote, and Jacks supposed that besides his clients, he didn't get many people stopping by to visit. The silence made the trip awkward.

They climbed out of Javier's truck at the bus stop, and everyone thanked him for his hospitality. Naturally, the Carina Express bus was nowhere to be found for its five o'clock departure.

Kwame gave Javier a hug goodbye, and Jacks and Farzan stepped over to Javier to thank him. Javier barely hugged them back. With just a parting glance at Kwame, he stepped around the truck, and the driver's door squeaked open and slammed shut. The red Chevy pulled away and gunned down the road.

Strange, Jacks thought. Javier hadn't come across as a moody guy. Daylight was fading, and the entire block, not to mention the bus stop, was deserted. Perhaps other travelers knew the five o'clock bus never really came at five o'clock. With their sudden privacy, Jacks told Kwame about his call to the N.S.A.

"They had to have recognized my name. The guy was pushing hard to get me to an embassy."

"At least they'll make some inquiries into Boca de Anjo," Farzan said.

Kwame dug into the pocket of his cargo shorts and brought out a folded sheet of paper. "I made some inquiries of my own while Javier was in the shower."

Jacks did a double-take. Kwame had been snooping around the house? He didn't realize he was so sneaky.

Kwame unfolded the paper. "I was curious about Javier's schedule. He told me his business was thriving, but meanwhile this does not make sense. He has the entire week free on the occasion that we arrive to visit, unannounced. Near the start of the dry season and a popular time for tourists. I found his email on his computer. He canceled all of his bookings for the month just this morning. He departs for Lisbon tomorrow." He showed Jacks and Farzan a printout confirmation of a flight from Caracas to Lisbon.

Jacks didn't want to believe it. "He told us we could stay with him."

Farzan took the printout from Kwame. "He lied to us. And it's a one-way ticket. For someone who's not planning on coming back. For someone who wants to get out of town quick. The departure time is ten o'clock tomorrow morning."

"I asked him again about his plans for the week when he

came out of the shower," Kwame said. "He said his schedule was free until the weekend."

Cold prickles crept up Jacks's neck. "There could be an innocent explanation. Maybe he would have rescheduled the trip if we told him we were staying. Maybe he's got private business he didn't want to share. Like a sick family member. Or a boyfriend in Portugal." Even as Jacks said it, his last glimpse of Javier's face returned to him ominously. That hardened expression was the look of a man resigned to doing something desperate.

"It's too much of a coincidence, Jacks," Farzan said. He held the printout in front of Jacks's face. "Look at the date and the time of the transmission. Ten o'clock this morning. Right before he came to pick us up. Right after Kwame called to tell him we were in town."

Kwame looked at Jacks. "Javier was never someone secretive. It must be he was afraid of being caught with us or in some kind of danger. Either way, I don't like it."

Jacks felt like the air had been socked out of his lungs. Farzan shifted around, muttering nervously. "He knew we had just come from Barbados. There was nothing in the news identifying us. He had to have heard it from the Glaring. He was trying to delay us so they could get to us."

"Let's chill, okay?" Jacks jostled his backpack in his hand. "We've still got the Báalam-Tet. If Javier wanted to help the Glaring, he would have tried to take it." He gathered his thoughts. "We should keep on the move. When we get back to Caracas, we'll check out of the hotel and head someplace else."

A tense and thoughtful silence fell over them until Farzan's voice rose up angrily. "It's a fucking ghost town out here. Where's the goddamn bus?"

A distant rumbling down the road drew Jacks's attention. Not a single car had come by the main byway through town

where they stood, and they had seen no men on military patrol.
The source of the rumbling came into frightening focus. Less
than a quarter mile away, a line of Jeep Wranglers sped toward
them. They were sporty off-roaders, no government-issued
vehicles.

As the Jeeps drew closer, a familiar odor reached Jacks's
nostrils. Peat and wild animal musk. Werejaguars from the
Glaring, clearly on a mission to intercept them. Jacks looked at
Kwame. He had puffed out his chest, readying for danger.
There were four Jeeps, and probably at least two hunters in
each vehicle. Bella howled from her carrier like she was being
assaulted by a veterinarian's scalpel.

Jacks quickly searched the street. They needed somewhere
to blockade themselves. There were too many coming to
fight off.

The only store open was the mercado where Kwame had
called Javier. Jacks pointed to the store, and they hiked their
packs on their shoulders, grabbed Bella's carrier, and sprinted
for the door.

Once they made it inside, Jacks braced his back against the
door and shouted to the cashier at the store's single counter.
"We've got to lock and bar this."

Kwame barked Spanish to the young male clerk. The dark-
skinned kid was in his own world, listening to Reggaeton on his
phone. But as soon as he noticed Kwame charging his station,
he jumped and jerked out his ear buds. He took a quick
account of the situation and reached beneath the counter, bran-
dishing a semiautomatic pistol. Its barrel fanned across all three
men who had burst into his store.

Kwame threw up his hands and said something in Spanish.
Farzan froze, and Jacks stepped slowly away from the door,
showing he meant no harm. For a moment, it looked like the
young man was trying to understand, though he was fright-

ened. He waved his gun at the door and shouted at Kwame with his teenage voice cracking, "Fuera de mi tienda."

The team of Jeeps screeched to a halt in front of the store. The cashier swung a wild, bewildered look at Jacks and pointed his gun at his chest.

Cold sweat dripped from Jacks's brow. "No hacer daño."

"Say something to him," Farzan pleaded.

Kwame desperately tried to explain to the cashier. But it was too late. Hyped up voices and an aggressive tomcat stench closed in on the store.

"Run to the back," Jacks shouted.

Farzan ducked into an aisle. The cashier swung the gun in his direction and blasted out a shot that exploded into a shelf of canned goods behind which Farzan had disappeared. In that precious moment, Jacks grabbed Bella's carrier and fled down the aisle.

He crouched in a huddle with Farzan and Kwame, who had made a break for it as well. The door burst open, and a hail of gunfire shattered Jacks's ears.

When the cartridge was spent, a jaguar growl carved through the store. The cashier screamed. Claws scrambled on the floor and up the counter, and a wild animal frenzy overtook the cashier's agonized voice until the only sound to be heard was the tinny gangster rap from the kid's earbuds.

Farzan trembled against Jacks. He had buried his head in his hands and made himself small on the floor.

Jacks unlatched the gate of Bella's carrier. He couldn't get her and her carrier to safety. She scampered out and scurried into a backroom curtained by vinyl strips. Jacks locked eyes with Kwame. They needed to transform to defend themselves, but how would Farzan escape alive?

*The back entrance,* Kwame telepathized.

Jacks nodded. He could hear the werejaguars fumbling out

from behind the counter. They would sniff out their location in seconds. He grabbed Farzan's cold hand and eyed him steadily. "C'mon." The three of them sprinted to the vinyl strip doorway and ducked into the backroom.

Kwame navigated their way through stacked crates and cases of beer, reaching a metal fire door at the far end. Bella was already scratching at it.

Jacks and Kwame stopped to listen for a moment and tune into smells. Jacks heard movement from the way they had come. Kwame shoved open the door, and they staggered out in the waning daylight.

A black Jeep blocked their way. Two built dudes in utility pants and camouflage T-shirts were posted on the side of the vehicle. Each of them had long, wide-barreled handguns that looked like they held tranquilizer darts. Jacks saw a way around them but the close quarters would leave a slender margin of error.

He loosened the straps of his backpack. They had no choice but to transform and try to overpower them. In a blink, Kwame reared into lion form and charged one of the guys, burying him with his heft. Jacks bore down on the magical spot in his diaphragm that set off his cougar shift. Before he could pounce on his target, the guy fired a dart into one of Kwame's haunches.

Kwame snarled and curled his massive, furry head toward his attacker. He had mauled the other guy to the point where he was barely twitching beneath him.

Two werejaguars burst out of the backroom door. Jacks turned his cougar attention to the pair of beasts. Another bullet popped, and he saw Kwame had been hit by a second dart. He was swiping with his forepaw to dislodge the darts, but he looked panicked and clumsy.

Jacks growled ferociously at the werejaguars who had come

out of the store. He had to hold his ground and protect Farzan. He was just two-thirds their size, and meanwhile there was that guy behind him with an easy shot to sink a dart into his hide. The stocky werejaguars arched their backs with their fur bristling. From the right vantage, either one could easily tackle Jacks

A hue and cry erupted behind him. There was a tussle and then the dreadful sound of the dart gun again. Jacks turned back to that commotion. The Glaring marksman had shot Farzan and was wrestling him into the Jeep.

He leapt at the guy and brought him down by the shoulders. He managed to dislodge the dart gun from the guy's hands and send it tumbling under the car. But that was the opportunity the werejaguars needed. One of them dove for Jacks, shredding the flesh of his hind leg. He swerved back to the werejaguars, bearing his fangs. He had to protect himself from being ripped apart. He wouldn't be any use to Farzan dead.

He charged at the werejaguar who had attacked him, buffeting him back and swatting his fore claw across his muzzle. The werejaguar cowered from that wound for a moment. His buddy snarled and hissed, judging a way to engage Jacks.

Jacks needed to get himself and his friends out of the situation quickly. Two werejaguars might be possible to hold off, but more would be coming. Even if the cashier had managed to take out a couple with his gun, there had to have been at least six in total in the Jeeps that came up on the front of the store. Kwame was down, and Farzan was tranquilized halfway in the Jeep behind him.

Another worry hit him. The Báalam-Tet was in his discarded backpack. Jacks leapt to grab it in his jaws.

The Jeep door slammed shut, and the engine revved. Jacks swung back in that direction. Kwame's lifeless lion body was gone. The tranquilizer darts must have shifted him back to human form, and the Glaring henchman had stowed both Kwame and Farzan in the back of the Jeep.

The tires kicked up dust, and the Jeep lurched down the alley. Jacks bounded after it with his backpack in his mouth. He had to stop the driver and free Farzan and Kwame. Though his injured leg hampered his velocity, he trailed the Jeep for a good fifty yards. Then it swerved onto a paved road and picked up speed, leaving him galloping helplessly in its wake of dust and exhaust.

Chasing after the vehicle had given him some distance on the werejaguars, though Jacks could hear them gaining ground. From the main road, another Jeep careened into his path with its flood lights blaring into his eyes. He darted into an alley between a row of houses, accelerating from a flood of adrenalin. The desperate rush of his feline pursuers fell away behind him. It gave Jacks a moment to slip his forelimbs through the straps of his pack and nudge it over his head.

He didn't know his way through town. His friends were gone. Though he had temporarily given the Jeep the slip, the werejaguars were more of a threat. He knew they would follow his scent. They wouldn't give up stalking him to get their hands on the Báalam-Tet. Any domestics he came across would likely give up his location. Now the Glaring had Farzan and Kwame as barter. He didn't have time to wrap his brain around that disaster. He had to get himself to safety and work out a plan for another day.

Grasping for some bearings in his head, he worked out that he had headed in the direction of Javier's house. He could picture the route down the main road to the dirt drive through the river basin brambles, but main roads were the worst place for him right now. He would have to cut through alleys and yards and use an inner compass to guide him. He could also pick up the dank scent of the river as a marker.

He scurried over a cross street and cut through a soccer field. Some local boys were practicing by the lighted goalie cage at the far end. Night had fallen fully in that quick transition of equatorial climes, which gave Jacks some cover. Meanwhile, he heard the menacing sound of Jeeps barreling around the town's grid of streets.

Across the soccer field, he spotted a narrow pass between two aluminum-board houses. He skulked through and onward for another few blocks. The residential neighborhood gave way to a blackened, silty field dredged of river floodwater. That made for a starkly dangerous stretch, but Jacks could see the shadowy border of the woods along the river beyond it. He scanned in all directions. Sensing no sign of pursuit, he scuttled through the barren field.

As soon as he broke into the cover of trees, he reached out telepathically for Bella. He had lost track of her in the alley behind the store, but he trusted her good instincts. She had to have made it into hiding while the big boys were fighting. He got a read on her location and a telepathic image. She was squatting beneath a shed in town not far from where he had left her. He beckoned Bella to follow him to Javier's house.

He stalked through the brush, keeping to the denser parts away from Javier's drive. A plan came together in his head. Javier must have driven straight for Caracas to make that trip overnight and catch his flight to Lisbon. But he'd left his boat. Jacks needed to break into his house, find a set of keys, and motor his way upriver to some remote spot where he would be out of the Glaring's detection for a while. If he was lucky, he had put enough distance between himself and his pursuers. He had never captained a motorboat, so he needed some luck to figure out its workings as well.

He scaled Javier's fence. The pent up energy that had kept him focused was fading. His wounded leg throbbed, and his whole body ached. He took it slowly approaching the house. Every window was dark, and Javier's truck was gone.

He went around to the back deck. The house door was locked, but its glass panel looked breakable. He relaxed the spot beneath his diaphragm, enabling his shift back to human form. Morphing his mauled hind leg into a human limb hurt like hell. Jacks slumped over himself with cold sweat pouring down his back. He took deep gulps of air and looked around the deck. A discarded cinder block caught his eye. Before pain and exhaustion claimed him, he picked up the block and hurled it at the glass.

It shattered, and a home alarm blared, loud enough to attract attention from a mile away.

Fucking hell.

He grasped the door knob on the other side to unlock the door. Inside the house, he stepped through broken glass and scanned methodically for every likely location where Javier could have left the key to his boat. Nothing hanging on the wall. Nothing on the kitchen counter. Nothing in the kitchen utility drawer. Jacks limped his way to Javier's bedroom.

He searched a cabinet while the alarm kept blaring. Then he spotted Javier's computer desk, pulled out a drawer, and discovered a ring of keys. He grabbed it and made his way through the house to the back door.

Bella met him on the deck, staring up at him like he had lost his mind.

"You know a better way to break into a house?"

She followed him down to the boat. He untied and threw off the ropes from the jetty, and then he planted himself in front of the console, trying to remember how Javier had operated the vessel. He found the ignition key and gave it a turn.

Jacks motored backward into the river inlet, and then he grasped the steering wheel to angle the boat around. He brought the throttle down and ferried the boat out to the main channel.

He didn't know where the headlight switch was, but his night vision was keen, and he figured it might be better to travel beneath the cloak of night anyway. He gunned the engine, imagining an ever-stretching distance between himself and Puerto Ayacucho.

# FIVE

JACKS MOTORED UP the Rio Orinoco deep into the night. The way upriver was even less developed than what he had seen on the tour with Javier. Though instead of jungle brush, the banks were burrowed by sand dunes and thatches of shrubs. Beyond, the river plain was a wild, night-shrouded savanna.

Occasionally, he glimpsed headlights from a highway far inland on the eastern shore. That had to be the route the bus had taken from Caracas to Puerto Ayacucho. He didn't like the idea of traveling near a road where the Glaring's Jeeps could follow him. When he spotted an inlet to the west, he steered the boat that way.

It occurred to him he was headed into Colombia. What implications that had, he couldn't say. Neither country seemed to be particularly concerned about people crossing the river border in the wilderness. Unless the Glaring's pack of hunters had access to motorboats, traveling into Colombia would gain Jacks some time and distance on their pursuit. He hadn't seen a single bridge since leaving Puerto Ayacucho, and the Colombian backcountry looked to be uncharted by roads.

Beneath the drone of the boat's engine, the only sounds Jacks could detect were chirping katydids and croaking frogs on the riverbank. As the threat of the chase eased, worries about Farzan and Kwame crept in. Jacks had to believe the Glaring would keep them alive. They had brought tranquilizer darts, not guns. Their plan had been to not kill anyone until they had the Báalam-Tet. But what would Tepe do now?

Jacks would gladly hand the codex over to get his friends back. He had to find a way to negotiate with Tepe. For a delicate moment, his lungs heaved, and tears threatened to overwhelm him. He was ashamed of not being able to protect Farzan. He was ashamed of being so helpless.

The engine coughed and lurched. A flashing red gauge on the console warned that the fuel tank was empty. Now he was going to be stuck in the middle of nowhere.

Upriver, he spotted a truss bridge that had been halfway constructed to ford the river. The bank beneath its deck was as good a spot as any to beach his debilitated vessel. Marooned at a bridge to nowhere. That fit his situation perfectly. Jacks steered the boat toward the bank. He had seen a cable for an anchor when he had unhitched lines from the jetty. Once the hull caught on the sand in the shallows of the river, he cut the fading engine and traveled to the fore of the craft to release the anchor. It was meant for mooring in deeper water, but dumping the anchor on the river shoal did an okay job keeping the boat near the bank.

He climbed down to the boat's cabin and investigated its kitchenette. In a cabinet above the sink, he found a half a liter of rum and a tumbler. Jacks grabbed the bottle and the glass and sat down at the cabin's dining booth. Screwing off the cap of the bottle, he poured himself a drink and stretched out lengthwise in his seat.

The gouge in his leg bloomed pink, but the pain had started to numb. His werecat physiology made flesh wounds heal pretty quickly. Still, Jacks felt like he had been shattered to pieces that night. He gulped back two fingers of the rum and poured himself another double.

Bella came around and nestled into the crook of his arm. Jacks raked through her fur to calm her while he took long pulls of his drink. They would hole up in the boat and maybe get some sleep. His skull was like corroded metal webbing, barely holding his brain together after everything he had been through. All he could do was hope to wake up in the morning with some inkling of what to do next.

A TICKLING SENSATION against his leg shook Jacks awake. Cradled in his arms, Bella stared at him, wanting an explanation for being jostled from her slumber. Groggily, Jacks put together that Farzan's cell phone was vibrating in the pocket of his cargo shorts. He had never given it back after he called the N.S.A.

He dug his hand into his pocket to retrieve the phone. His first thought was that the Glaring was calling to collect their ransom. Farzan could have given them his phone number. Jacks felt like a fool for not having anticipated that. He had drank himself to sleep when he should have stayed awake for the kidnappers' call.

The call disconnected before he could answer it. The incoming number showed as a private caller. Jacks called back the number, and it went straight to a generic, automated voice-mail message in English. He sat up in his booth seat and carefully maneuvered Bella onto the table. "Hey, it's Jacks. Call me back."

That felt strange. But what was the appropriate message to leave for a terrorist holding hostages?

Diffuse light washed into the cabin from the steep stairwell to the deck. He remembered that the deck was covered with a screen, and he had beached the boat beneath a bridge. The phone clock read 10:45. The last slender bar of its battery flashed red. Jacks itched all over. When the phone died, so did his chance for contacting Farzan's captors. The charger for the phone was in Farzan's bag.

The boat rocked gently, and he heard the caw of shore birds. He went to look out from above deck to orient himself in the daylight. The phone buzzed in his hand just as he placed his foot on the first step of the stairs. He nearly dropped it in his jumpy state. "Private caller" flashed from the screen. He picked up the call.

"Hello?"

There was silence for a moment.

"Jackson Cherokee?" It was a man's voice and familiarly American. Based on the looks of all the guys who had ambushed him and his friends at the store, he had expected the Glaring's thugs to be South American.

"Yeah, it's me. Who's this?"

Another pause. "We've been looking to talk, Mr. Cherokee. How about we make some arrangements?"

"Where did you take Farzan and Kwame?" He knew he should be playing it cool, not giving away how desperate he was. He held the phone away from his face and sucked in a deep breath.

"Let's take it one step at a time," the caller said. "I need you to do a couple of things for me. Number one is to keep a level head. Can you do that, Mr. Cherokee?"

"What do you want? The phone's about to die, so hurry up."

"You're getting ahead of yourself, Mr. Cherokee. I need you to listen and follow a couple of simple instructions. The two of us have to trust each other here. You show me some trust, and I'll do the same for you."

Jacks bit down on his lip. He was nowhere near trusting the guy on the other end of the line. His phone warbled, reminding him that the battery had just about kicked. "What do you want me to do?"

"That's better. You and I are going to get along just fine. I can tell. The second thing is: I need you to get out of that boat you stole, unarmed."

How did the guy know he was in the boat? He drew up flush to one side of the cabin stairwell to try to peek out of the hatch. He had no angle to see anything beyond a few feet of the deck. The only thing that mitigated his paranoia was that he didn't smell werejaguars. But they could be scouting him from a distance, waiting to close in as soon as he stepped away from the boat. Maybe they wanted to lure him out so he couldn't make another escape.

But he was out of gas. He was totally trapped.

"Did you hear me, Mr. Cherokee?" the voice came back. "Step out of the boat. No guns. No weapons. That's the only way we're going to do this safely. If I've got to come to you in that boat, the outcome is going to be a whole lot more unpredictable."

"What about Farzan and Kwame? Are they with you? I'm not doing anything until I have a guarantee that the two of them go free, unharmed."

No answer came back right away. He heard a staticky voice in the background, which brought to mind an image of the caller wearing a headset, relaying information to another party.

"I'm afraid that's a no-can-do, Mr. Cherokee. I'm going to give you a chance to follow my instructions one last time. Come out of the boat unarmed. We've got a lock on your location, and the next step is to bring in a squad with a round of tear gas aimed at your cabin. It doesn't have to be like that. I just want to help you sort things out rationally."

His adrenalin spiked. That wasn't a bluff he could risk calling, was it? Jacks rifled through his backpack and brought out the Báalam-Tet. He could hide it in the waistband of his shorts with his T-shirt covering it in the back. In the kitchenette, he had seen a long-necked stove lighter. He grabbed it and stowed it down the front of his shorts. This would be his last stand. If the bastards wouldn't release Farzan and Kwame, he would burn the book to ashes.

Bella drew up at his feet, sensing the tension. He picked her up and gave her an urgent message. She was his one last hope for Farzan and Kwame's lives. He made her promise that if he didn't make it through this exchange, she would find them and help them escape. He told her to stay back in the boat until the coast was clear. He kissed her on the crown of her head. Then he climbed up to the deck.

The boat rocked gently as Jacks took a look around. The peacefulness of his surroundings was eerie. The river shore was deserted in all directions, just sand dunes with tufts of beach grass. No boats were on the waterway, and no roads could be seen on land. The worry was what might be waiting for him at the top of the steep escarpment that supported the bridge. He couldn't see anything up there from his position.

"How are you doing, Mr. Cherokee?" the caller spoke in his ear.

"I'm on the deck, going to the shore."

"Good."

Jacks stepped to the bow of the boat. Below was the shallowest place to disembark, though the drop down would still have him splashing into a foot of water. He climbed over the railing. Using his feline agility, he leapt from the bow onto a dry spot on the beach. He stood up from his crouch. Still no sign of anyone in the vicinity.

He was beneath the shade of the bridge. The only place for the caller to come out of hiding was above him. Based on his sense of smell, he still couldn't detect any werecats, though the morning was a bit blustery. He didn't smell any living thing except the shore birds. What the hell was going on?

"I'm out of the boat. What now?"

"I need you to climb up to the bridge. That's our rendezvous. You're doing great. Just get yourself up here, and we'll have a talk."

Jacks looked to the river escarpment, working out a good place to ascend. That blind approach had him worried. "You're alone, or have you got people with you?"

No answer. The fucking phone had kicked. Jacks tried to control his panicked breathing. He stashed the phone in his pocket. He had to go up to the bridge and make whatever sacrifice needed to be made for Farzan and Kwame's lives. He had to believe in miracles. The Glaring might ambush and kill him, but Farzan and Kwame might escape. Bella could help them. Maybe the Glaring would take him hostage instead of killing him. Could he somehow play up his knowledge about the codex?

He climbed up the bank to the top of the bridge. The vast and brilliant morning sky blinded him for a moment. There was no cover for miles, just shallow brush as far as he could see outward from the river bank. A dirt road led from the unfinished truss bridge into the infinite countryside.

A solitary figure stood at the far end of the bridge platform over the water, a sandy-haired man wearing sunglasses, a navy blue suit, a white button down, and a red tie. He had a Bluetooth device in his ear, and he mumbled some words into the receiver. The stranger wasn't from the Glaring unless, for some ridiculous reason, they had operatives who dressed like Secret Service agents.

"Mr. Cherokee," the man called out. "I'm Agent Dickerson. We spoke on the phone yesterday."

It had been less than twenty-four hours since he'd made the call, and the guy had found him? Through his cell phone? Jacks felt like he'd been stripped bare.

"What do you want from me?"

"I want to help you," Dickerson said. "You've got information of national importance. You've also got a hefty file with the New York City police, the FBI, and international authorities."

Dickerson pushed his sunglasses up to his crown of cropped, tidy hair. He stepped toward Jacks a foot or two, playing things like a companionable guy. "You're on Colombian soil now, Mr. Cherokee. The U.S. has full authority to take you back. You're not going to get away. But if you cooperate and let me take you into custody, we can work out something to make your problems go away."

That sounded like bullshit if Jacks had ever heard it. He held his ground. "The Glaring took two of my friends. Where are they?"

Now that Dickerson's sunglasses were off, he could see he was challenged by the question. Like he had no idea what he was talking about.

"We're going to take a trip together to a place where we can sort everything out," Dickerson said. "But we can only do that the nice, easy way if you follow my instructions. I asked you to come up here with no weapons."

He was looking at Jacks's shorts. The long stove lighter formed a bulge that looked like a concealed knife or possibly a pistol. Jacks sized up the situation. No way was he going anywhere with the federal agent. He had to free Farzan and Kwame. Even if Dickerson had tracked him down for information about their operations, he would be slowed up by an interrogation at the least. More likely, he'd be locked up while Farzan and Kwame could be getting tortured and possibly killed.

"You're making me antsy, Mr. Cherokee," Dickerson said. "I need you to take that weapon out of your shorts and place it on the ground."

Jacks glanced at the countryside. He could outrun the agent as a cougar. When he looked back at Dickerson, the guy was reaching for a gun holstered beneath his jacket.

Jacks pulled out the Báalam-Tet, clenched it in his teeth, and he bore down on his gut to burst into cougar form.

A gunshot pounded into the ground, inches from his hind foot. The rapid, freakish transformation must have thrown his aim off. Jacks charged inland with the codex clamped in his mouth, leaving Dickerson on the bridge. A second shot whirred through the air, lancing the underbrush on his right. He scrambled forward. No destination in mind. Just as far from the agent's range as he could get.

He heard the guy talking loudly into his Bluetooth. How long did he have until sharpshooters mounted on Humvees closed in on him from some hidden position? It looked like scrubby fields for miles, but he had to figure Dickerson came prepared with backup. He barreled through the field, not finding any hiding place up ahead. No woods. No country village where he could find someplace to hole up for a while.

An aircraft shrieked through the sky from a distance. Reflexively, Jacks tore faster through the underbrush, though he couldn't tell what direction the hostile aircraft was coming from. A familiar chopping sound gained up on him. It was a military helicopter, some state-of-the-art menace that could close distances in seconds. He sped into panic velocity, but the helicopter quickly shadowed him overhead with its whirring blades churning up a cyclone on the field.

He swerved from one side to the other, anticipating gunfire. He was like a rabbit caught in a giant's shadow, and the aircraft was pressing down on him. Military toughs shouted at each other in the cabin. A metal mesh net fell from the sky and buried Jacks. He wiped out in a tumble, feeling like the air had been socked out of his lungs.

More shouting broke out overhead, and then there was a pop, and a needle stabbed into his exposed haunch. The dart's tranquilizer stung through his flesh from that point of entry. The poison gripped his lungs, and he was out.

# SIX

JACKS BROKE OUT of a leaden sleep. His body was weak and dehydrated. Lifting his head brought on a wave of vertigo. Panicked, he looked around to sort out his surroundings, though the effort made him feel like he would vomit all over himself.

He managed to sit up and take some deep breaths, which tempered the dizziness and nausea. He had been stripped of his clothes, which he was usually able to teleport back on after his transformation. The tranquilizers had knocked that ability out of him. He was on a metal bunk bed welded to a concrete wall. A noisy, industrial air conditioning system saturated the room like a meat locker. He stood, but that quickly sent things into seasick mode again. The whitewashed prison cell spun and tilted in his vision. Jacks took some more deep breaths to hold things still.

He could nearly touch the wall across from him. Not far away, a seatless toilet and a tiny sink were installed in one corner. A third wall had a metal door with a service port and a slat viewing window, and no knob or handle. The back wall of the cell had a high window of thick, impregnable polyurethane, bringing filtered light into the room.

Jacks made fists to pump some strength back into his hands. He must be in some U.S. military detention center. Anger washed away the vestiges of the tranquilizer they had shot into his body. The fuckheads had no right to take him prisoner. He had contacted them so they could look into the Glaring's base of operations, but they were wasting their time with him.

He noticed a neat pile of clothes on the concrete floor by the door: a short-sleeved shirt and elastic waistband trousers, both in bright orange. The bastards had handled him naked to lock him up. They must have taken the Báalam-Tet.

He sprung to his feet, pressed up to the door, beat against its metal panel, and hollered. Looking out of the viewing window, he could see the door of a cell across from him and a small portion of a pre-fab barracks hallway. He shouted louder, beat harder against the door. He needed to find Farzan and Kwame. He had to convince somebody they had made a mistake taking him into custody.

The unsealing of a heavy gate and a hail of movement echoed down the hallway. Jacks stepped into the detainee pants and watched at the door window. A soldier in gray fatigues appeared and then a man in a navy blue suit. The service port slid open. It was big enough to slip a pair of hands through.

"Mr. Cherokee, you think you're ready to try some conversation now?"

Jacks couldn't see the man's face so well, but he recognized the voice. Agent Dickerson.

"Put your hands through the door. We'll get you cuffed and bring you out for some air and something to drink."

He held down some choice words. He had no bargaining chips, but he was still a cougar shifter. Getting out of the cell could give him an opportunity to escape. He shoved his hands through the port, and a pair of cold metal handcuffs were clipped around his wrists.

The door lock clanged free, and they let Jacks out into the hallway where the soldier braced him with ankle cuffs chained to the handcuffs. Smart on their part. Shifting while in shackles would be extremely painful at least, if not impossible. Jacks glared at Dickerson hatefully, but he didn't flinch. He gestured down the hallway toward a barred gate, and Jacks shuffled along between him and the soldier.

They passed through a guard's station and on to another metal door, which the soldier unlocked with a key from an old-fashioned ring. The place was not particularly high tech. He noted mounted security cameras here and there, but they were the kind that could be ripped down by their hinges from the ceiling. He didn't smell many people around.

Beyond the lockup, they entered an administrative wing with austere, military offices. They led Jacks down another hallway and out to a yard enclosed by a chain-link fence topped with barbed wire. A half dozen wooden picnic tables were scattered around the yard. Cigarette butts littered the grounds, which was more dirt than grass.

Dickerson took a seat at a picnic table and gestured to Jacks to sit across from him. That was impossible to do facing the guy. When Jacks parked his butt on the bench, the soldier came around and unlocked his handcuffs from his leg cuffs so that he could swing around.

Beyond the detention enclosure, he saw a garrison of military tents. Farther afield, the arid country landscape was not much different from the spot at the bridge where he had been captured.

"You want a bottle of water? Soda? Coffee?" Dickerson said.

"Water."

Dickerson glanced at the soldier, and the guy left. He leaned one elbow on the table and tried to catch Jacks's gaze.

"This your first time in a lock-up?"

Jacks scowled at him. "Yeah."

"I wasn't sure. Something about Jackson Cherokee sounds like an alias."

"Where am I?"

Dickerson sat back. "Tolemaido. It's a U.S. military base."

"Am I still in Colombia?"

"Yes, sir." Dickerson smirked. "You thought we hauled you back to the States? You've only been out for six hours."

Close up, Dickerson looked younger than Jacks had originally presumed. An Irish or British complexion. Slate blue eyes that took things in with precision and gave away nothing of his own thoughts and feelings. Not bad looking, though that Bluetooth pinned to his ear pretty much killed his prospects for being considered sexy. He was probably a military academy overachiever under thirty.

"You realize this is bullshit?" he said.

"How so?"

"I'm not a threat to national security. The people you're looking for, the ones responsible for New York and Bridgetown, they're in Brazil."

"The group you called the Glaring?"

"Yeah. I told you that over the phone. They're operating out of Boca de Anjo. Did you even check it out?"

The soldier came back with a bottled water and set it down in front of him. Jacks unscrewed the cap and lifted the bottle to his mouth with some limitation owing to his handcuffs. He chugged down half of it in one long draw and carefully placed the bottle on the table. Dickerson glanced at the solider, and the guy left them again.

"We're working on that tip, Mr. Cherokee," Dickerson said.

"The U.S. doesn't have quite the same partnership with Brazil as we have here in Colombia."

"What's with the Mr. Cherokee bullshit? Is that some kind of interrogation technique to make me feel like I'm back in high school?"

"What would you prefer to be called?"

"Jacks."

"All right, then. Jacks, what can you tell me about Benoit Guichard and a British national who went by the name Bernard Fahey?"

Jacks skirted his gaze. He was reminded of the possibility of double murder charges. Bigger than that, his shifter nature would make him the subject of scientific investigation. It had been easy to forget for the past few days that 99.9 percent of the world didn't know about feline shifters. Things that were normal for him had to be totally bizarre to Dickerson. Now, Jacks wondered if his bottled water had been spiked to make him pliable to questioning. Nothing about the world felt predictable.

"This is the problem, Jacks," Dickerson said. "We've got a promising informant, but he happens to be a fugitive from two murder investigations. Do you recall a pair of NYPD detectives by the names of Robbins and Faraday?"

Jacks said nothing. They had interrogated him after Benoit's murder. They hadn't had any evidence to arrest him since the murder scene had looked like a big cat attack, but he knew they had been suspicious of his vague account as a witness.

"They remember you real well. And given that both Guichard and this guy Bernard were mauled by a big cat, and you got caught by my team hauling ass on all fours, the feds are not particularly keen on giving you a free pass from the investigations."

"One thing has nothing to do with the other. Don't you see? The Glaring organized those attacks in New York and Bridgetown. They're the U.S. security crisis. They kidnapped two people in Puerto Ayacucho. One of them is a U.S. citizen. Why aren't you investigating that?"

Dickerson maintained his infuriating composure. "You're talking about Farzan Mohammed?"

"Yes."

"That's the guy you were living with in Richmond Hill at the time of Guichard and Bernard's murders? Who left the country to meet you in Barbados?"

A cold curtain fell over Jacks. He had to shut down. Should he ask for a lawyer? Did he even have that right? But he didn't have that kind of time. Jacks had to free Farzan from the Glaring. What if they had already hurt him?

Dickerson brought out a wallet-sized notepad from his pocket and paged through it. "Mr. Guichard's holdings at the Beechfield Bank of Barbados were claimed by a Donovan Heathcliff on August 29th." He set down his notepad. "You want to tell me how a passport and a bank card under that name ended up in the wallet you were carrying in your shorts?"

Jacks bounced his knee under the table. He said nothing. Dickerson took up his notepad again. "We found a Donovan Heathcliff on a flight manifest for American Airlines, JFK to Bridgetown, the morning of July 27th. Farzan Mohammed, we've got on flights from Albany to Miami and Miami to Bridgetown on August 19th."

Dickerson flipped another page. "Both guys booked rooms at the Primrose Guesthouse, about twenty miles outside of Bridgetown. Neither one has been seen since the morning of August 29th." He looked up at Jacks. "The 29th being the day wildcats went berserk at the Beechfield Bank of Barbados, where Mr. Guichard had accounts totaling fifteen million dollars and a safety deposit box."

They held a silent standoff. Jacks had to give Dickerson credit for keeping everything procedural. A series of shifter attacks must have aroused disbelief and terror. Had he underestimated the guy's knowledge of shifters? He wasn't sure if that made things better or worse.

Dickerson broke the silence. "You want us to nail the Glaring? You're going to have to level with me, Jacks. Because right now I've got a half dozen U.S. agencies and the Barbadian Department of State telling me the number one priority is to haul you in for criminal charges."

With his arms unchained from his ankles, could he morph and make a leap over the barbed wire fence? No one appeared to be watching him besides Dickerson, and he had only seen a few guys in fatigues traveling around the grounds of the military base beyond the fence. A barrier wall enclosed the perimeter of the base, and no doubt it was guarded in places by soldiers with rifles. They also had that hellish helicopter to pursue him. But even if he got killed trying to escape, at least he would have tried to save Farzan. Otherwise, he was headed back to lock-up and eventually a laboratory for study and experimentation.

The brown hills in the distance called to him. A beep and a staticky voice interrupted his thoughts. Dickerson turned in his seat and spoke into his Bluetooth. Jacks scoped out the fence for a workable route with the least amount of barbed wire.

Before he could shore up the courage to shift, Dickerson ended his call and faced him.

"A colleague of mine just arrived on the base. I think he's someone you'll want to meet." A smug phase passed over the agent's face. "He'll probably have more luck getting through to you."

Jacks didn't like that. As seconds ticked by, dread accumulated in his veins. It started with a faint whiff of wild cat musk. There was a tom, somewhere on the base, and by the strength of his scent, he was closing in. Jacks glanced around. He was hardwired to loathe other cats with which he was not familiar. It was fight or flight, and given his restraints, he'd be dead in seconds through either option.

Dickerson stood up from the table to greet someone coming through the door of the yard. Jacks swung around. He saw a tall, well-built guy with silky, black hair pulled back in a ponytail, wearing the same G-man uniform as Dickerson. A werecat federal agent?

"Jacks, meet Agent Sowanake," Dickerson said. "Sowanake, this is Mr. Cherokee. But he prefers being called Jacks."


THE U.S. GOVERNMENT knew about werecats. They had even hired at least one. Jacks couldn't wrap his brain around what that meant in terms of his prospects for getting help rescuing Farzan and Kwame. On the face of it, maybe the situation was encouraging.

But just as his feline instincts told him to distrust other werecats, his human instincts had always been hardwired to distrust authority. A crazy conspiracy occurred to him. What if the U.S. government was in league with the Glaring? That was the kind of nightmare you had to consider when you had been hunted down, shot with tranquilizer darts, and restrained with hand and ankle cuffs.

Sowanake took a seat across the table from him. He had unmistakably Native cheekbones and russet undertones in his complexion. Tattoos peeked out from the cuffs of his shirt and his collar. Every species of cat had a distinct odor, from the earthy jasmine of werelions to the swampy peat of werejaguars.

Jacks couldn't place the guy's ancestry at first. Besides his sharp tom scent, he seemed to have no odor at all.

Then it hit him. The guy's family scent was so similar to his own, it nearly passed right by him, a sort of musky sage. He had never met another werecougar before.

"How are you doing, Jacks?" Sowanake said.

Jacks reached to rake his hair back on a nervous reflex, but he couldn't do it with his cuffs. He snorted absurdly. "Right about now, I've got no fucking idea."

"You've probably got a lot of questions."

"I do. But the problem is, I don't have time for them." He stared firmly at the agent. "My boyfriend was dragged away by the Glaring. There's nothing going to happen here until you let me out of this place so I can find him."

"We want to bring him back safely as well. We're on the same side, Jacks. But we need your cooperation."

Jacks scowled. "How are we on the same side?" His eyes flared with rage. "I was shot down with a dart gun and caged in a cell by your buddies."

Sowanake rapped his fingertips on the table, betraying a chink in his composure. Ferociousness rose up in Jacks. He telepathized to Sowanake: *I want to rip out Dickerson's throat. I want to kill every goddamn person on this base before I break the fuck out of here.*

The agent glanced away, formulating a new tactic. "Jacks, you're not going to threaten me. And no one's giving clearance for you to run free. We know you've got valuable information about the Glaring. We can work together to rescue your boyfriend. The sooner you tell us about what happened with Benoit Guichard, Bernard Fahey, and the situation in Barbados, the sooner we can proceed."

Jacks noticed the American flag pin on the pocket of Sowanake's jacket. Though it was a sultry day, his jacket was closed, probably hiding recording equipment. "Why?" Jacks said. "Tell me that. What could make it worth it to you to work for people who committed genocide and put us in reservations? People who hunted down our shamans to extermination?"

Sowanake came back at him, unchastened. "How are you making the world a better place, Jacks? By running fugitive from two murders and cleaning out your ex-boyfriend's bank account?"

"I acted in self-defense and to try to get ahead of what the Glaring is doing. You think your friends would have given me a fair hearing? What world are you living in?"

"*I'm* giving you a fair hearing."

"You're a real stand-up guy. So, this is just you and me here, and I'm imagining all the barbed wire and the guys walking around with rifles."

"I can help you, Jacks. It's a complicated situation, but the feds are willing to work with you if you tell us what happened."

*All this is being recorded, right? So they can nail me as soon as I break?*

"It's standard agency procedure," Sowanake said. "You don't get any special treatment because the two of us happen to be werecats."

Jacks scoffed at that. He had a feeling that Sowanake had never been the sort of guy to give special treatment to any of his werecat kind. A traitor. Somewhere between desperation and wanting to throw hot oil in the guy's face, Jacks let it all go.

"All right. I killed Benoit. I killed Bernard. I don't give a shit about what the feds want. So you can tell that to your boss, Dickerson, and he can get on with the gas chamber, or maybe you'd prefer for the two of us to have it out like we do in the wild so you can impress your buddies." He added with a sneer. "Though I doubt you've got the balls for that."

"What were you going to do with the Báalam-Tet?"

"Trying to keep it away from the Glaring, you fucking idiot."

Sowanake sat back from the table with a bedeviled grin. "This charming attitude of yours go over well with the boys? Bet you had them beating down your door back in New York."

That clever jab disarmed him for a moment. It wasn't homophobic. It was more like a pal-to-pal sort of dis, which got Jacks thinking that maybe Sowanake was gay, too. In a blink, Jacks despised him even more. "What's the point of this? Dickerson brought you in to get a confession out of me? You got it. And right now, two people are being held hostage, and the only way they're going to make it out alive is if their kidnappers hear from me. You all are pretty good at tracking people down. So how 'bout letting me save some people who are no threat to anybody, and you can fucking televise my execution afterward."

"You think you can negotiate with the Glaring alone?"

Jacks bounced his knee beneath the table again. He looked up at Sowanake. "I don't know. But you've got to let me try. You tell me you're just going to keep me here, doing nothing, I might as well take a leap for that barbed wire, praying for gunshots. I can't—" Tears of helplessness welled up in Jacks. He turned away from Sowanake, trying to withstand the thought of Farzan being hurt.

Sowanake stepped around the table. "I know what you're dealing with, Jacks. The Glaring has been on Homeland Security's radar for the past two years. That's why they brought me in. Their ringleader Tepe is at the top of the F.B.I.'s most wanted list. He's a merciless and indiscriminate killer. Before his night of terror in New York, there were several other incidents we kept out of the media. Yosemite Park, August 2010. Eight families of campers killed in one night. Marianna, Florida, July 2011. Fourteen people killed heading home from a fireworks display on July Fourth. That's minor compared to what Tepe's Glaring cells have done throughout Latin America.

"Tepe is an expert at being elusive. We've barely made any progress tracking him. Our best try was recruiting a werecat civilian to infiltrate his organization. Six weeks in, our guy ended up double-crossing us. Radicalized by Tepe's propaganda. He called in an operation in Baja California. Said he had a location in the desert where Tepe was passing through. It was a bloodbath. Twenty-four Special Forces soldiers were killed. I was lucky to make it out. If anyone wants to take Tepe down as much as you, it's me."

Jacks looked up at him through blurry eyes. "I don't care about revenge. I just want to save Farzan and my friend Kwame."

Sowanake reached across the table and gripped his shoulder. "Let's figure out a plan then."

LATER THAT NIGHT, they brought Jacks into a conference room in the military base. Twenty-some federal agents and military officers sat in front of laptops at a long, oval table. A dozen others had video-conferenced in from other locations, creating a mosaic of talking heads on the room's big screen. Jacks was ushered to a seat between Dickerson and Sowanake. A military general named Gainsway helmed the meeting.

He tried not to bug out from how surreal the situation was, not to mention how shoddy he looked in an orange jumpsuit. They had brought him in without restraints, but he was still a flashing neon sign: werecat detainee. He was startled to recognize some of the people on the screen, like a ruddy-faced guy with an unfortunate comb-over who was the Secretary of Defense, and a middle-aged Black woman with a tidy helmet of hair and a pearl necklace who was the president's Chief of Staff.

Gainsway handed the floor to Dickerson, who had put together a presentation. Based on Jacks's tip, they had done some surveillance on Boca de Anjo, and Dickerson's slides included satellite images. It looked at first like the little tropical village had been abandoned after a hurricane. The streets were barren, and storefronts and windows were boarded up. Cars on the streets had been picked over for scrap.

Dickerson said the two ways into town had been bunkered: the first, a bridge over the Purus River, and the second a road to a highway through the Amazon rainforest. Drones had taken photos of guerrillas guarding those byways. Dickerson said the Brazilian president denied any incidents in the region. But the families of two college students from the University of Denver were petitioning Washington to find their sons, who had been to Boca de Anjo in July. State departments in Britain, Australia, Chile, Denmark, and Germany had all received requests to investigate missing persons who recently visited the town.

Jacks looked away when an image of a mass grave appeared on the screen. "This is a photo from yesterday, 5:30 p.m., at a schoolyard on the edge of town," Dickerson said. "Based on the decomposition of the bodies, we can place the Glaring's siege at two to three weeks ago, mid-August. We can also safely assume most of the residents and the tourists in town were lost."

A series of photos of mini-trucks and Jeeps passed over the screen. "The dissidents are supplied by the Fronteras drug cartel in Bolivia. Light artillery and anti-aircraft missiles. Meat and bottled water. Basic hygiene supplies. In return, the Glaring provides Fronteras with a cocaine trafficking route through uncharted riverways and roads in the Western Amazon. The drugs head to Ecuador and onward to Southern

California and Asia by plane and boat. Our colleagues at the D.E.A. estimate that two-thirds of the North American cocaine supply originates from Fronteras's plantations."

Jacks recalled Javier's supposition that the Glaring had alliances with drug lords. The scope of the organization was staggering.

A grainy photo of a bearded man in a snap cap came on the screen. "Some of you will remember this photo of Tepe," Dickerson said. "Though it was taken by an operative who later went rogue, we believe it's the only reliable image of the man who heads the Glaring organization."

Jacks stared at the photo. The man looked thirtyish or fortyish? Latin or possibly Asian? It was hard to make out much from it. Dickerson cued up a new slide that showed a two-story, concrete hotel with a wraparound balcony. A man in guerrilla fatigues, carrying a rifle, patrolled the grounds.

"This is the Hotel Tropical on the northside of Boca de Anjo. It's the town's biggest structure. It was its largest hotel before the Glaring took over. We believe it's the organization's center of operations and Tepe's residence."

Dickerson looked over the room. "We have a rare window of opportunity to strike Tepe's location. For over ten years, he's been notoriously elusive and enigmatic, engineering attacks around the globe by sleeper cells that disappear without a trace. Recent intelligence indicates he's holed up with hostages in order to retrieve a lost artifact he tried to acquire from the Beechfield Bank of Barbados. That artifact is now in our possession. And with the help of Mr. Jackson Cherokee, we can arrange a hostage negotiation that will give us access to the most wanted criminal in the world."

The Secretary of Defense was the first to raise a question. "Captain Dickerson, can you take us through how your proposed operation would proceed?"

Dickerson clicked forward to a map of the surrounding region. "For the integrity of the mission, Mr. Cherokee will need to make the negotiations and enter the compound unescorted. The safety of the hostages is a prime concern. We start by airlifting Mr. Cherokee to Pucallpa, Peru. He will drive into Brazil and enter Boca de Anjo via the Purus River Bridge. Tepe has never seen the artifact, so Mr. Cherokee will carry a counterfeit. We'll have drones to monitor the exchange. As soon as Mr. Cherokee and the two hostages return to the bridge unharmed, we'll launch an airstrike from Pucallpa that will take out Tepe and his base of operations. General Gainsway has already mobilized a force of Apache missiles and stealth fighters from the Navy's nearest fleet of aircraft carriers in the Pacific. A reconnaissance chopper will meet Mr. Cherokee and the hostages on the other side of the bridge to bring them safely back to Pucallpa."

"Who are the hostages?" the Madam Chief of Staff, Myrna Diallo, asked.

"One is Mr. Farzan Mohammed, a U.S. citizen and a medical student from New York City," Dickerson said. "He was traveling with Mr. Cherokee when the Glaring attempted to take the artifact in Puerto Ayacucho, Venezuela." Dickerson glanced at Jacks. "The other is a French national who goes by Kwame. Also a traveling companion of Mr. Cherokee's."

"Has the French Directorate-General been informed?" Ms. Diallo said.

"No, madam," Dickerson said. "Our understanding is that Kwame has not been a resident of France since the early 1990s." He looked at Sowanake, seeking some support. "Like many of his kind, he abdicated nationality and lives his life off the grid."

Ms. Diallo frowned. "Still, don't you think it would be appropriate to notify the French?"

Dickerson nodded and looked to one of the military officers who was typing notes on his keyboard. "We'll make arrangements directly."

"What communications have been made with the Brazilian president?" Ms. Diallo said.

"His office is disinterested in anything related to Boca de Anjo," Dickerson said. "As you are aware, the Bolsonaro regime disavows the existence of the Glaring, which they say is a conspiracy dreamed up by their socialist political opponents. But we received assurance from the Brazilian National Central Authority any action against the dissidents will be uncontested. A report from the director of the CIA suggests Bolsonaro is just as eager as we are to get rid of the Glaring, but he won't go on public record to acknowledge his massive security failure. Nor does he want to give political fodder to the far left faction in the Congreso Nacional, which has voiced some sympathy for the Glaring's efforts to thwart international real estate developers in the Amazon."

"What is this artifact that is the subject of the hostage negotiations?" the Secretary of Defense asked.

Dickerson gestured to Sowanake. "I'm going to defer to Special Agent Sowanake on that item. He's been our expert on shifter ethnography for the past two years."

Jacks studied the faces around the table and on the screen as Sowanake stood to address the room. Besides a collegial smile from Dickerson, the men and women regarded the werecat agent with a touch of morbid curiosity. Dickerson had talked about the Glaring in the routine language of counterterrorism. Did the U.S. military understand their enemy? Did they prefer to skirt around the fact that they were dealing with a non-human threat?

"Secretary McCuthers, the artifact is called the Báalam-Tet," Sowanake began. "It is a codex written in Olmec hieroglyphs. This ancient book was believed to be a folk legend until it was brought to us yesterday by Mr. Jackson Cherokee."

The Secretary broke in. "Olmec? As in prehistoric Mexico?"

"Yes."

"So, what is the codex?" the Secretary said. "Another Mayan doomsday calendar?"

A gale of nervous laughter fluttered through the room.

Sowanake smiled graciously. "We are in the process of having it studied by an expert in Mesoamerican archeology. Dr. Philip Reyes from Arizona State University has agreed to help us with the translation. With Mr. Cherokee's permission, the Báalam-Tet will stay in the care of the U.S. Department of State while its contents are analyzed and transcribed."

"That is to say, you don't know what it is," McCuthers said tartly, frowning. "I suppose it doesn't matter. If Dickerson's operation is successful, we'll have the book in hand and have eliminated Tepe." McCuthers shuffled through some papers in front of him. "But with regard to Mr. Cherokee, we read in your report that he acquired the book from the Beechfield Bank of Barbados, claiming to be the sole successor to a Mr. Benoit Guichard." He looked up from his notes. "I understand that it is your proposal, and Captain Dickerson's, that Mr. Cherokee be granted temporary clemency from a long list of state and international criminal investigations. You are suggesting that our return on that gamble will be the elimination of our greatest threat to national security. That would appear to be a compelling argument. But I would like to hear from Mr. Chero-kee. What is your speculation on why Tepe wants this book, the Báalam-Tet, so badly?"

Jacks cleared his throat and chose his words carefully. "We won't know exactly what's in the Báalam-Tet until it's exam-ined by an expert. But it's pretty obvious that Tepe's mission is to exterminate humans. The book must have instructions on gaining more power to do so."

The room fell silent. He chose not to explain the Sim Ru prophecy. Probably, most of the heads of state and military higher-ups would think it was bullshit, but if they believed him, he didn't trust what they might do.

A fiftyish white guy in a business suit broke into the discussion from the video-conference screen. "General Gainsway, this is sounding like a delicate operation. You'd be sending a civilian into an enemy camp to negotiate the release of hostages who may be injured or even incapacitated. What contingencies do you have in place?"

"First and foremost, Senator Newsome, we will attempt to conduct the exchange on neutral ground. What Captain Dickerson has laid out is a Plan B, if you will, based on our best guess on the terms which Tepe will offer. But we'll be able to monitor the situation and tailor a response accordingly. If the exchange does not proceed as planned, we'll be able to shell the site to create a chaos scenario in which Mr. Cherokee and the hostages can escape. No missiles will be launched on Tepe's compound until we have confirmation the civilians have safely removed themselves from the building."

The Madam Chief of Staff spoke. "Has there been communication with Mr. Mohammed's family?"

"Our position is that communication is not indicated at this time," Gainsway said.

"Could you elaborate on that?"

Gainsway glanced at Dickerson, nudging him to respond. "Madam Chief, officially, Mr. Mohammed is a suspected accomplice to Mr. Cherokee's activities, which are under investigation by the F.B.I. Our intelligence is that Mr. Mohammed has not had any contact with his family for several weeks. They believe he's engaged in a medical internship in the Caribbean."

"So, they don't know that he's been kidnapped?"

"That's correct. He'll be debriefed after the operation, and we'll proceed with communications with his family, corresponding to his disposition."

Jacks thought he saw the slightest glint of fearful knowledge passing over the Chief of Staff's face. "We'd like to be kept up to date on that."

"Of course, Madam Chief," Gainsway broke in. "The entire mission will follow a top-level security protocol. Every partner has a stake in handling the matter with discretion. The highest imperative here is conducting the operation as though it never happened."

Jacks was sure there were contingencies not being spoken about. Should Farzan be killed in the strike, the military would have a story for his family, some spin on the events to cover up their failure to protect him. The hostage negotiation wasn't much more than a pretext for destroying the Glaring. The military wanted revenge for the ambush in Baja California. His own life hardly mattered to anyone. He was an outlaw of no value. Farzan and Kwame were pretty much the same.

But to have a chance to free them, well, Jacks had to grasp it. He was a detainee, and several of the high ranking officials at the conference looked like they would prefer to nail him to a cross for the unsolved murders in New York. It's not like he had another choice.

# SEVEN

AFTER THE MEETING, Dickerson and Sowanake took him to a small interrogation room for a low-level briefing on the next steps of their operation. Then Dickerson handed Jacks the cell phone they had confiscated. He wanted him to use it to contact Tepe.

Jacks stared at Farzan's phone like it was booby trapped. Based on Dickerson's high tech work to track him down in Venezuela, he had no doubt they pulled out the call history, voicemails, searches on its browser, and everything else stored in the SIM card. Both Dickerson and Sowanake put on Bluetooths so they could listen in on his call.

He sat at a table with Dickerson while Sowanake stood off to the side. Dickerson showed him a voicemail from 10:58 that morning. Dickerson had contacted him around 10:45, and since then he had been in custody. The kidnappers had just missed him.

The hairs on his forearms stood up as he listened to the message. The caller said he was Tepe himself. His voice was deep and authoritative, and his English was tinged with a Brazilian accent.

"Bring us the Báalam-Tet. You have twenty-four hours."

His hand trembled, and he fumbled redialing the number. They'd already had a practice run-through, but now he had to make it sound perfectly convincing. Farzan and Kwame's lives depended on it.

After three rings, someone picked up. It was a man's voice, but not the one he heard on the voicemail.

"It's Jacks. I'm calling about the Báalam-Tet." An exchange ensued in the background. Spanish or Portuguese. His heartbeat drummed in his ears so loudly, he couldn't tell.

Another man took over the conversation. "You're running out of time, Jackson Cherokee. Did you go to the authorities?" The voice was as halting as a feline growl, so aggressive, it seemed to reach inside his head to grasp his thoughts. Jacks licked his lips and cleared his dry throat.

"I've got what you want. But I need to know that Farzan and Kwame are alive."

"You didn't answer my question."

"It's just me."

"Where are you, Jackson?"

He exchanged a glance with the agents. "I needed to get settled. That's why I couldn't call earlier. How are we doing this? You coming to me?"

That made Tepe pause for a moment. Jacks eased back a little in his seat. Keep him off balance. Toss him a question for a question. That had been Dickerson's coaching.

"You really are an arrogant fool," Tepe said. "We have your mate and your best friend. Which would you like delivered back to you first wrapped up in butcher's paper?"

A sharp pang of fear sunk into his stomach. Maybe he wasn't so good at this. Sowanake hovered at his side.

"You'll never see the Báalam-Tet if you hurt them. I'll take it straight to whoever wants to use it against you." He drew in some confidence. "After you fucked things up in Bridgetown, you've got a whole lot of people looking for you. You won't stay under the radar for long. You need the book. All I'm asking is to set my friends free."

Dickerson gave Jacks a thumbs up.

A cold chuckle fizzed from the phone. "You still think humans are your friends, don't you, Jacks?"

"We meet on neutral ground. Colombia or Peru. Take your pick."

Tepe came back at him forcefully. "You do not tell me anything. You bring me the book, and we'll see about your friends going free."

"That doesn't sound like a good deal for me. Why should I bring you the book if I don't know you'll keep up your end of the bargain?"

*You don't, Jacks. But you haven't any choice, do you? You killed the only person who could protect you.*

Jacks shut his eyes, trying to expel Tepe from his head. It felt like fighting a demon trying to take possession of his mind and body. All werecats could telepathize, but Tepe's ability was more powerful than any he had experienced, even Benoit's. They were something like 1,000 miles apart, connected by a cell phone signal, yet Tepe could bore into his head as easily as a werecat could control a domestic.

"Where?" Jacks said. Mercifully, speaking out loud seemed to break their mental connection.

"We'll text you instructions. You have until eleven o'clock tomorrow morning."

Jacks looked at his companions helplessly. Dickerson rolled his hand for him to keep Tepe talking. "You don't even know where I am. I'll need time. To rent a car. I don't know how long it will take me to drive to you."

Tepe sucked his teeth, hissing through the receiver. "Unless you turned to the U.S. for help, like a coward, you can't have made it far from Puerto Ayacucho. How soon can you get the Caracas airport?"

The agents stared at Jacks. He knew he had to bide for time. "A day, at least."

There was a brief pause on the other end of the line. "I have more faith in you. Make it twelve hours. We'll send you an itinerary from Caracas. We'll be watching you, Jackson. Any sign of interference, and we'll be feasting on your mate's liver. Good night."

"Wait. I won't do anything unless you put Farzan on the phone."

Tepe hesitated. In a burst of rage, Jacks sent his voice traveling on a missile sharp psychic course across the miles into Tepe's head. *Put him on the phone or I'll destroy the book right here and now.*

It sounded like the phone was muffled. Sweat dripped down his brow. He needed to hear Farzan, but when that voice finally came, Jacks shrank inside.

"Jacks, is it you? Jacks, I'm scared. I don't want to die."

AFTER THE CALL, Dickerson and Sowanake paced around, discussing their next move. Jacks stared down at the table. He hadn't even had the chance to tell Farzan he loved him. The phone had cut off seconds after Farzan's voice registered. Had he been beaten? Had the bastards tortured him? He wasn't sure if he could handle his emotions. One million times he wished it was him instead of Farzan being held hostage.

He was distantly aware of the agents' discussion. A series of text messages had chimed in, and they were poring over them and studying a map stretched out on the table. Periodically, Dickerson called in questions on his Bluetooth to a communications unit in another part of the compound.

"This is going to be tricky," Dickerson was saying. "He's got you on an itinerary from Caracas to Manaus, Brazil, and then to a little town in the Southern Amazon called Porto Velho. That's a lot of places they could intercept you." He rechecked the screen of Farzan's phone. "Tepe wants you on a flight from Caracas at 9:30 tomorrow morning. It doesn't give us time to get men on the ground at each airport."

"It's suicide," Sowanake said. "They'll know where he is every step of the way." He pointed to the map. "Besides, Porto Velho is a long trek through the jungle to Boca de Anjo. Bringing him to their headquarters might not even be their game, let alone releasing hostages."

Dickerson drummed his fingers against his sculpted chin. "I don't think so. It's a plan designed to throw off interference. Look at the map. Porto Velho is the nearest town with an airport in relation to Boca de Anjo. But they don't know we know Boca de Anjo is where they're hunkered down. It's far enough away to escape attention. There's thousands of acres of jungle around Porto Velho where they're picking him up. They're protecting their location, making us guess where they're taking Jacks from the last place he lands."

"They've got us thrown off from the point of Manaus," Sowanake argued. "They could be waiting to intercept him there."

Dickerson shook his head. "Look at the time frame. It's almost eleven o'clock. Jacks will be in Manaus by 11:30 tomorrow morning. Unless they've got private aircraft, they could never make it all the way to Manaus by then. It's a two, maybe three day drive from Boca de Anjo."

"They don't need private aircraft. They've got satellite gangs all over Brazil like the one who did the ambush in Puerto Ayacucho."

"I've got a different instinct about this." Dickerson stepped around the table. "Why go to all the trouble with the itinerary? Just to screw with our heads? It doesn't make sense." He looked back at the map and pointed. "They've got him zigzagging through Brazil in case he's being monitored. They want to make this trade. Otherwise, they'd tell him to go back to Puerto Ayacucho and call it a day. We can make this work. We just need to figure out how to stay a step ahead of Tepe."

Sowanake sighed. "We could also mobilize a strike right now while he's waiting for Jacks. Take out the bunkers by the highway and the bridge. Get copters and Special Forces in there to rescue the hostages."

That broke Jacks out of his cocoon. "No way," he told Sowanake.

Dickerson glanced at Jacks. "I agree. We've got two objectives here: rescue the hostages and immobilize Tepe. A raid on their compound leaves too much room for error. We need Jacks to draw Tepe and the hostages out. You heard him on the phone. The guy's got a serious grudge. He wants to meet Jacks face-to-face. That'll give us a lock on his location. With a ground operation, Tepe could escape into the jungle. We don't have time to deploy the kind of force we'd need to surround the town."

Sowanake pushed up from crouching over the table, clearly unsettled. Bizarrely, Jacks found himself on Dickerson's side, albeit for different motivations. Dickerson wanted a clear shot at killing Tepe. Jacks didn't trust anyone but himself to break his friends free from the kidnappers.

"What about sending a unit to Porto Velho for when Jacks

makes his rendezvous, just in case?" Sowanake told Dickerson. "There's time."

"I'll talk to Gainsway," Dickerson said, pushing up from the table. "But they'll need to deploy pronto."

Dickerson rifled off some instructions in his Bluetooth. Sowanake glanced at Jacks. Jacks wasn't sure what to make of it. Sympathy for the doomed mission they were setting him up for?

"You've got to promise me you're not going to blow this," Jacks told him. "They see I've got an army trailing after me, they'll kill Farzan and Kwame."

"That's not going to happen, and we'll be with you every step of the way," Sowanake said. "We'll be able to trace you from your phone."

Jacks worried about that. Tepe was already suspicious. Wouldn't Tepe want him to get rid of his phone before leading him to his secret location? Worse to think about, the guys might want him to wear a wire. As soon as Tepe discovered that, Farzan would be dead meat. But he would need some way to signal it was safe for them to launch their air raid from the military base in Peru. Otherwise, he, Farzan and Kwame could be buried in the attack.

It hit him—Bella. The past twelve hours had been such an ordeal he had forgotten about her, which made him feel terrible. He shuttered his mind from the room's fluorescent, overhead lights and the spray of conversation Dickerson was having through his Bluetooth. Jacks concentrated on reaching out to Bella.

They had bridged the distance from Barbados to New York City to make a psychic connection before. Could he find her? She couldn't have gotten too far from the Colombia-Venezuela border where he had left Javier's motorboat. Though Jacks had no idea where he was in relation to that.

He imagined a homing beacon radiating out and scouring everything for miles. The brown Colombian hills beyond the army base. His recollection of the Orinoco River plain. In the tunnel of his mind, a familiar mewling called back to him. Jacks grinned. The cat was one tough cookie. He didn't doubt Bella had held her own traveling through terrain with anacondas, crocodiles, and bigger cats.

He joined his mind with hers. She showed him a river bank, and he could hear the nocturnal sounds of the country-side. She'd been waiting by their river landing until she received a psychic signal from him.

Dickerson broke off from his conversation and turned back to Jacks and Sowanake. "It's a no-go on Puerto Velho. Washington won't do it. The Brazilian president agreed to U.S. military maneuvers in Boca de Anjo and nothing more." He looked at his oversized, utility watch and then up to Sowanake. "We've got to get Jacks moving. He can catch the last flight out from Bogotá to Caracas at 1:00. You want to take him in the Apache?"

"Sure."

"Wait," Jacks said. "We've got to make a stop before Bogotá."

He explained things quickly to the two agents. They needed to pick up Bella. If anything went wrong with tracing Jacks through his cell phone, he could keep them informed of his location by telepathizing to Bella. There was no way he was risking wearing a wire. Besides, Bella was a much more secure "wire." Jacks could message her, and then she could relay it to Sowanake. It was a perfect, detection-proof system.

Dickerson gave him something like a shrug and turned to Sowanake. "That sound good to you?"

His reaction pissed Jacks off. Dickerson had zero curiosity about feline telepathy or anything related to werecats. He just wanted to see through his operation and get the credit for eliminating the Glaring. He probably didn't give a shit if Jacks came out of it alive.

THEY BROUGHT JACKS his T-shirt, his shorts, and his sneakers. Jacks happily traded out his jumpsuit for his old clothes. Dickerson handed him a hastily issued U.S. passport and a printout of the flight itinerary they had booked for him to Puerto Velho. He got his wallet back, which had been trimmed down to one hundred U.S. dollars, and his backpack, in which they had stowed a counterfeit version of the Báalam-Tet. He had to quickly follow Sowanake out to the base's airfield.

A high-speed Apache helicopter awaited them, churning up the wind. Sowanake led Jacks ducking and climbing into the back cabin where there were benched seats with harness straps to belt up in. They put on headsets to communicate with each other and the pilot. Jacks told the pilot they needed to retrace the way back to the unfinished bridge at the border of Venezuela where they had picked him up. He would scan the bank of the river telepathically to locate Bella.

It was a harrowing lurch up from the airfield, and then a breakneck flight over night-shrouded, marbled terrain. Once Jacks's stomach had settled down from his throat, he got the dummy Báalam-Tet out of his backpack. Sowanake switched on an overhead light so he could examine the book.

The substitute which Jacks was to hand to Tepe looked aged and Mesoamerican. But it was made from tree bark, and the grainy vellum contained faded, painted hieroglyphs that looked nothing like the characters in the Báalam-Tet. The two books were constructed entirely differently.

"We got lucky with that," Sowanake said. "We were able to requisition a sixth century Mayan codex from a museum in

Guatemala, and the guys in our lab created the replica you're holding. Looks pretty good, right?"

"The Báalam-Tet is written in Olmec."

"That shouldn't be a problem. Tepe has never seen it. He doesn't know what to expect. Unless he's been studying Mayan hieroglyphs as a hobby, it's going to take him a while to make sense of it. Your job is to get in and get out before he does."

Jacks carefully folded up the book. He wasn't feeling so optimistic. Tepe had learned Benoit had the Báalam-Tet months ago. He had been trying to track it down ever since. Who could say whether or not he had found out some things about the codex? As Benoit had uncovered, there were Zapotec mystics who had knowledge of the authentic text.

A nearer worry occurred to Jacks. "It's not bugged or booby-trapped?"

"No."

He studied his companion. Sowanake was so focused, in his easy manner. It bothered Jacks.

"What happens to the Báalam-Tet?"

"It will be analyzed. Decoded. If it's as dangerous as you say, they'll want to keep it in an undisclosed facility."

"I guess what I mean to ask is, what happens to us?"

Sowanake's amber eyes sparked. It was the most feline Jacks had seen him look before. In that moment, Jacks could picture Sowanake's lithe body morphing into tawny hide and his head elongating into a snout with deadly jaws. Though he doubted that happened very often. The federal agent kept his wild side tightly wrapped.

The agent glanced away casually. "Nothing happens, Jacks. We go on living our lives."

"You think that after everything that's happened in the past few months, the U.S. government is going to just forget about our existence after this mission?"

Sowanake didn't answer.

"I could feel it in that conference room," Jacks said. "People don't want to know about us. They're afraid. Didn't you feel it? They're afraid of you."

"People need time to get used to differences."

Jacks snorted out a humorless laugh. "It's been five centuries since Europeans made contact with indigenous Americans and discovered our shaman tradition. They still call us savages and demon-worshippers."

"We're not living under colonial rule. Times have changed. The world has changed."

"I see. You think the world is ready for werecats living side-by-side with humans?" Jacks gave his companion a crooked grin. "You think we're ready for a werecat president?"

Sowanake shirked off his sarcasm. "I think we're better off without a faction representing the worst that we can be."

"You prefer a kinder, gentler approach? To show humans we're just like them?"

"We are just like them. In every way that matters."

"Is that why you got into working for the government? To demonstrate how normal werecats can be?"

Sowanake drew back from the conversation. Jacks hadn't meant to be so confrontational, exactly. He genuinely wanted to understand.

"I enlisted in the army when I was nineteen," Sowanake said. "I was a high school dropout. Living in a little town in California near the oil fields." His tone turned more candid. "On the wrong side of the tracks like they say. People there had no ambition to make anything better of themselves. They laughed at anyone who tried to get an education or a good job, and they dragged them down to the same hopeless pit of poverty and crime. I'm talking about gangs and drugs. I got caught up in that for a while until my older brother OD'd on heroin. That was my wake-up call. I knew if I didn't get out I'd end up dead or in prison.

"The army gave me everything: a G.E.D., a college degree, decent friends, and a career. I made sergeant in two years. NCO in three. As soon as I got my bachelor's degree, I applied to the C.I.A. academy, and that led to a job in Homeland Security. In October, it'll be my two year anniversary."

Jacks took a sidelong account of his companion. Sowanake certainly had cleaned up well from the origins he had described. A tailored suit. A fancy chronograph watch peeking out from his sleeve. Probably made good money, and Jacks could understand the pride in that.

"When did you become a werecat? Before or after?"

"During." Sowanake let that hang in the air. For a while, Jacks wasn't sure if he was going to elaborate.

"My third year in the service, I was deployed to an army base in Panama. It was an easy gig after my tour of duty in Afghanistan. Most of us had come straight from ground operations there. Some were rattled pretty badly and probably should have been sent home on medical leave. There was a town a few miles from the base where a few of them liked to cut loose. Things could get rowdy at a particular cantina down there.

"One night, I was ordered to go into town as part of a squad to bring back some guys who had gotten into a brawl. We had no idea what we were walking into. The inside of the cantina had been demolished. A local woman had been hurt badly. A mob of locals was gathering to take care of the soldiers who had disrespected their town and their women. A drunk private, nineteen years old, was at the center of it all, and he had beaten unconscious one of his friends who tried to intervene. He broke free from my colleagues, and I went chasing the guy down the street. He made it to the outskirts of town and into the forest.

"There were some other guys chasing him, but the locals wouldn't set foot in that wild and darkened expanse. I thought I had a good read on his path, so I went in after him. That turned out to be a bad idea real fast, but I was angry enough to drag the guy by his throat back to base. I lost my bearings in the brush. I was panicked and stumbling in circles. I heard a growl, and then something about twice my weight buried me. It must have come down from a tree."

A werejaguar, Jacks figured. And a wereshaman. It occurred to him that the werecat who had reared Sowanake could still be alive. If Sowanake served in Afghanistan, the attack couldn't have happened more than maybe ten years ago, twelve at the tops. He held back from saying it, but he was encouraged that there had been a wereshaman in existence so recently. He had never met a werecat who had been turned less than thirty years ago. Everyone seemed to believe that weremagic in the Americas had died with Benoit. Unless...

"Do you know who it was?"

"Benoit Guichard."

A cold draft passed through Jacks. It was quickly dispelled by his anger. "Why didn't you tell me before?"

"It's not relevant."

"We're like, what, blood-brothers?"

Sowanake reassumed his stiff demeanor. "Our relationship is strictly professional."

"That's such bullshit. You wouldn't have brought it up unless you wanted me to know."

"It doesn't change anything."

Jacks scowled. "Guess you're right about that. I certainly didn't miss out on any quality brother-to-brother time."

Sowanake said nothing.

"We're fucking werecougars, Sowanake. Native American

blood. Reared by the same weremaster. You don't feel a connection from any of that?"

"I don't base my associations on race or being werecat versus human. You want to lecture me about Native American blood? Awfully woke for a guy who looks like he stepped out of an Abercrombie & Fitch catalog. You been to a lot of pow-wows? Leave your ribbon shirt back in New York?"

Jacks didn't know what to say to that. He was something like three percent Cherokee, which he'd only known since April of that year. Sowanake looked far more Native than Jacks with his darker complexion and silky hair. So what, though? It still meant something that they shared a tribal past, didn't it?

"You're definitely the most human werecat I've ever known," he said. "Actually, you're more like a robot." A dreadful thought occurred to him. "Did you and Benoit—"

"No," Sowanake quickly answered. "I'm aware of your past relationship with Guichard. It wasn't like that."

"Thank fucking god," Jacks muttered. "Would have been awkward, huh?" A little glow of humor grew inside him. "Seriously though, you missed out. Benoit was a-MAZ-ing. Werecat sex is like Molotov cocktail orgasms." He glanced at Sowanake crookedly. "But I suppose a guy like you doesn't know much about that. First duty being to your country and all."

Sowanake drew up his mouth, and he pointed his steely gaze in the other direction.

"I was just ragging on you," Jacks said. "You're so serious. You ought to lighten up."

"I don't choose to advertise my sex life."

Jacks picked up on an intuition. He had noticed just the faintest aura of sexual energy from Sowanake and something he could read in his eyes. "I get it," he told the agent. "Just because we both happen to be werecats and we both happen to be gay doesn't mean we're buddies."

Sowanake said nothing.

"I knew it! Every male werecat I ever met was gay. Except that fucker, Bernard. Why is that? Is the werecat gene and the gay gene on the same chromosome or something?"

"I have no idea what you're talking about."

"I think I've got you figured out. A gay, Republican, Native werecat. They'll probably have you stuffed and lacquered so future generations can see you at the Smithsonian." Jacks laughed while Sowanake did not. He kept riding him, "Do you wish you were normal like your idol Dickerson?"

"I don't define myself by any of those characteristics."

"But you wish you weren't a werecat."

"I didn't say that."

"Is the military working on some kind of sick lab to turn werecats into humans? I bet you'd be the first one to sign up for it."

"You're not going to get a rise from me, Jacks. You're the one who needs to lighten up."

Jacks backed off for a moment, though he'd never been good at sitting in tense silence. "How did you manage to stay in the military after Benoit turned you?"

"My team found me in the jungle the next morning. I looked like I'd been mauled by some kind of animal, but I was still alive. I spent a few days in the infirmary, and I recovered quickly. It wasn't until I went on furlough that I discovered what happened to me."

Despite Jacks's contempt for Sowanake, he remembered his own rearing and the strange and frightening period he'd gone through afterward. "That's rough. You must have had to hide it from everyone."

"No. There was an officer who had become a good friend and a mentor to me. I told him everything. He helped calm me down and figure things out. It was nobody's business but my own, so there was no reason why I couldn't continue with my military service and move on with my career." He added, pointedly, "Not everyone is against us, Jacks."

Jacks rolled his eyes. "Sure. So long as you act like them and hide your feline soul." In truth, he was impressed Sowanake's army pal hadn't bugged out. "Though I guess you must have come out at some point. That's why Dickerson recruited you to help with his project against the Glaring, isn't it?"

"When I found out about the Glaring, I talked to my mentor, and he helped me work out a meeting with Dickerson where I volunteered to join his team. I'm doing my part to protect national security."

Jacks thought about telling him what he had learned from the Báalam-Tet, but he decided against it. Sowanake was like the dickish older brother he never had or wanted. The guy would definitely go straight to his superiors with any information he shared. The Sim Ru prophecy was going to freak people out big time. The archeology professor the military had brought in would discover things eventually. Hopefully not soon enough for Jacks to figure out a plan to disappear.

"If they ask you to round up werecats for detention, will you do it?" he said.

"If they're a threat to America, I'll do whatever's asked of me. If they're law-abiding citizens, they'll have no problem with law enforcement."

A typical tool response. Jacks tried a different question. "Let's say I make it through this mission alive. What's going to happen to me?"

Sowanake hesitated. "That's for the Secretary of Defense to decide."

In other words, he was screwed.

"If you pull this off, there'll be respect owed, Jacks,"

Sowanake said. "Keep your focus on the operation. You get ahead of yourself, things can go south really quickly."

He wanted to believe that, but he had serious doubts. Sowanake was either brainwashed by the military, or, just like a cat actually, he'd glommed on to the military as a means to survival. Anyway, Jacks was back to the place where he'd started. He had no choice but to do what he was told. However long the odds, it was his only way to rescue Farzan and Kwame.

He heard Bella's plaintive mewl, and he peered out the window and concentrated. He got an idea of her location and radioed the pilot to land on the river bank.

As soon as they touched down, he unbelted and shoved open the cabin door. Bella emerged from the brush, staring warily at the noisy, flying contraption. Jacks climbed out of the cabin and sent her gentle, encouraging images. He had never been so glad to see someone he could trust. She took a tentative route toward him with her ears pinched back. He scooped her up and gave her a big, smacking kiss on the forehead.

He brought her into the cabin where she nearly fought her way out of his hold from the sight and smell of Sowanake. Jacks reached one hand to the side to shut the door. He explained the situation to Bella.

*That's Sowanake. I know. He's kind of a tool. But he's all we've got to help us now.*

# EIGHT

JACKS WOKE AS the single row, regional plane lurched and plummeted to a descent. He had managed to doze off on the flight from Manaus, unable to sustain a state of hypervigilance through three legs of flights and two customs inspections with a bogus passport and the strange cargo in his backpack as his only luggage.

He wiped his face. It was oily from sleep and going through so many climate changes. He cleaned up as best as he could with a cocktail napkin and smoothed out his cotton T-shirt. Squinting out of the cabin window, he saw a patchwork, rural landscape and a coppery river, snaking through the countryside. The deep green Amazon rainforest dominated the land, but they were approaching a little enclave of plotted houses and commercial buildings. Puerto Velho. A tiny city scooped out of the jungle.

Jacks brought out his cell phone from the pocket of his cargo shorts to check the time. He had left Bogotá at one in the morning, and it was now 4:40 in the afternoon with the extra hour he had accumulated crossing time zones. He guzzled from a half-bottle of complimentary water. Showtime was approaching. He had instructions to find the shuttle bus queue outside the airport, and a van would meet him to take him to the place where Tepe wanted to make the exchange.

The plane touched down on the airport's single runway and taxied to a halt. Cold sweat dampened his brow and armpits. He felt for the counterfeit Báalam-Tet in his backpack, as though it might have magically disappeared, and he checked his phone in case he missed any new messages from Dickerson and Sowanake. Then he shoved the phone back into his pocket and waited to deplane. An airport crew wedged the wheels and rolled over a stairway to the cabin door.

Emerging from the cabin, Jacks locked in on something strange right away. A crew member was directing passengers across the airfield to the tiny airport while two toughs in snap caps and fatigues were scouting the line of people disembarking from the plane. Beneath the acrid stench of jet fuel, exhaust, and asphalt, a familiar swampy musk hit his sinuses. Tepe had switched things up. What could Jacks do? He climbed down from the stairs and looked at one of the werejaguar reconnaissance men.

A dark-skinned guy with a Sideshow Bob mop of hair bushing out from his cap waved him over. His partner was lighter-skinned, scruffy, and looked more European. They escorted Jacks farther down the sunbaked tarmac. Another pair of Glaring padrinhos stood at the stairs of a single-engine, piston plane. They gave Jacks snide looks. He returned that attempt at intimidation with a bit of swagger. Tepe had sent four hunters for the job. Their capitán respected what he was capable of.

"Where's Farzan and Kwame?" Jacks asked.

They didn't answer. The toughs had cocksure faces. They probably wouldn't mind roughing him up as repayment for killing one of their pals in Puerto Ayacucho. Jacks remembered with an itch of worry that Kwame had also mauled one of the guys before they had taken him out with a tranq gun.

At the plane, one of the guys turned him around, stripped his pack off his back, and patted him down from his ribs to his thighs. Since his capture by the U.S. military, Jacks was more than a little touchy about being poked and shoved around. The aggressive tom energy surrounding him amplified his urge to claw and bite back his attackers. He fought against it. He had to play it cool.

A hand pulled the phone out of his pocket, and then he heard it drop to the tarmac and crack under the weight of a steel-tip work boot. They wrenched his arms behind him, and they bound him with nylon cuffs. Then a hood swallowed his head, and a finger jabbed him between his shoulder blades.

A gruff voice said, "Mova-o."

ABOUT AN HOUR later as best as Jacks could figure, the piston plane began its descent to what would be his fourth landing that day. Tepe wanted him to have no idea where he was going and to throw off any intelligence agency that might be tracking him. It was a smart move. Dickerson was expecting the rendezvous in Puerto Velho to lead to a nine-hour drive on back country roads to Boca de Anjo. Jacks had no idea how that might affect the military's plan to swoop in and rescue hostages and blast Tepe with missiles. His captors might not even be taking him to Boca de Anjo.

The only good thing about wearing a hood was that his captors couldn't tell when he was concentrating to reach out psychically. Early in the flight, he had messaged Bella that he'd been smuggled onto a plane. He had received back an image of Sowanake by locking into Bella's vision.

"Stay calm, Jacks." Sowanake looked like he was traveling in a military vehicle. He and Dickerson were supposed to be directing operations from a base in Pucallpa, Peru, and now they were behind schedule. "We're going to get a satellite feed on the area around Porto Velho, and our control tower at the airbase should be able to pick up your aircraft on radar. As soon as you have details on your location, report them back."

Jacks prayed Tepe was bringing him to Farzan and Kwame. The fact that he was still alive was a little bit encouraging. Tepe could've had his thugs dispose of him as soon as they grabbed his backpack with the counterfeit Báalam-Tet. He was keeping Jacks alive for a reason. Maybe until he could authenticate the codex. Maybe so he could kill Jacks himself.

The plane hit the ground and gradually skidded to a halt. Fast-paced banter broke out among the foursome of Brazilian werejaguars, and one of them grabbed his arm and led him out and down from the plane.

The decaying smell of the jungle dug into his nose. He could smell and taste the scent of birds and monkeys in the trees. He pictured the dense rainforest surrounding him, a giant hunting ground for big cats.

They put him into a utility vehicle and motored down a bumpy road. The route got smoother, suggesting a paved street, and the vehicle accelerated. Jacks tried to hold on to every detail—a bend in the road here, an incline there. Wherever they were taking him, he could tell it was far removed from civilization. They didn't pass any cars or any people. The only things he heard were the car engine and the primordial chatter of the jungle.

Shortly after a gruff conversation in Portuguese, the car stopped, and they prodded Jacks out the door. One of the guys insisted he shuffle forward with his hands bound behind his back. It took every fiber of Jacks's self-control not to head-butt or body-check him in reprisal. The stink of dozens of aggressive toms made his shoulders tense and his hair stand up. He bore down on his fear. He tried to breathe through his repulsion. It was good the place was populated by werecats. That meant they had brought him to their stronghold. It was where he wanted to be. He just had to bury his wild cat impulses that told him to break free and get as far away as he could from the other werecats, though it was like forcing himself to drive his hand into a meat grinder.

As he went along blindly with someone's firm grip on his arm, Jacks noted the taste of indoor air and the texture of a carpeted floor against the tread of his sneakers. They had entered a house or a building. He could smell Naugahyde furniture and cloying mildew. That didn't provide much information, but he sent his impressions to Bella.

Sowanake's face and voice came back to him. Now the agent was in some military control room at the base in Peru. Air traffic consoles flashed and bleeped in the background.

"We couldn't find you by satellite. We had some technical issues. There was also a delay with the airstrike team getting down here. They're getting the missiles operational, but we need more time. As soon as you have a confirmation on your position, let me know. Try to slow Tepe down as long as you can. Let me know when you get confirmation on the hostages. I'll give you instructions."

Sowanake's face was shiny with sweat. Jacks swore underneath his breath. It wasn't the confidence-building conversation he'd been hoping for. He wished he could connect directly to Sowanake and vice versa, but their psychic bond wasn't strong enough to bridge distances. Bella was the only cat with whom he could link when they weren't face-to-face. He sent her an urgent message. *You better not start launching missiles until the three of us are out of here.*

A short while later, Sowanake's reply came to him.

"We're with you, Jacks. No one's launching anything until you guys are safe. We'll have an Apache aircraft pick you up as soon as we get visual on your position. Two units are going airborne as we speak. They can get anywhere in a 600 kilometer range of Puerto Velho in 45 minutes. Your flight time corresponds to a landing in Boca de Anjo. They'll be hovering around that region to make an even quicker pickup."

Jacks took a dry swallow. He hoped they wouldn't be hovering too close and giving away the plan.

He returned his attention to his surroundings as the man leading him clamped his arm and barked for him to stop. Movement shuffled around him. He tried to get a scent of Farzan, but the fug of werecat musk overwhelmed everything in his ken.

A door swung open, and a dreadful presence entered. Jacks had only spoken to Tepe over the phone, but he was certain it was him. The chilling aura and hyperaggressive pheromones could only belong to the most powerful werecat in the world.

Someone pulled his hood off, and he winced as his eyes adjusted to the indoor lighting. He had arrived at some dining hall decorated in tropical pastels. Chairs and tables had been moved to the periphery, and faded, yellow curtains were drawn across the windows on two walls of the room. One of the thugs from the airport stood at his side. Sideshow Bob. Tepe's lieutenant apparently. Directly facing him, there was a tall and broadly built man with a snap cap over his shiny black curls. He had a bronze complexion and an anchor beard and mustache.

*Jackson Cherokee,* Tepe purred into his head. *We finally meet.*

He had little creases around his eyes, which sparkled like hazel gems, and he wore khaki military fatigues. But he was more of a Latin heartthrob than a hardened werecat capitán as

Jacks had pictured. He held Jacks speechless for a moment. Tepe was dangerously charismatic.

"I brought you the Báalam-Tet," Jacks said. "Where are my friends?"

Tepe closed the distance between them, smiling like a pirate carrying a knife in his teeth. "You impress me, Jackson. Not many of our kind would risk their lives to save their friends. How is it that you can be so loyal to some yet a traitor to your race?"

"I came here for Farzan and Kwame. They've got nothing to do with your gripe."

Tepe stood so close, his warm, purring energy thrummed through Jacks, a thrill on the edge of terror and a turn-on. That was how it had been with Benoit, melting down his mistrust, as though he understood his nature better than he knew himself. Maybe Jacks was hardwired to be attracted to werejaguars. But he had grown a lot since he had allowed himself to be pushed around by alpha males.

"There are no innocents, Jackson," Tepe said. "It's been a war between humans and werecats ever since the conquistadors invaded our territory. With the Báalam-Tet, we will turn that war around. Traitors must be held accountable. Your friend Kwame murdered three of our revolutionaries in Bridgetown. Farzan is a human enemy who helped you steal the Báalam-Tet. Why should I let them live?"

Jacks sweated over what to do. Free of his hood, he could have given Bella a visual of Tepe and the room. But he still needed them to bring Farzan and Kwame out of whatever hold where they were keeping them, and he hadn't seen the outside of the building to describe a target for the military.

"I think you brought me here because you're a man of honor," he said. "You know the three of us pose no threat, now that you have the Báalam-Tet."

Tepe stepped around him. "I learned some things about you. Reared as a werecougar by a powerful weremaster Benoit Guichard. Vanished from the world because you feared what your family and friends would make of you. You even took on a new name, Jackson Dowd."

Jacks shifted his weight. Neither the police nor U.S. intelligence agencies had figured out his past. But Tepe had spying strays who must have informed him.

"I think you did the right thing," Tepe went on. "Humans and werecats can't coexist. That's why you took off as a fugitive. But why, Jackson, would you kill the shaman who reared your beautiful feline soul? He was your mate." He leaned in close, inhaling Jacks's scent. He might as well have captured his balls in his hand.

Jacks turned his head away from him. Murdering Benoit had been the start of the Glaring's grudge with him, though Tepe sounded genuinely intrigued. Was he satisfying his curiosity before he killed him? Or was Tepe planning to have his way with him before he did that? He was like a cat playing with wounded prey, and Jacks considered for a desperate moment that giving into Tepe might provide a chance for Farzan and Kwame.

He pushed that desperate thought out of his head. "I had to kill Benoit. It was me or him. I told him I wouldn't stand by while he killed humans indiscriminately. He couldn't handle that."

Tepe backed off a bit, and his eyebrows rose. "I heard about the brawl. An admirable feat for you to overpower a two-hundred-year-old weremaster."

"He taught me to be fearless. I guess it backfired on him in the end."

"Fearless and ambitious. With Benoit dead, you took the Báalam-Tet for yourself."

"That wasn't why I killed him."

A playful phase passed over Tepe's face. "Oh yes. I've heard this part as well. Your pristine incorruptibility. You took the Báalam-Tet so that it wouldn't get into the wrong hands. Do you really expect me to believe that?"

Jacks shrugged. "Believe what you want. It's the truth."

Tepe smiled, a full set of big, white teeth. "You're a good liar, Jackson. A good liar or you're too young to know what you want. A desire for power can be a tricky thing. It can make some men strike out too quickly, underestimating their enemies. Others turn away from the temptation in fear of what they might achieve. Which type are you?"

"I just want to live my life."

A snarling voice pried into his head. *I don't believe you. You want more.*

He glared at Tepe. "Stop that."

*With the Báalam-Tet, you could be a weremaster. You could have werecats and humans bowing at your feet.*

Jacks felt like his skull had been cut open, and Tepe was plucking at his brain. He forced back Tepe's telepathy like an invisible claw swatting Tepe's probing voice away. "I told you to stop it."

Tepe drew back with a ghost of a smile on his face. "Does it bother you, Jackson, that werecats are a dying species?"

He didn't reply. With every ticking second, he felt like he was sinking deeper into quicksand. If he demanded Tepe release Farzan and Kwame, he'd just delay things more to fuck with him. What the hell did Tepe want?

"The weremasters have been exterminated," Tepe went on. "In Phnom Penh, the last Suea Saming Skinwalker priest was killed in 1970. In South Africa, the last White Lion shaman was murdered by bounty hunters in 1987. The Waghia and Ashanti weremasters succumbed to the same fate in the early twentieth century. All at the hands of the imperialistas."

Tepe rounded Jacks again, a panther sizing up his adversary. "With the exception of Benoit. You killed the only living magi." Jacks met Tepe's gaze for a second, then looked away. "I don't condemn you for that," Tepe said. "I should thank you, actually. Benoit's death gave us a rallying call. The Glaring now has hundreds in our fold. We are werecats from every continent, united to make a final stand against humanity. With the Báalam-Tet, we will be victorious."

"Look. If you're trying to convert me, you're wasting your time. I'm neutral on this. I just want my friends. We'll be out of your hair like this never happened."

"Do you know your history, Jackson? The Cherokee were an honorable people. They took in runaway African slaves when the British and Spanish laid siege to their country. After the United States was established, Andrew Jackson declared war against them to drive them out, but they resisted. When the Spanish gave up their territory in the South, many of your people evaded execution by resettling in the Caribbean, and others stayed on to fight the white invaders. The U.S. spent more money battling the Cherokees than they spent in the War of 1812. They lost hundreds of men. Yet, in the end, the story is always the same. The white imperialistas offered a treaty with the false promise of giving them land farther west, and they marshaled your people to camps where they could be controlled and die off from hopelessness. The Americans reserved a special cruelty for the shifters of your kind. They were rounded up and bound to totems so soldiers could use them for target practice and run at them with bayonets. The ones they called berdache were raped with Bowie knives before they were executed."

Those images made Jacks's stomach cramp and burn, and

he held down bile. He forced a hardened look at Tepe. "Get your revenge. I'm not standing in your way." He peeked around the room. It was just him, Tepe, and Sideshow Bob, though he could smell dozens of other werecats in the building. The military had verified the town had been taken over by the Glaring. "You said yourself, you've got plenty of people to help you already."

"What do you plan to do? Run off to some deserted island to live happily ever after with your human boyfriend?"

Jacks snorted. "That actually sounds pretty amazing right now."

"Based on the tremendous chivalry you've shown Farzan, I have a hard time picturing you sitting by idly while his family is torn to shreds."

He had hit on a compelling point, but at the same time, Jacks hit on an idea. "I studied the Báalam-Tet. I can tell you what I found. But I need to know that Farzan and Kwame are okay."

Tepe scratched his bearded chin. He had to think he was in an inviolable position. What harm was there in showing Jacks his friends were still alive? Jacks meditated on that as though the idea could be channeled into Tepe's brain.

Tepe and Sideshow Bob exchanged words in Portuguese. Jacks thought he heard the word livro and something that sounded like prisoners. Sideshow Bob left the room, and Tepe went over to a table where there was a pitcher of water and some plastic cups.

Sowanake was still waiting for confirmation of his location. The room could have been a dining hall for a cheap hotel or even a dingy office building. Jacks wondered if he could work a question into conversation. It would take infallible guile. Tepe had taken care to disguise where he had taken him. He wasn't apt to blab about it.

Jacks noticed printed cocktail napkins on the table where Tepe was pouring himself a glass of water. They were too far away to read, but it looked like they were imprinted with a logo. When Tepe turned to him to offer a drink, Jacks nodded his head. By the grace of the gods, Tepe brought over a napkin with a cup of water. He helped Jacks take a drink since his hands were bound behind him. After Tepe fed him a long swallow, he wiped Jacks's face. Jacks locked in on the lettering: Hotel Tropical. It was the place in Boca de Anjo Dickerson had mentioned.

While Tepe brought the empty cup back to the table, Jacks zoned in on Bella and reported where he was. He also sent her a visual of Tepe. Then Tepe started up conversation again.

"You know, Jackson, we are not as mercenary as you might think. Your human pet could be overlooked if you chose to join us."

"Exterminate humankind, but keep a couple around as exotic curiosities?" Jacks said. "Wasn't that what the imperialistas did to our people?"

Tepe grinned though his eyes remained cold. "To the victor go the spoils. Though it wouldn't have to be so barbaric. We could arrange for Farzan's family to be spared. They could live comfortably."

"Why would you even want me on your side?"

"To renounce the sins of your past and show the world our cause is just."

He understood then what Tepe wanted. He was a political opportunity—a scrappy werecougar who had fought off werejaguars, and if he came around to embrace the Glaring's cause, that would be a compelling endorsement. He was also the very last werecat who had been reared, a sort of final legacy and a symbol of werecat pride. Maybe Tepe hadn't united werecats under the Glaring's banner as well as he had claimed.

He was rocked out of his thoughts by a vision blowing up in his mind's eye. "We got your confirmation of the Hotel Tropical." It was Sowanake. The control room was filled with shadowed heads at air traffic monitors. "We're locked in for a strike. Have you made contact with the hostages?"

Jacks's face ticked. *No. I need more time.* He shook off his connection with Bella. He had to pay attention to his surroundings and not give anything away.

"You want me to be your poster boy? Fuck, I'll do it," he told Tepe. "But show me Farzan and Kwame are unharmed. I'm not agreeing to anything until I know they're safe."

That seemed to be what Tepe wanted to hear, though his grin was hard to read. The door to the dining hall swung open, and two of Tepe's padrinhos rough-handled a pair of prisoners in hoods and rope cuffs into the room. Jacks's heart bled like it had been shot by a crossbow bolt. He recognized Farzan's trembling body, clad in the same T-shirt and track pants he had worn back in Puerto Ayacucho. Kwame looked clumsy and depleted from some cruel torture.

Farzan's voice grasped out into the room. "Jacks?"

Jacks staggered to him, wrenching at the nylon bonds around his hands. All he could do was press against Farzan. "It's me." Tears sprayed from his nostrils and his mouth. He nuzzled against Farzan's hooded face and strangled words came from his lips. "I'm so sorry, baby. But I'm gonna get you out of here."

Sideshow Bob came at Jacks to pull him away. Just then, someone roared in his head.

"Get that fucking cat out of here."

He saw an image of the control tower with men frantically working at the consoles. Bella was scampering over panels of keyboards and switches, trying to confuse the military operators. Disembodied voices filled his head.

"Patriot One is launched and on target."

"We've lost feed on Patriot Two and Three."

Jacks placed Dickerson's voice. "You get those fighter jets in the air pronto. If the missiles miss their target, we'll need a sweep of that compound before anyone gets out."

"For Christ's sake, there's two Americans in there." That was Sowanake.

"Stand the fuck down, Sowanake. General Gainsway's orders were that the mission proceeds as soon as we have a lock on their location. You want to be of some use? Get that cat out of the tower."

Jacks shivered back to his surroundings just in time to catch his footing as Sideshow Bob shoved him to the other side of the room. One missile was headed for the hotel in how many seconds? Two more had been thrown off course, but how far? Fighter jets were on their way to raze everything to rubble. He was momentarily paralyzed. No Apache helicopters were coming to rescue them. Just as he had feared, Dickerson had been using him all along to put a bull's eye on the Glaring. But Jacks had to get over that fast and think of some way for the three of them to make it out alive.

The padrinhos pushed Farzan and Kwame toward the door they had come out of. Jacks needed his hands free to wrangle them out of the hotel before they were locked up in a room to be blown to bits by missiles. He needed a goddamn miracle. All three of them were bound by the hands, and Tepe and his three henchmen could easily overpower him if they tried to escape.

He bore down on the magical place in his diaphragm. His shift was explosive and painful, but with his cougar strength, he shredded the nylon bonds around his forepaws.

A shriek knifed through the air overhead, and then the world exploded with a deafening kaboom and a hail of smoldering wood and concrete.

The blast threw Jacks clear across the room into a wall. For a moment, it seemed like a curtain of night had fallen over everything. He fought against his shattered reflexes and vertigo. It felt like the missile had landed on top of him, but that couldn't be. Through a foul fog of dust and smoke, he saw the far wall of the room had burst to cinders. The missile must have carved through a higher floor and blown away the opposite side of the building. Bodies and remnants of tables and chairs had been thrown helter-skelter.

Jacks relaxed his diaphragm in a delicate spasm. He had to shift back to human form and rescue Farzan and Kwame from the wreckage.

He crawled along the cracked and buckled floor in the direction of the door where the two had been headed. He spotted Farzan splayed out face down and weakly twitching. Jacks gently grasped Farzan's sides, sensing the warmth of his body and the faint and rapid beating of his heart. He carefully removed Farzan's hood and unknotted the ropes from his wrists.

"I've got you now," Jacks told him. "We're going to be okay."

A distant explosion reverberated through the floor. A second missile struck nearer, shaking the foundations of the battered building.

Fighter jets were on their way to decimate the hotel.

He lifted Farzan to a limp stand and leveraged his weight on his shoulder. Farzan was dazed and possibly deafened by the explosion, but besides some scrapes, he had no serious wounds Jacks could see. They had to get out of the hotel and far out of town. There was a way. But first, he had to help Kwame, who had been thrown on his side a few yards away.

Jacks shouldered Farzan in that direction. Mercifully, Kwame was already raising himself from the floor. A shattered wood beam had torn into the back of his thigh like a stake. Judging that Farzan had gained enough strength to stand on his own, Jacks knelt beside Kwame and removed his hood.

Grimacing, Kwame bore down to summon what had to be an excruciating shift. His lion forelegs were bent behind his back, but they wrenched free from his bonds. The morphing of bone and muscle in his hind legs expelled the stake of wood from his thigh.

Jacks scanned the bodies strewn around the room. He could make out one man who was curled, bloody and lifeless, having taken the brunt of the shattered wall. Sideshow Bob was clawing the floor for traction with lame legs dragging behind him. That accounted for two of the four men who had been in the room. Tepe was nowhere to be seen. Maybe he had fallen through the shattered wall into the smoldering gulf where the missile had blown through the roof.

He staggered over to Sideshow Bob who was trying to crawl his way to safety. Either him or the other guy had the keys to the truck. Jacks dug his hand into one of Sideshow Bob's fatigue pockets, then the other. Sideshow Bob growled but was in too bad a shape to resist. No keys. He shuffled over to the guy who looked to be dead from the blast.

He struck gold the first pocket in. An SUV key fob plus a money clip with a wad of Brazilian reals. Jacks grabbed both and gathered Farzan and Kwame. They had to get to the parked truck outside the hotel.

Jacks led Farzan by the hand, and Kwame limped behind him. Farzan was still shocked speechless and pliable. Kwame's feline eyes showed some awareness of the situation though he was panting and choking out coughs. Heading down a dusty and smoky hallway, Jacks found the hotel lobby and a shattered glass door leading out to the street.

They hurried out of the building. An angry cloud of smoke

still hovered above the roof where the missile had struck. A pair of padrinhos with rifles slung over their shoulders rushed toward them.

Jacks steered Farzan and Kwame around the corner of the hotel. The rebels ran into the hotel lobby, hardly taking account of them. Their headquarters had been attacked, and they must have been in a panic over whether or not their leader Tepe was alive.

Another pillar of smoke rose up from a house down the street. Shouts in Portuguese echoed through the town—people trying to make sense of what had happened. Scanning through the murk of twilight, Jacks could see Boca de Anjo was an even smaller outpost than Puerto Ayacucho. Beyond the hotel's commercial block, it was all wood-paneled bungalows that must have been turned into barracks for the Glaring.

A truck revved and rattled through town, getting louder by the second. The rebels would be organizing an evacuation of the hotel, and it wouldn't be long before someone took notice of them. Jacks glanced around the side of the hotel and spotted a black SUV parked clumsily by the curb. He clicked the fob he'd stolen, and a two-tone bleep answered back. Jacks glanced at Farzan and Kwame. "C'mon."

There wasn't time for conversation, though Jacks worried about Farzan. He was looking at Jacks as though he held his life in his hands. He probably badly needed water and something to eat, not to mention a Valium. Jacks guided Farzan into the passenger seat, and put Kwame into the back. He ran around to the driver's seat, shoved the key into the ignition, and started the engine.

The truck he had heard careening through town came up behind him and nearly sideswiped his vehicle before stopping in front of the hotel. A troupe of men jumped down from its bed and three others from its carriage. Some ran into the hotel, and some stayed back with their rifles.

Jacks pulled the vehicle around the truck and gunned it down the road. He heard shouts, but luckily the revolutionaries had bigger worries than someone hijacking one of their vehicles.

A blood-curdling screech ripped through the sky. Dickerson's fucking fighter jets. Jacks had no idea where he was going, but the main road had to lead out of town. Up ahead, the road declined to a river and a truss bridge. Dickerson had said a bridge was one of Boca de Anjo's entry points. He stepped on the gas pedal. The bridge was maybe half a mile away.

A boom and a fiery blast erupted from someplace behind him. Like bolting out of a burning building, Jacks didn't look back. He kept his eyes on the road and the goddamn bridge ahead. He heard the familiar sound of a chopper, which would no doubt take an interest in a vehicle barreling out of town. He glanced at Farzan. He was mechanically strapping himself in with a seat belt. Jacks hiked up a grim look of reassurance. He would get them out of the war zone and to safety.

Nearing the bridge, he saw bunkers of sandbags cutting down the passage to one narrow lane. Only two men with rifles stood guard. Anyone else assigned to the checkpoint had probably been sent back to the hotel to gather the troops and high-tail it out of there. Jacks punched down harder on the gas pedal. The guardsmen stood in the gap of the bunkers, staring at the vehicle hurtling toward the bridge with no sign of stopping.

One of the guys waved his arms and shouted. The other took up his rifle and fired a warning shot that zipped by the driver's side of the truck. Jacks steered a course straight at them, and they leapt out of the way. The SUV pounded into the sandbags, dragging them forward and grinding over them.

Once clear, Jacks gunned it over the bridge and onward to a two-lane country highway.

Night had fallen, and thick brush lined both sides of the road like a dark tunnel. He resisted hitting the flood lights. That would make them an easy target for Dickerson's Special Forces bombarding into Boca de Anjo to sweep the town clean. He used his feline vision to navigate the winding road, praying they had made it out unnoticed.

# NINE

DEEP INTO THE night, Jacks spotted a roadside cantina and pulled into the gravel parking lot. The open-air, cinder-block pavilion glowed with hanging lanterns. Lively Brazilian pop music reverberated from well-worn speakers. A guy was behind a counter tending the bar and grill with about a dozen patrons hanging around the picnic tables.

He parked the SUV and eased back in his seat. The muscles of his arms and neck throbbed and burned. He had been driving for more than two hours, all the while gripping the steering wheel and scanning the way ahead like some RPG commando in night vision goggles. No one in the car had uttered a word.

He had glanced at Farzan and Kwame from time to time, just to check that they were still breathing and reasonably comfortable after the explosion and whatever abuse they had endured. Now, they were in the middle of a dense jungle. No passports. With a hundred dollars, whatever small cash Jacks had stolen from the dead Glaring hunter, and a quarter tank of gas. Escaped from a U.S. military mission meant to kill them and every werecat in Boca de Anjo.

He dropped his head against the steering wheel and sobbed.

Farzan gripped his shoulder. "Jacks."

"I'm sorry." Jacks wiped his eyes on the sleeve of his T-shirt.

"What are you sorry for? You saved our lives."

He couldn't stop himself from weeping. He felt so small and useless. "None of this would have happened if it hadn't been for me."

Kwame leaned in from the back seat. He had shifted into human form along the way. "Javier betrayed us," he told Jacks. "Why blame yourself?"

"You don't understand. I should have given Tepe the book. Even if he murdered me, it would have been better. They're going to round up and exterminate every werecat alive."

"All of us need something to eat and a stiff drink," Kwame said, firmly. "C'mon."

Jacks took a deep breath to steady himself, and he followed them out of the car. Farzan waved Jacks over, and they huddled on the passenger's side of the SUV facing away from the cantina. He looked his companions up and down. "This isn't exactly the Rainbow Room, but we can't walk in there looking like this."

Jacks was heartened. Farzan still had his sense of humor. And he was right. Their faces and their clothes were covered with dirt and dust. Minor cuts and abrasions scored their heads and arms. Farzan took a peek over the roof of the SUV. Then, he quickly stripped off his T-shirt.

"No shirts required in the dress code," Farzan turned his shirt inside out and used it to wipe his face, his arms, and his hands. Kwame pulled off his shirt and did the same, and Jacks followed suit. They helped each other find dirty spots on their heads and backs, and they beat off the dust from their shorts and sneakers. Kwame had already healed pretty well from the gash to his thigh, though he would have to walk into the cantina with a big tear in his shorts, stiff with dried blood. He stepped out of his shorts and put them on backwards so the rip was on the back of his leg. Farzan rolled up his track pants to his knees so the worst of his dirt-caked and frayed pants didn't show. As for the welts on their torsos from being thrown by missile fire, they had to hope for favorable lighting.

They opened the hatch of the SUV and threw their shirts into the back. "Maybe we can find a river in the morning and beat them clean against a rock," Farzan said. Jacks and Kwame chuckled.

"All right," Farzan said. "We don't look like we dynamited our way out of a prison anymore. We just look like we woke up from a subway grating."

"I'll take it," Jacks said. "You guys must be starving." He could smell fried fish cooking at the cantina and realized he was starving, too. He pulled the wad of reals out of his pocket. "It's all we have. Besides a hundred U.S. bucks we'd have to exchange."

Farzan took the money and examined it beneath the interior light of the car. "Three thousand real. That's about eight hundred dollars."

For about the millionth time, Jacks was astounded at his knowledge.

"I did some research back in Caracas," Farzan said. "In case we ended up crossing borders." He handed the money back to Jacks. "Just don't order the filet mignon."

They stepped around the truck and walked up to the cantina, taking up spots casually at the bar. The patrons watched them, but they didn't look unfriendly. Things didn't get more local than the cantina. Jacks hadn't seen a house or a gas station or any businesses on the road for miles. Most of the men were shirtless and dark-skinned with Amerindian features. They were tossing back bottles of a local beer called Brahma. A foursome played dominoes while a girl with straight black hair and tribal tattoos on her chin and her cheeks looked on.

The bartender wandered over looking mystified. He was barely more than a kid, short and scrappy, with oversized shorts and rings of beaded necklaces.

Kwame spoke to him in Portuguese, and their conversation proceeded with lots of repetition. They were deep in the Brazilian back country. People probably spoke a local dialect. Kwame managed to communicate three orders of fried fish and cassava chips, a liter of water, three shots of rum and three beer-backs. The bartender got straight to business at the frying drums behind the counter, and in minutes, he brought over a banquet of food.

They clinked their shot glasses and tossed back a heavenly dose of alcohol. Then they each attacked their plates and took slugs of precious water while they chewed it down. The food was gone almost as quickly as it had been prepared.

Farzan let out a croaking belch. Jacks raised his eyebrows.

"What? In many cultures, it's a tribute to the cook to burp after a meal."

Kwame mustered up his own prodigious belch. The bartender looked over at the guys with a grin.

Rehydrated and with a full belly, Jacks felt a little looser. There were things he needed to know. He took a slug of his beer and looked at his companions.

"What was it like?"

Farzan and Kwame eyed each other.

"Could have been worse," Farzan said. "The trip down

from Venezuela was the hardest part. They had us bound and gagged in the back of a mini-truck. It was like being slow-cooked in a crockpot."

"Some of the padrinhos got rough with me in the beginning," Kwame said. "They wanted revenge for attacking their friend. They separated us when we got to the hotel. They kept me in a cage in one of the rooms."

"Not knowing was the worst part," Farzan said. "I had no idea if the two of you were alive. I had no idea what they were going to do to me. I gave them my cell phone number so they could call you, and then days dragged on, and they wouldn't tell me anything." He looked at Jacks. "I thought if they found you, you'd be dead. I tried to hold on to the hope that they were keeping me alive for a reason."

Jacks sloppily polished off the last of his beer.

"It's not your fault, Jacks," Farzan said. "Look at what you did. I don't know how, but you found us and broke us out of Tepe's base of operations."

Kwame nodded and waved over the bartender to order another round of shots and beers.

"I had to get you guys back," Jacks said. "But the Báalam-Tet is gone. It's in U.S. custody." He told them about his abduction by Dickerson and the mission he had been duped into. When the bartender brought over the shots, Jacks gulped the stinging rum. Anger was rising inside him.

Farzan watched Jacks dubiously. "You think it would be better if Tepe had the Báalam-Tet?"

"I don't know." He pushed back his hair, which left a gritty mix of dust and oil on his hands. "But we can't trust the U.S. government. They were willing to sacrifice the three of us so they could take out Tepe."

"The book belongs with werecats," Kwame said. Jacks nodded.

"What are we supposed to do? Infiltrate the U.S. Department of Defense to get the book back?" Farzan shook his head. "We leave well enough alone. We escaped a strike zone. Now we just have to hope they don't have marshals looking for us. Where to? North Korea? Antarctica?"

Jacks remembered what Tepe had told him. Would he run away to a deserted island while werecats and humans battled it out? Even if that was possible, it was cowardly. How could he sit back like his ancestors had while his own kind was destroyed?

"We don't have the book, but we know about the Sim Ru prophecy," he said. "If we can figure that out, maybe there's a chance for werecats to live."

"How?" Farzan said. "We lost the book. We lost Benoit's notebook. Even if we had them, the Sim Ru prophecy spoke about the summoning of a sabretooth god that will destroy humankind. Is that what you want?"

Jacks hung his head. "I don't know what I want." He looked up at Farzan and corrected himself. "Of course I don't want mankind destroyed. But I need to understand why this happened. How our gods could let this happen."

"Jacks, what if there are no answers?"

Coming from Farzan, who never gave up trying to understand things, the question got Jacks's attention.

"I've been thinking about this a lot," Farzan said. "Though I wasn't sure you wanted to hear it. People have been looking for guidance from ancient texts for hundreds of years, and what has it accomplished? They find rationalizations for slavery, war, and every abomination you can think of. Books are written by men, making up stories about what they think their God, or gods want us to do."

"No. The Báalam-Tet is different. There was a time when men and werecats co-existed peacefully. It was in the book."

"That's what I'm talking about, Jacks. It was in the book. A story. Like the Garden of Eden and an Islamic heaven for the righteous. We have no idea who wrote the Báalam-Tet. How can you believe it represents an objective truth?"

"Benoit believed it was the truth. He spent a hundred years trying to learn from it."

Farzan gazed at him compassionately. "I know you want to believe you'll find answers. But if Benoit couldn't find them in a hundred years, you have to consider maybe they never existed."

Jacks took a long swallow of his beer. He knew what Farzan was driving at. He had assumed that Benoit had locked away the Báalam-Tet because he had discovered an unstoppable prophecy. But there was an alternative scenario. Benoit had discarded the ancient codex because he discovered it was useless. Werecats had no special purpose. Their lives were just as meaningless as any other being in the world. That could have pushed Benoit to give up on controlling his wild nature just as much as if he had believed there was a way to arouse a terrifying feline god.

"What do we do now?" he said. "We can't return to the U.S. We'll be hauled off to detention so that their mission in Boca de Anjo doesn't get out." He pulled his cash out of his pocket and flipped through it. "We've got money to live on for a couple of weeks."

"We start with a shower and a good night's sleep," Kwame said. He wandered away to the patio of the cantina. Jacks was too weighted down by his thoughts to wonder why. Farzan laid his hand on his and tried to get him to meet his gaze.

Kwame returned in a buoyant mood. "We're in luck. I spoke to a man, and there's a campground just down the highway. A two-bed cabin and a shared bathhouse for one hundred real a night."

THAT NIGHT, AFTER burrowing into a one-room cabin in the forest and squeezing in with Farzan on a twin-size cot, Jacks plunged into a glorious abyss of sleep. Though later, as his mind stirred with peculiar illusions, he felt vaguely alive and transported to another realm.

He was surrounded by diffuse light like rays of sun strangled by fog at the crown of the world's highest peak. A ferocious wind whipped at him, and he stumbled around a blank, barren place. He could not see the ground nor his feet. His only awareness of himself came from a sense of breathing and the impatient drumming of his heart.

A bank of fog lifted from his path, and he saw a platform of stone jutting up from an unseen land mass. It was a netherworld embanked in clouds. Ozone filled his nostrils and his lungs, inciting a wave of vertigo. He was weightless and exposed, but though his body cringed, he could not turn his eyes away from the sight atop the stony dais.

Supine on its fours towered a giant cat the height of a horse, its body thick and muscled. Its tawny hide was lightly camouflaged with dark chestnut spots, which brought to mind the primordial fields of sedge where it made prey of any creature in its dominion. The monster seemed not to have taken notice of Jacks at first, seated statuesque on its throne with its head turned away in a distant stare. But then its short, dog-like tail craned to attention.

Jacks watched, paralyzed. The cat shifted its bearded muzzle toward him. Horn-sized, twin fangs hung from its jaws. Its amber eyes appraised Jacks as though anticipating a question. Jacks sank down and prostrated himself.

A single word filled his head in a husky growl. *"Time."*

Jacks woke drenched in sweat. He propped himself up on his elbows and glanced around the overheated cabin. For a frightening moment, he thought he had been returned to a detention cell.

The walls seemed to press in on him. The cabin was a rickety shelter built to contain the two cots and not much else. A high window was unshuttered, and the door was wedged open, but that did little to relieve the tropical swelter. The scents of vegetation, soil, and moisture saturated the room. A cacophony of insect buzzes and chirps surrounded the cabin.

At some point in the night, Farzan had moved to the other cot. He lay beneath a coarse blanket that had come with the cabin, and he was turned away from Jacks. Kwame was out and about. He spotted a bottled water on the floor between the cots. Had they picked up water last night before checking into the campground, or had one of the guys bought it in the morning? Jacks grabbed the bottle and twisted off the cap to relieve his thirst.

Heavy steps creaked up the short stairs to the cabin. Kwame appeared at the door with a striped beach towel tied around his waist. His thick chest and arms had returned to a healthy, dark honey sheen, showing that his body had thoroughly repaired itself. He gave Jacks a white-toothed smile, but then he pointed a troubled glance at Farzan's cot.

Jacks climbed out of his bed and hovered over Farzan. His brow was beaded with sweat, and his body trembled weakly. Color had drained from his face as though he had aged twenty years overnight. A rolled, wet towel mantled his neck.

"What is it?" he asked Kwame.

"Last night, I heard him vomiting outside of the cabin. He called it blunt force trauma, a delayed reaction to the explosion. I propped him on his side like he told me, and I went out to find water and ice. I hope you didn't mind me taking the car and your cash."

"Of course not."

"He told me to check on his breathing and his color every half hour," Kwame said.

Jacks noticed a Styrofoam cooler on the other side of the cot. He couldn't believe he had slept through everything. "Why didn't you wake me up?"

"You needed to rest as well."

That was hardly as important as Farzan's condition. Jacks gently stroked one side of his head. "Baby, how are you doing?" Farzan nodded faintly, acknowledging his presence. His eyes were shut, and agony showed on his pale, clammy face. Did he need to go to the hospital? Why hadn't they thought about this happening before? The missile strike at the hotel had been as brutal as getting thrown through the windshield in a car collision. Farzan didn't have the self-repairing ability Jacks and Kwame had.

"Before I left him, he told me he should be all right with rest and icing his neck," Kwame said.

"He doesn't look all right to me." Jacks stepped around the bed, carefully removed the towel from Farzan's neck, and went to the cooler to wrap up more ice.

"I spoke to the clerk at the store down the road," Kwame said. "There is a hospital in Rio Branco, but it is two hours away. We will need more gas, and the closest station is an hour in the opposite direction."

Jacks scooped ice cubes into the towel, wadded it up, and crouched over the bed to dab Farzan's forehead. A frigid droplet of water rolled down his arm to his bare shoulder. They'd all stripped off their clothes before bed so they could wash them in the morning, but modesty meant nothing while Farzan looked like he was clinging to life.

Farzan spoke to him in a thin voice, "Jacks."

"It's me, baby. I'm gonna take care of you. Tell me where it hurts."

"Everywhere."

Jacks grimaced. Farzan was wiped out by that brief vocalization. They needed a doctor to check him out. But moving him and driving four or more hours on a bumpy country road would be excruciating. What if it made his condition worse? They might get lost trying to find the hospital. Could they send for help? He reached under the blanket and squeezed Farzan's feverish hand. Farzan gripped back weakly.

"Baby, I need you to help us to decide what to do," Jacks told him. "But I don't want you to wear yourself out by trying to speak. Can you squeeze my hand for yes?"

Farzan squeezed.

"Good, baby. That's all you have to do. Now, do you want us to take you to a hospital?"

He waited. Farzan shifted his head painfully back and forth in defiance.

"Okay." Jacks bit his lip. Farzan had made it through three years of medical school as a straight-A student, but could he diagnose himself?

"I'm better off here than at a disease-infested medical clinic," he croaked.

That familiar grouchiness was a good sign, but Jacks wasn't entirely convinced. "I know you're tough, baby. But that was a hard fall you took at the hotel. You sure that icing and some bed rest is gonna be enough?"

Farzan took a dry swallow. "Percocet."

"Then, baby, we've got to go to a hospital."

Farzan slowly shook his head again. "Won't do anything you can't do for me. Wake me every two hours in case there's a concussion. Feed me ice."

Kwame stretched into the conversation. "All they had at the store was ibuprofen. But I met a man who offered to bring a local remedy. It's called chuchuhuasi."

Farzan gave a little nod.

"Really?" Jacks said.

"It is a natural pain reliever," Kwame said. "Made from tree bark. He sounds better than when I last checked on him. I bought towels, bathing trunks, and T-shirts at the store. Why don't you get washed up in the bathhouse and have something to eat? There's corned beef and eggs."

Jacks needed a shower badly, though he didn't want to leave Farzan's side. If only there was a way of transferring his healing ability. He glanced at Kwame then back to Farzan.

"I'll be right back. You'll be okay for a little while?"

Farzan squeezed his hand.

Kwame handed Jacks a beach towel and a pair of nylon, elastic-band, fluorescent blue trunks. Jacks tied the towel around his waist, and they stepped out of the cabin down the stairs to the forested campgrounds.

Palm and rubber trees dwarfed the humble campsite where a half dozen hut-like cabins had been pitched. Each cabin was equipped with a fire pit and a rusted grill caked with grease drippings. Kwame had parked the black SUV nearby at the end of a dirt trail leading from the highway. He showed Jacks the way through the woods to the bathhouse.

"He doesn't want to go to the hospital," Jacks said. "But what if he's being stubborn?"

"He knows his own body. I think we have to trust his intuition. This is a good spot to rest and not have to worry about what we might run into on the road."

"What do you mean?"

"There is an Indian village nearby and not much else.

These are good people. I spoke to some of them at the store. But they told me a lot of drug-running passes through here. From a cartel in Bolivia. People who would kill to take an expensive SUV if they spotted it."

Jacks remembered Dickerson's report. The Fronteras cartel had a pact with the Glaring to move drugs through the Amazon. Could they have been alerted to what happened in Boca de Anjo and be headed up their way to check it out? The forest felt suddenly like a precarious place.

"How much money is left?"

"Three thousand real and your hundred dollars." Kwame hesitated, then spoke. "It is a long drive, but the money could get us to Salvador on the Atlantic coast, when Farzan is able to make the trip. From Salvador, we could call Maarten to pick us up."

"No way. I'm not begging Maarten to take us back on his yacht. He hates me."

"I had a feeling you would not like the idea. But what other choices do we have?"

Jacks could think of nothing, but he wasn't ready to agree. He needed to run something else by Kwame.

"The mixing of blood for the rearing ritual unleashes a powerful magic. What would happen if a human drank our blood without the intermingling? Could they get a dose of our healing power?"

"There are stories of such things, but I have never seen it myself."

"If it doesn't work, it wouldn't cause harm, would it?"

"I cannot say." Kwame grinned at Jacks crookedly. "Though there's never been harm from the intermingling of other body fluids."

Jacks supposed that was encouraging. All they truly had

was supposition. Even Farzan's medical knowledge wouldn't help them.

They reached a wooden stall attached to a steel water tank, and he went into the shelter. He hung his towel and trunks on a hook on the wall and stepped under the shower head and pulled its rusted chain. A feeble stream of tepid water trickled down on him. He found a bar of soap to lather up his oily hair and his grimy body. It was hardly luxurious, but after a few pulls on the shower, he felt stripped clean of the filth and toil of the past few days.

A piercing mewl split through Jacks's head. Bella. His heartbeat quickened. She was still alive and talking to him. Based on the strength of that psychic cry, she was near.

A familiar wild sagey odor reached his nostrils. He threw on his swim trunks and pushed through the stall curtain. Kwame had stayed back to wait for him, and he looked at Jacks curiously.

"No fucking way," Jacks muttered. He tramped through the campground, following the smell of smoldering sage. Kwame kept up with him. He had picked up the scent as well and was scouting the area. When they returned to the cabin site, a black SUV trundled down the trail from the highway. Jacks strode toward it and put himself in the middle of its path.

The car came to a halt, and the engine cut off. The driver's side door creaked open. Sowanake stepped out of the SUV in military fatigues.

Jacks came at him like an NFL linebacker. "Give me my cat and get the fuck out of here."

Sowanake raised his hands to buffer him back. "Take it easy, Jacks. I just came to talk."

Jacks got in his face. "You think I want to hear anything from you? You snitching, lying, dirtbag piece of shit?" His arm tensed, readying to pound his fist into the guy's face. Bella scampered out of the truck and raced to the safety of the cabin.

"Calm down, Jacks. You know I tried to call things off," Sowanake said.

"You put us in the middle of a hellstorm."

"I'm glad you made it out. Thanks to Bella, most of the missiles went off-course. Her interference at the control tower in Pucallpa paid off."

He stared flames at Sowanake. "You must really think I'm an idiot. What is it, Sowanake? You thought you'd just show up to congratulate me for escaping the airstrike? For pulling my friends out of the rubble? You want to tell me it was all part of your plan?"

Kwame swaggered up behind Jacks. The federal agent was masked in aviator sunglasses, but a little nervous energy in his body betrayed his calm demeanor. He and Kwame could rip Sowanake to shreds. His feline soul thirsted to do it. More complex, human considerations held him back. Farzan was in a frail state. They needed to know what the fucker was doing there, and what that meant.

"Where are your buddies? Getting ready to swoop in with jets and helicopters? You got us on surveillance?"

"I came alone. I caught an airlift to Boca de Anjo. As soon as Bella determined you made it out of town, I snuck off with her in the truck to look for you."

Jacks snickered bitterly. He thrust his hands into Sowanake's chest. "Fucking liar. Bella would never lead you to me."

Sowanake stumbled back and righted himself from the shove. "I'll let that go because I know you're angry." He smoothed out his shirt. "But she did, Jacks. She understands the danger you're in."

Jacks stalked around him, menacingly.

"You intend on getting physical with me, the U.S. government will have an airtight rationale to hunt you down," Sowanake said. "I can guarantee you my absence from the base won't go unnoticed for long."

"They already want the three of us dead. 'Sweep the town clean.' That's what Gainsway ordered, right? That's what Dickerson was happy to do. Doesn't make a whole lot of difference if we take you down with us."

"It was a covert plan between the Secretary of Defense and Gainsway from the start. I was duped as much as you."

"You were duped as much as me," Jacks repeated thickly. "No one was duped as much as me." He backed the agent against the car. "You fucking led me into a plan to kill my friends."

Sowanake shielded his face with his forearm. "I came to help."

Jacks gasped beneath his breath. He took a step away to cool down. Facing the shiny, black SUV, a warped and murky silhouette of himself reflected from the door panel. He drove one side of his body into the car, collapsing the panel with a satisfying metallic groan. He caught his breath and swung back to Sowanake. "What help you got, big man?"

They stared at each other in a tense stand-off for a moment. The federal agent appeared to be unarmed in his tucked-in shirt and flat-pocketed cargo pants. Still, Jacks locked in mentally on the spot below his diaphragm if he needed to quickly shift.

"I've got friends on the inside. I can get you settled in neutral territory. Someplace the U.S. government won't bother you ever again."

"Where's that?"

"Micronesia. They're sovereign states in the Pacific with

limited U.S. authority. You can have your pick of Samoa, Vanu-
atu, or a dozen other islands."

Jacks glanced at Kwame. The big guy looked impressed. He
didn't appreciate the bullshit Sowanake had put him through.

"How's that going to happen?"

"We get you passports and put you on a flight from Lima.
But the clock's ticking, Jacks. Everyone assumes you're dead,
but they're taking inventory of bodies in Boca de Anjo.
They're already pretty sure some survivors escaped, including
Tepe."

Tepe survived? Jacks wasn't sure how to feel about that. It
actually touched a spiteful place in his heart. The Glaring were
terrorists, but they were werecats, and he couldn't deny he was
glad the U.S. had failed to eliminate them completely.

Sowanake drew up closer to him. "I can get you cash to
start new lives. There's a medical school in Samoa for your
friend, and they need MDs." He glanced at Kwame. "You can
get jobs in the tourist industry. It's not a bad deal, Jacks."

"Why would you do that?"

Sowanake took off his sunglasses in a gesture of respect.
"We let you down. I haven't said that once in my twelve-year
career. I never had to. I still believe the cause was just, but
sometimes the ends don't justify the means."

It was probably as close to an apology as Jacks could expect
from the patriotic prick, but why would Sowanake go to the
trouble to track him down unless it was some kind of trap? The
military had done so many things to deceive him. Yet, on the
other hand, they didn't need Sowanake to make a solo visit in
order to detain him again. He could have come with numbers,
and he'd brought back Bella.

He pushed back his wet hair from his cheek. "Farzan is in
some kind of physical shock from your just cause. He needs
medical attention."

"We'll get it for him. We can make a stop on the way to Lima."

"What about his family?"

Sowanake hesitated. "The Secretary of Defense is working on that. They're going to inform the Mohammeds that Farzan was kidnapped and killed by a drug gang. They won't be interrogated. We know they weren't involved in any of this."

Jacks's mind spun. When would the nightmare end? For simply trying to do something good, Farzan got kidnapped and then nearly shattered by bombs, and now his family had to mourn his death, and he could never see them again?

"I'm going to make sure they get some compensation from the Department of Defense's victim's fund."

"You're a real fucking prince. A real hero," Jacks said bitterly.

"I can't change the circumstances, Jacks. The three of you came down here thinking you could negotiate with a terrorist organization. However good your intentions may have been, you were out of your league, and there are consequences."

"Yeah, yeah, yeah. Enough of that bullshit. What about the Báalam-Tet?"

"It's in the hands of the Department of State."

"And you're cool with that?"

"That's where it belongs. It'll be studied to ensure it doesn't pose a threat to national security."

"What about the security of werecats?" He fixed on Sowanake. Sowanake didn't flinch. "Yeah, stupid me. You don't give a shit. You'll keep lapping Dickerson's balls while some archaeological lab figures out how it can be used to exterminate werecats. That's pretty fucking sick, but I guess you've made a career out of self-hatred."

"I'm offering you a Get-Out-Of-Jail-Free card, Jacks. And I'm leveling with you, man-to-man. This is where we're at. I can get the three of you to safety, but I don't have a lot of time to pull it off."

Jacks looked at Kwame. His alternative plan was to go back to Maarten's yacht, if Maarten would even accept them. It would be a miserable situation for Farzan, and they would constantly be in danger of being caught by the authorities. He had to think about what was best for Farzan. Jacks would be fine living as a fugitive, giving Sowanake a big fuck-you for his offer, but it wasn't fair for Farzan to have to keep living on the run.

# TEN

JACKS STRODE OVER to Kwame and motioned to follow him into the cabin while Sowanake waited outside. They needed to decide on things in privacy.

But first, he checked on Farzan and gave him some ice cubes to suck on. Bella had nested herself in the crook of Farzan's arm, playing nurse in her mysterious way. Jacks gave her an affectionate rub, and he sat down on the other cot with Kwame.

"I can't believe I'm even contemplating this. That mother-fucker made a goddamn fool of me."

"The problem is, if you don't accept his offer, you could have U.S. agents trailing after you, not to mention Tepe."

He hadn't thought of that. Tepe had escaped the airstrike. Whether or not he could rebuild his organization, revenge would be his first priority. He looked at Farzan. "How's he supposed to travel like this? He needs something for the pain."

"If your friend is true to his word, he will help Farzan get medical attention," Kwame said.

"He's not my friend."

"I do not know this man. But he took a risk to bring Bella to you. His superiors wanted you dead. If this is him following their orders, they are making it an elaborate game. They could have come with helicopters and a truck full of soldiers."

Jacks mulled over that logic. The big guy was quiet for a moment. Finally, he told Jacks, "It is a good deal for you and Farzan. I think you should take it."

"What about you?"

Kwame eyed him soberly. "Maarten, César, Som-Suea, and Nicolas are my family. They are where I belong."

Emotions pressed down on Jacks. "I thought we were family."

"I wish I could have it both ways." Kwame placed his big hand on Jacks's shoulder. "You will always be my brother. I followed you down here to claim justice for the murders of Annika, Thierry, and Lars and to stop Tepe from getting the Báalam-Tet. It was an honorable mission. It played out in a way we had not expected. But our lives are branching now. I promised Maarten and the others I would return."

Though it hurt like hell, Jacks understood. How would Kwame be happy, stuck on an island in the Pacific for the rest of his life? How would he and Farzan be happy for that matter? "Will you stay with us until Farzan recuperates?"

"Of course. That medicine man from the village should be here soon with the chuchuhuasi. They had such herbal remedies in Côte D'Ivoire. I have seen them heal men with very serious injuries."

Jacks looked at Farzan languishing on the cot. Maybe the chuchuhuasi would help, but what if it didn't? He had to do something to stop Farzan's suffering. He stepped over to the side of the bed facing Farzan and knelt down beside him.

He gently laid his hand on the side of Farzan's clammy

face. "Baby, I need to give you something to help you heal. You're not going to like it, but you have to trust me."

Farzan stirred faintly. Kwame stood to watch what was coming.

He had nothing to puncture his skin. Shifting into a cougar so he could bite himself seemed like far too much drama. But Bella had sharpened claws. He laid his wrist beside her.

He concentrated on a blue, raised vein. He joined with Bella mentally, commanding her to strike him. She growled in defiance, but Jacks bore down on his command. The tabby's olive eyes glinted red, and she swatted her forepaw, shredding the pale skin of his wrist in three puffed up and bleeding slashes.

Jacks bent his wrist toward Farzan's mouth. It smarted, but much more importantly, Bella had ripped open a vein. He pressed his bleeding wrist to Farzan's lips. Farzan's eyes quivered behind his lids, and he put on a fussy resistance to the strange sensation.

He clasped the back of Farzan's head and told him tenderly, "Drink. It'll make you strong. Take all the pain away."

Farzan's mouth sealed over the wound, and he drank. If it worked as well as Jacks hoped, Farzan would be back to normal in a matter of hours.

BY NIGHTFALL, FARZAN could sit up in his bed and feed himself warmed corned beef hash from a can. A fog of disorientation still blunted his speech and his demeanor, but his strength had returned, and a darker, warmer color had overtaken the pallor of his face. They didn't speak about the transfer of blood.

Sowanake pushed them along to embark on the trip to Peru. Jacks told the federal agent Kwame had decided to return to France, and the story raised no qualms or questions. He figured Sowanake understood Kwame posed no threat to national security. Besides, if Sowanake was successful with his insider plan, all three of them would be presumed dead and taken off the C.I.A.'s persons of interest list. He had no choice but to take Sowanake at his word. He and Farzan needed to go off the grid of U.S. intelligence, and they needed Sowanake's help to do it.

Kwame said goodbye to Farzan, who was able to embrace him for a delicate hug. Bella regarded him with feline umbrage, and Kwame gave her a playful ruffle on the head nonetheless. Jacks insisted Kwame take his cash. He would need it for his three-day drive to the Atlantic coast, and they could spare the money. Sowanake promised Jacks $15,000 to get him and Farzan settled in Samoa. It was the same sum they had taken away from him, a gesture to call things even, though Jacks would say they owed him a lot more than that.

He walked Kwame to the SUV while Farzan and Sowanake stayed back in the cabin. When they were beyond earshot, he told Kwame, "You'll visit us, won't you?"

Kwame patted him on the back. "As soon as I can convince Maarten, we'll make a trip to the Pacific. Could be a month or more, but we'll find you again."

Jacks looked his friend over. "I feel like there's unfinished business. Benoit mentioned a Zapotec mystic in the Yucatán. I want to find him. To understand. To see if there's a way for werecats to live free. Not hiding, like Sowanake. Not fighting, like Tepe. Do you think it's possible?"

"If anyone can do it, you can," Kwame said. "I will talk to Maarten. We will do whatever we can to help you."

They hugged, and Kwame climbed into the SUV with his handful of belongings. It was a sad moment, but Jacks was overcome by a wry grin. A 220-pound West African embarking on a cross-country drive through the Amazon, outfitted like he was headed to the beach. He had no doubt Kwame could handle the dangerous trek. Knowing Kwame, he would probably meet a handsome Brazilian along the way and make a little pit stop.

He watched Kwame back the SUV down the road, make a three-point turn, and disappear into the night. The world seemed to be tilting again, sending Jacks sliding to a new destination. Everywhere he went, he felt like he was barely secured to the ground by shallow roots. He wondered if he would ever find a place where he was settled and could call his home. He could handle living on the run, but would he be any good at staying put?

# ELEVEN

WHEN JACKS ARRIVED in Samoa, it occurred to him that he could no longer consider himself a temporary visitor to the tropics. The climate and the scenery had become a lifestyle, if not quite a home. The main island of Upolu had the familiar trademarks of the Caribbean isles he had run through: palm trees, white beaches, and a rugged inland lush with greenery. Ocean-facing, high-rise hotels were hedged around the coastline. With an eternal blue sky above and an endless Pacific seascape, every vista was postcard-ready. The equatorial sun was vigorous, but the drier, breezy South Pacific climate gave the island an easier, more welcoming feel than the Caribbean or the Amazon.

He and Farzan found a furnished, second-floor apartment near the sports stadium in the capital city of Apia. It was modest, local-style accommodations, living above the landlord and his family, and the rent was $1,500 per month. Everything they needed was within walking distance or reachable by the island's rustic buses, which were painted in bright, primary colors. That helped a lot; they wouldn't need to buy or rent a car. With his light skin and American accent, Jacks quickly got a job as a waiter in a casino resort. Most weeks he brought home $1,000 in salary and tips.

Meanwhile, Farzan ordered electronic transcripts from New York and filed an application to the regional medical school, though he was chagrined to discover he would have to repeat some of his coursework due to their transfer policies. Worse, the tuition, which was necessarily out-of-pocket due to his foreign status, was so steep, their entire nest egg of $15,000 wouldn't even cover the first two semesters.

Jacks insisted Farzan move forward with his application. He picked up extra shifts at the casino and applied for a second job at a beach club. The school was perfect for Farzan. He could take his classes online and complete his clinical work at a teaching hospital in town just two miles from their house.

Figuring these things out left little time to take in the island's attractions or to deal with each other for that matter. Though they inhabited the same space, they went about their days possessed by their respective inner worlds. Jacks searched out answers, but he pursued that issue quietly in stolen moments at the laptop they had bought for Farzan. His internet searches returned no news about the operation in Boca de Anjo, the discovery of the Báalam-Tet, or anything else related to werecats beyond the old coverage of the attacks in Barbados and New York City.

That got Jacks paranoid. The U.S. government had pulled off one hell of a cover-up, and General Gainsway and Secretary McCuthers could be plotting another operation to destroy his kind. He couldn't talk to Farzan about that. He didn't want to trigger his trauma or start an argument. What he needed to do was rebuild some semblance of a normal life. So, he searched for answers alone, paging through conspiracy blogs and losing himself in endless search returns on Zapotec mystics with the slender hope he would find a lead on the man who had bequeathed the Báalam-Tet to Benoit.

Meanwhile, he left Farzan to his distant, preoccupied mood, though Jacks worried about what he was thinking. At home, they lavished attention on Bella, the only child of two daddies who had lost the language to communicate with each other. Even christening their bed on their first night in the apartment, the sex had been careful on Jacks's part, mindful of Farzan's physical and psychic wounds, and mechanical on Farzan's part. It had been an inevitability more so than an exchange of feelings for each other, and neither one had reached out for the other again.

One night when Jacks came home from work around two o'clock in the morning, he found Farzan sitting on the back porch of their apartment, staring toward the town's light-spangled, crescent harbor in the distance. How long had he been sitting there in the dark? Farzan's face was shadowed, but Jacks could feel his desolation. Bella had nested herself in his lap.

He stepped near and spoke quietly. "Hi, Honey."

Farzan wiped his face, but he didn't look up nor respond. Jacks crouched beside him. "Everything okay?"

"I don't know how to do this."

Jacks felt ice compacting in his chest. He knew that hollow tone. Two months ago, a huge fight had started the same way when Farzan found out he had been on a party cruise with Maarten for three weeks.

"It'll get better." He clasped the side of Farzan's arm. "Once you get back into school, doing what you love, things will start to feel normal again." Farzan was dead silent. "Did you Skype with your parents tonight?"

Farzan nodded. He had contacted his brother Sammy soon after they arrived in Samoa and explained their situation. Sowanake had told them they could never return to the U.S., but Farzan could have discreet contact with his family. Sammy and his mother were already planning a visit in December.

"Am I enough for you?" Farzan said.

Jacks looked at him in the face. Shouldn't Farzan have known the answer to that after everything they'd been through? Yet Farzan stared back at him, searchingly.

"This isn't a vacation. It's not running around the world, fighting to stay alive. This is you and me living together on a remote island in the South Pacific for the rest of our lives."

"Yes, you're enough for me. I love you. That never changed."

"But things have changed. Every day from hereon in, it's going to be this, just you and me, separated from everyone and everything we've ever known."

Jacks rubbed his arm. "It'll get better, baby. It just takes some time."

"Will it get better?"

The forcefulness of Farzan's voice, and his pained expression triggered Jacks. He leaned back against the terrace wall. "What do you want me to say? I'm sorry. I pulled you into my fucked up life, and now we're stuck together."

"That's not what I meant."

"How is that not what you meant? I feel it from you every day. You lost your scholarship from medical school—my fault. You can never see your family—my fault too. We've got no friends and no money to do anything—my fault. What else?"

"I never said any of that."

"You don't have to. It's always there. Every lousy thing I dragged you into. And I'm sorry, Farzan. I really am. I'm trying the best I can. Is it really that bad? Do you have to be sad all the time?"

"I'm trying, too. But I can't pretend this is the great, big life we planned together so you won't feel guilty."

Jacks buried his face in his elbow. He felt like his world was collapsing. If this was Farzan's way of leaving him, he would be utterly alone. There would be no purpose to live.

"Do you realize that next week, it'll be exactly seven months since we've known each other? That's not that long, Jacks. We went from friends to boyfriends in a month, and the rest of the time was running from the police or running after the Glaring."

"Do you not want to be with me anymore?"

"I want us to finally talk about this instead of going through the motions every day. Neither one of us signed up for this kind of commitment. Can you honestly tell me this is what you wanted all along?"

"I couldn't have known it would turn out like this, but I want us to be together. Isn't that what matters? We make it work because we love each other." Jacks swallowed hard. "Maybe it's been too much for you. Maybe it changed you, and you don't love me anymore."

"Jacks, I think it changed both of us."

He looked up at Farzan through blurry vision. Then he hugged him and buried his head in his chest. "I couldn't stop them from taking you. I couldn't stop the missiles before they hit."

"You can't blame yourself for that." Farzan combed his hand through Jacks's hair. "You rescued me."

"When I look at you sometimes, I wonder if a part of you got shattered, and I don't know how to fix it."

"It's PTSD. I get heart arrhythmia and panicky feelings. Sometimes it makes me depressed."

"What can I do to make it go away?"

"Jacks, you can't just make it go away. And I'd much rather talk about how you're really feeling than watch you walking on eggshells around me. I'll get better. I made an appointment to see the hospital psychiatrist who can give me antidepressants. I guess your blood repaired the muscles and tendons in my neck, but it didn't have an effect on my brain."

That plunged the conversation into scary territory. He made Farzan drink his blood without his consent.

"It probably saved my life. I could have gone into neurogenic shock if you tried to move me. I never would have made it to Peru."

"It was the only thing I could think to do."

"You did the right thing." Farzan chuckled mildly. "It didn't make me sprout whiskers and a tail. When I have access to a lab, I'd love to take a look at a blood sample under a microscope."

"You're not angry at me?"

Farzan held his chin and looked him in the eyes. "No." Bella scurried away, and Farzan pulled Jacks into a tight embrace. They kissed, long and deep, for the first time since they arrived in Samoa. Quietly, Farzan told Jacks, "It was the most loving thing you could have done for me."

Jacks nuzzled against Farzan. He'd been needing his physical reassurance so badly. "Thank you."

"For what?"

"For accepting me for who I am."

"That goes both ways."

Jacks glanced up at him. "I love who you are. But after all you've seen, maybe it's not as easy for you."

Farzan pantomimed weights in his hands. "Neurotic control freak? Cougar shifter?"

Jacks grinned. "I love neurotic control freaks."

"Good." Farzan traced his ear with his hand. "You drive me a little crazy with your hero complex and aversion to communicating, but I guess that's what you get when you fall in love with a man with a feline soul."

The latter part warmed Jacks's heart, but the former...
"Hero complex?"

"You take on every wrong in the world like it's your responsibility to fix it."

"I'm just trying..." Jacks cut his thought short. If he tried to tell Farzan about the allegiance he felt to his kind, it might not come out right. Meanwhile, Farzan took his hands in his.

"We're not so different that way. I've got plenty of generational traumas I'm still working through."

"I'll do better with communicating. It doesn't always come naturally to me. You know my family wasn't great at expressing their feelings. I mean, talking about them."

Farzan squeezed his hands. "I know you're trying." He wrapped his arms around Jacks's back. "I like *this*. I never stopped feeling like divine justice lost track of me for a moment, and I ended up with the hottest boyfriend I didn't even know existed."

Their embrace was getting more sensuous, beckoning both of them to take things further. Jacks stood and led Farzan by the hand into the apartment, through their living space, and into their bedroom. They undressed each other, laid down on the bed, and made love urgently, as though to repair their respective hurts. Afterward, Jacks clung to Farzan, chest-to-back. Being with Farzan like that felt like a blessing from another world.

Farzan turned to Jacks and pushed back the sweaty locks that stuck to the side of his face. "There's something else we should talk about. I think you should look for that man who gave Benoit the Báalam-Tet."

Jacks supposed he'd been deluding himself, thinking Farzan hadn't picked up on what had been on his mind. But Farzan only had to retrieve the search history on his laptop. He erased it most of the time, though perhaps, subconsciously, he'd been a little sloppy.

"You said it wouldn't make a difference."

"It would make a difference to you."

He shifted away a bit. "What're you saying? You want me to try to find Benoit's contact? I'd have to travel to Mexico."

"I'm saying, if we're going to make this work, we have to respect the things that are important to each of us. I don't want you to resent me for keeping you from trying to find connection to your kind. You should never feel ashamed of who you are."

He appreciated that, and his mind opened up to possibilities. But how was it supposed to work? "I can't just leave you here."

"My mom and Sammy are coming next month. They'll want to see you, but you don't have to stay for the entire visit. It would be a good time for you to try to find what you're looking for."

Jacks shook his head. "I need to work. We need money so you can go to medical school."

"It'll be fine, Jacks. We have my first semester of tuition, and we'll take things as they come. I'm working on a dozen scholarship applications. One of them is bound to work out. Believe me, I'm not crazy about the idea of you going away, but I'm even less crazy about you feeling trapped here." Farzan caressed his face. "I know you want to find answers about your werecat family. Everyone deserves to find where they belong."

Jacks wasn't sure how to feel. He was grateful to Farzan for being so understanding, but he couldn't say what would happen when he explored the gaping hole in his identity. The thought of losing Farzan tore at him. But he was right. Jacks couldn't pretend he didn't need to find out more about his kind.

IN DECEMBER, THEY brought Mrs. Mohammed and Sammy home from the airport, and it was like the early arrival of Christmas Day. They had brought two extra suitcases loaded with gifts, clothes, and Mrs. Mohammed's home cooking. Jacks and Farzan's quiet apartment was quickly filled with spirited voices and laughter.

While Mrs. Mohammed appropriated the kitchen, Sammy told Farzan and Jacks about all the goings-on back in New York, which amounted to his favorite subjects like the Jets and his plans for making big money on Bitcoin. Though three years older than Farzan, Sammy was the brother who had never grown convincingly into an adult. He shucked his sneakers and nested his husky, football jersey-clad body on the Naugahyde couch with his socked feet on the coffee table as though he had visited the place a hundred times before.

When the food was ready, they sat around a fold-out table that the guys had bought for the special visit, and they had a feast of rice with lentils and raisins, stuffed eggplant, meatballs, and roasted chicken. Jacks poured wine to toast the arrival of their guests, and he toasted a second time to Farzan's acceptance to Oceania University's School of Medicine where he would begin his studies in January.

Mrs. Mohammed had always seemed to him like the kind of mother who showed affection through service around the home and hectoring her sons more so than hugs and kisses. She had survived the Islamic revolution in Iran, relocated to a foreign country, and raised three sons while her husband had worked for petty wages. But Jacks noticed her tiny chin trembling and her eyes getting misty as she looked at Farzan. Farzan stood up from the table to embrace her, and her tears came freely.

His eyes burned, watching them reunited. He'd never truly know that feeling that passed between them. His own mother had lost him to the clutches of Satan, in her own words. That was years before his feline soul had been reared, which had to place him several fathoms deeper in the pits of hell according to his mother's beliefs.

Sammy broke into the sentimental moment. "What? It's not like he won the Nobel Prize for medicine."

That stirred up nervous chuckles, and Mrs. Mohammed gave Farzan a kiss on the cheek and sent him back to his seat.

After dinner, Farzan and Jacks cleared the dishes, and Farzan tried to negotiate cleaning up so his mother could rest.

Mrs. Mohammed pushed her way into the kitchen. "You clean up after yourself every day. When do I have the chance to do the dishes for my son?"

Sammy's voice hailed from the living room. "You wash my dishes every night."

"What's to brag about?" she called back. "Twenty-eight-years-old and still breaking your old Maman's back cleaning up after you. You need a job and a wife."

Sammy sucked his teeth in reply. Some things hadn't changed. Sammy had never gone to college, and he worked shady jobs like forging fake IDs. Jacks told Farzan to visit with his brother, and he stayed back in the kitchen. He grabbed a hand towel and presented himself to Mrs. Mohammed who was getting to work on a mountain of pots, pans, and plates in the sink.

"House rules. You wash, I dry."

Mrs. Mohammed shrugged, and they went about the routine.

"Is it always this hot?" she said.

"Pretty much."

"In Persia, they had heat like this." She made a gruesome face. "But they didn't have all of these lizards."

Jacks grinned and took a plate from her. At night, green

geckos found their way to the windowsills. He noticed one had perched up on the high frame of the kitchen window.

"Doesn't your cat do her job keeping them away?" Mrs. Mohammed said.

"I'm afraid she's outnumbered. But they're harmless." Bella had snuck into the kitchen to watch them wash the dishes. Mrs. Mohammed took notice of her with the same mild look of authority she displayed to her sons.

"I have always believed that it is good to have a cat in the home. Did you know there is a famous story about a cat who was very dear to our prophet Mohammad? It is said that one morning when he rose to prayer, he found her sleeping on the sleeve of his prayer robe. Rather than wake her, he cut his sleeve so he could leave her untroubled. This is said to be an example to his followers that the cat is to be treated with kindness and respect."

He had heard the story from Farzan before, and it made him smile again the second time. He told Mrs. Mohammed that and then retreated into private thoughts. She took a high view of cats, but what would she make of him being a werecougar?

Mrs. Mohammed was quiet for a spell. From the adjoining room, a blast of Japanese instrumental music and a clash of swords announced that Sammy had cued up an action movie on his tablet. The brothers bantered about the volume, and it dampened to a reasonable level.

"My son is under the impression that the three of you are sleeping in the living room and I'm sleeping in your bed," Mrs. Mohammed said. "You must disabuse him of this nonsense."

"He just wants you to be comfortable."

"There's no need. We spent two years living in a one-bedroom apartment in Hoboken." She raised her tan, slender finger instructively. "That was before Farzan was born. He only suffered his first six months in that awful tenement before my husband could afford to buy our house in Queens. The pull-out couch is perfectly suitable for me and Sammy."

Jacks had barely cleared his throat before she spoke again. "It would not be proper to impose. This is your home."

Farzan had never told his mother about their relationship. He thought his parents had no inkling he and Jacks were more than friends, though Jacks gave them more credit than that. They had done nothing to hide the fact they shared the same bed, and Farzan had vowed to explain things to his mother in time. The conversation caught him by surprise. He didn't feel it was his place to confirm or deny anything.

Mrs. Mohammed continued while her back was turned to him. "You take good care of my son. A mother sees these things. And there is no greater joy than seeing one's son happy." She set down her iron wool for a moment. "I can't say this is what we wished for, Farzan's father and I. But if it must be, I am grateful it is you Farzan has chosen to share his life with."

"Thank you," Jacks managed to say.

She turned to him. Motherly concern had drawn up on her face. "He tells me that your family turned you away."

A dry gulp split down Jacks's throat. He nodded.

Mrs. Mohammed frowned and shook her head. "I do not wish to know their reasons. It is an abomination to turn away a child." She looked at him squarely. "You'll always have a family now." She patted his hand with her thin, bony palm.

He ached to hug her in gratitude, but sparing just a slight smile, she turned back to her washing, satisfied enough had been said about the matter. He changed the subject.

"You'll be here four weeks. What would you like to do first?"

She frowned. "I never cared for the beach, but I suppose it's unavoidable. I would like to see the school where Farzan will be studying."

"The hospital is just down the road. There's a good market in town if you're interested in traditional Samoan crafts. Or, you might like to see the Robert Louis Stevenson Museum. There are tours of the rainforest as well."

Mrs. Mohammed nodded vaguely. "I am sure my son has planned an exotic itinerary. And I shall follow wherever I'm led because I know it pleases him. But simply being here to visit with the two of you is enough for an old woman like me."

She was probably in her fifties, which wasn't so old, though Jacks knew better than to argue the point with her. A pang of guilt crept up on him. "I cleared my schedule for most of the week. I'm just working at the casino Friday and Saturday night." He shifted his weight a bit. "Then next week, I expect I'll be heading out of town for a short while."

Kwame had talked to Maarten and tracked Jacks down. They were en route in Maarten's yacht with an estimated arrival of one week. That was handy but delicate timing. Jacks wanted to make his trip to the Yucatán while Farzan had his mother and his brother to keep him company. But he was worried about what Mrs. Mohammed would think about a flashy entourage of guys whisking him away for a secret trip.

"I can't expect your life would come to a halt on our account," Mrs. Mohammed said. "I just wish it didn't have to be like this. The two of you living on the other side of the world."

"I know." Farzan's family had been told he and Jacks had to be relocated for a witness protection program because they had identified members of the international gang that had stormed the bank in Barbados.

Mrs. Mohammed must have had questions, but Jacks was grateful she seemed happy washing the dishes in their moment of privacy. He was also grateful that she didn't seem to blame him.

"Where is it you'll be going?" Mrs. Mohammed said.

"I have some friends I haven't seen in a long while," he said, trying to keep his tone even. It wasn't entirely a lie. "They're kind of like my family. Or really, they are my family. More so than my own family ever was."

Farzan's mother eyed him curiously.

"One of them has a boat. They're picking me up here, and we're sailing through the islands."

She wrinkled her nose. "I do not like boats. But that sounds like a good adventure for a young man. And nothing to feel guilty about. I can see on your face how happy it makes you."

His cheeks burned even warmer.

Strangely, Mrs. Mohammed brightened gleefully. "I'll tell you something, Jacks. But it must be sworn in confidence to the Almighty, or whatever god you worship."

He looked at her soberly.

"There are times when I wish Farzan's father would take a trip with his friends. Just to give me some breathing space. It is only healthy for a marriage." She retreated, uncertain of her words. "Healthy for any sort of relationship." She looked at him with a bashful glow. "Besides, absence makes the heart grow fonder, they say."

# TWELVE

NATURALLY, FARZAN DID have a full itinerary planned for Sammy and his mother, and each day proceeded with a hearty breakfast cooked by Mrs. Mohammed and a day-long excursion into town or to the beach or to one of the island's points of interest. Jacks came along when he could. Their money was tight, so it didn't hurt when they could save the extra bus fare or the extra cash for admission to this or that. One day, he splurged and rented jet skis for Sammy and himself while Farzan and his mother lounged beneath the shade of a thatched umbrella on the beach. They jetted across the north shore of the island and saw sharks and dolphins and coral reefs. Sammy talked about their adventure for days.

One early morning, later in the week, Jacks awoke to the drone of his cell phone. He reached groggily to the bedside table, but he was too slow to grasp the phone before the caller gave up.

*Maarten's Boat Phone* splashed on the screen. He slipped out of bed, taking care to not disturb Farzan, and he stepped lightly out to the back porch with the phone in hand. Before he could hit redial, Bella's ragged mewl caught his attention. She was clawing at the screen door.

They locked eyes knowingly. Maarten's yacht had anchored at the harbor ahead of schedule.

He rushed to make his way down to the harbor in the dawning light. Luckily, they'd left yesterday's wash on a clothesline across the back porch, and he quietly slipped into a swimsuit, T-shirt, and his flipflops. He took the back stairs and jogged downhill to the port. He had to intercept the guys in case they were thinking it would be funny to show up at his doorstep.

The town's narrow streets were vacant, and its tourist stores and restaurants were shuttered. Jacks hurried along. Having to introduce Mrs. Mohammed to Maarten would be a nightmare. He'd told Kwame they needed to avoid that when his yacht arrived, but now, he didn't trust that conversation. He particularly didn't trust Maarten, who liked to get a rise out of Farzan. He broke into a run when he sighted the marina.

A long pier serviced cruise ships on one side, with a shorter pier on the other for a dozen or so recreational boats. Amid the little boatyard, Maarten's Pride stood out like a swan amid her cygnets.

As Jacks gained on the piers, it looked like the double decks of the imposing vessel were desolate. Then, tramping down the dock, he breathed in a familiar and exhilarating musk that made him grin. It felt like he hadn't been among his kind for ages.

When he stepped onto the gangplank, the main cabin door slid open, revealing Kwame, half-clothed in a sarong and bearing a great big white-toothed smile. He came out to the deck and captured Jacks in a feet-off-the-ground hug. Som-Suea, César, and Nicolas emerged from the cabin, eager to give him a brotherly hug.

"It's great to see you guys," Jacks said. "Christ, you traveled halfway around the world."

"The worst of it was from the Galapagos to the Marquesas," Kwame said. "Fourteen days, nonstop. We all got a little bit stir-crazy, but we played cards to pass the time."

César, a tall and elegant, sandy-haired Spaniard, threw a question at Jacks. "You know Truco?"

Jacks shook his head.

"We teach you." César rifled off some words in Spanish to Kwame.

Kwame translated to Jacks. "César is happy now, because we have an even six players for three teams."

Jacks smiled, though it sank in sadly how much the group had dwindled. Annika, Jean-Luc, Thierry and Lars—all dead. He had a ball of nerves in his stomach about facing Maarten again. Just then, the playboy werelion appeared at the cabin door in a bathrobe.

Everyone turned silent. Maarten's last words to Jacks had been vicious, and he had threatened to make a meal out of Farzan. His expression was hard to read, but if he still hated Jacks, he wouldn't have come all the way to Samoa, would he?

He took a step toward Maarten and offered his hand. "Thanks for coming." His hand hung in the air, unacknowledged.

"I had no choice." Maarten didn't look at Jacks. "Kwame has an annoying preoccupation with telling me how you saved his life."

Kwame nodded to Jacks encouragingly. He drew his hand back to his side. He supposed it was too soon to expect their friendship to be repaired, if that would ever happen. But conversation without threats was a step in the right direction.

"It was a mess," Jacks said. "In trying to stop Tepe from getting the Báalam-Tet, we ended up endangering all of us.

The codex is in U.S. custody now. Being studied." He glanced around the guys. "If wereshamans are really wiped out around the world, we could be the last of our kind. That's why tracking down the mystic Benoit got the book from is so important. They may have knowledge that can help us get ahead of the authorities so that our kind doesn't die with us."

Maarten looked him over blandly. "We'll need a few days to get the boat in order for the voyage back. I expect you'll be ready to go at our earliest convenience."

"For sure."

Maarten turned around and disappeared into the cabin.

Kwame came around to his side. "We had very bad cell phone service most of the way."

"I know. Your messages were all dead air." He had tried to engage Kwame in texting, but none of the guys had adapted very well to technology. Besides Nicolas, a French diplomat's son, who grew up in the 1990s, they had been born decades before the invention of the cell phone, and in any case, they rarely had to communicate with anyone besides each other.

"After we spoke, from Grenada, we charted a route to get here as quickly as we could," Kwame said. "You heard what happened in Boa Vista?"

Jacks shook his head. He had no idea what Boa Vista was.

"It has begun," Kwame told him soberly. "Three weeks ago now, an American Special Forces unit raided a house in a little Brazilian town near the border of Guyana. The U.S. was able to keep Boca de Anjo out of the news, but there were witnesses to this attack. People recorded video that is making rounds on South American news channels. Tear gas grenades. Servicemen shooting down the evacuees. The U.S. issued a statement to say it was an urgent mission to thwart a bioterrorism plot aimed at American cities. We picked up the story from an independent press in Brazil."

Apparently, the story hadn't made the BBC, which had been Jacks's only news source. "You think it was another attack on the Glaring?"

"I do. No one has been able to identify the victims with the exception of one man who had been reported missing from the Amazon. In 1961. I believe they were werejaguars in hiding, whether they were affiliated with the Glaring or not."

"How do you mean?"

"There's more. We stopped in Aruba on the way to the Panama Canal, and we visited my old friend Sterling who owns some property in Miami. He told us that two of his tenants were taken into custody by the police, and Homeland Security impounded their condominium, pending an investigation."

"Werecats?"

Kwame nodded. "With no affiliation to the Glaring."

"How do you know for sure?"

"Sterling is a good man. I have known him for years. He would not lie to me."

"Maybe he didn't know his tenants were involved."

"I do not think so, Jacks. Sterling would never do business with anyone associated with the Glaring. He's...like you. He met his human husband Rafael in Aruba, and they have been together for thirty years."

"So, what is it? They're rounding up any werecat they can get their hands on? How are they even finding them?"

"This I do not know. Sowanake? Some other werecat they coerced to sniff us out? Something they learned from the Báalam-Tet? Whatever it is, they are on a hunt."

Jacks had had paranoid thoughts about U.S. intelligence agencies before, but hearing them come to life left him stunned. Then he was disgusted with himself. None of this would have happened if he hadn't made that phone call to the N.S.A. back in Venezuela.

"I'm sorry, Jacks," Kwame said. "I did not mean to throw this at you all at once."

"It's all right." He stepped over to the railing of the deck to cool off for a moment. Words burst out of him. "I'm just so fucking angry."

The guys gathered around him.

"It's genocide," César said. "We are all fucking angry." César was a werelion of proud Spanish and Zulu heritage.

"Sterling also had some information on that man you're looking for in the Yucatán," Kwame said. "You remember Benoit spent some time with us a year ago in Barbados?"

Jacks nodded.

"After he left us, Sterling and Rafael put him up for a few nights at their guesthouse. He told them he was on his way to Mexico to visit a friend who lives in an artist's colony outside of Valladolid. When they teased him that he must be looking up an old flame, Benoit said it was nothing like that, just a psychic he consulted from time to time. A psychic Zapotec." Kwame passed a smirk to his friends. "They must have caught Benoit in a good mood, or gotten him good and drunk. He barely spoke a word about his personal life to any of us."

Jacks's hopes lifted. "That has to be who gave Benoit the Báalam-Tet. Let's hope he's still alive." Jacks puzzled over what Kwame had said. "But I thought Benoit was talking about a wereshaman. What do you think he meant by a psychic?"

"Could be he was being cagey. Could be his friend is both. I have never met these people, the Zapotec. Could be they know of an entirely different form of magic."

# THIRTEEN

THAT NIGHT, AFTER Sammy and Mrs. Mohammed had gone to bed, Jacks sat up with Farzan in their bedroom, trying to explain things. Though Farzan had encouraged him to seek out knowledge about his heritage, it still felt like a minefield conversation. Farzan had good reasons to worry about him running off with Maarten and his friends. The last time, he had gotten caught up in their carefree lifestyle and been unfaithful. Now, the U.S. was killing and detaining werecats domestically and internationally.

Farzan got on his laptop while Jacks was talking and pulled up entries from his search engine. He stopped talking when Farzan got quiet and studious. It looked like he hit on something of interest.

"There's a press release about Boa Vista on the U.S. Secretary of State's website," he told Jacks. "They say it was an anti-terrorism investigation that had the full backing of the Brazilian government." Jacks scooted up close to him at the head of the bed so he could look at the screen while Farzan scrolled through some news coverage. "Looks like most of the world bought it," Farzan said. "News outlets covered it for a day or two in November. It didn't even make headlines. That's how we missed it."

Jacks was relieved Farzan wasn't going ballistic about him traveling to the Americas, at least not yet. "Check out N.S.A. activity in Miami," he suggested.

Farzan keyed the words into his browser. A new list of items came up on the screen, and Farzan's mouth hung open. "Did you know what N.S.A. also stands for?"

Jacks squinted at the screen. It looked like a directory of personal ads.

"No Strings Attached," Farzan said. "We're looking for counterterrorism operations, and we found everyone in South Florida who's looking for hook-up sex."

Jacks reached for the mouse pad to open a Man4Man listing. "Could be interesting. And educational."

Farzan shooed him away and tapped in a new search. "Let's try something more specific: suspected terrorists Miami." He studied the refreshed list of returns and opened a news article from the *Miami Herald*. "'Two men arrested in connection with terrorism investigation,'" he read. "That sounds like the story Kwame was telling you about."

Jacks nodded encouragingly.

"Manuel Ponce and Ivan Syarrudin of Coral Gables," Farzan read. Jacks scanned the short article while Farzan read the rest of it to himself. "Listen to this," Farzan said. "Two officers were injured when they entered the suspects' apartment and were attacked by a house cat."

Jacks glanced across the room at Bella who was grooming herself in the far corner of the room. "At least someone's fighting back." Peeking in on the shit-storm happening back in the U.S. made him antsy. He climbed off the bed and crouched down by Bella to rub the back of her neck.

Farzan watched the two of them. He keyed a new combination of words into his browser. After a few moments, he raised his voice. "Jacks, you've got to see this." Jacks hurried over. "It was just a hunch, but look at these attacks by domestic cats. All from the past few weeks. San Diego. Missoula, Montana. Fort Meyers, Florida. All across the country."

Jacks leaned in, and his eyes bugged. They jostled a bit to get a good view of the screen. Farzan read aloud, "'No connection between feline attacks in two parts of the state, according to Health Commissioner.' This is from Colorado. One fatality. An off-duty police officer Janice Deets. Another attack on an Assistant District Attorney Peter Shapiro." He clicked open another article that was emblazoned with a photo of two victims. "'*Pet Sematary*-style ambush on customs agents in Niagara Falls,'" Farzan read. "This is crazy, Jacks."

A fierce pride welled up inside Jacks. "The Glaring has a network of hundreds of thousands of domestics and strays. That's how Tepe knew so much about me. Now those cats are fighting for their masters."

Farzan huddled over his laptop, doing more research. "There are approximately ninety million domestic cats in the United States. This could be a bloody war."

Jacks sat up against the headboard. "It could be a massacre. They'll round up the domestics just like they're rounding up werecats."

"Someone should call them off." Farzan added quickly, "Not you. You know you can't go back to the States."

More thoughts stirred in his head. "Domestics choose their masters, but their loyalty can be manipulated. Just like Bernard lured Bella away from me."

Farzan glanced at him, not understanding.

"Do a search of Special Agent Dickerson," Jacks told him.

Farzan tapped away at his laptop. A few items down a list

of search returns, he pointed out a press release from the Secretary of Defense Matthew McCuthers. Farzan called it up, and Jacks stared at a photo of Dickerson, looking polished in a navy blue suit and wearing his too-cool-for-school smile. He was standing between McCuthers and General Gainsway, receiving some kind of commendation.

Farzan read the caption, "'Andrew Dickerson, former Navy Seal Captain and Special Agent to the Central Security Service, receives Ulysses James Memorial Award for his work on counterterrorism operations in Latin America, and an appointment as director of Secretary McCuther's new Bioterrorism Research Agency.' It's dated November 19th." He looked at Jacks, still at a loss.

"The operation in Boca de Anjo earned Dickerson a big, fat promotion. It had to be him behind the supposed preemptive strike in Boa Vista, and now he's looking for werecats in the U.S., like the two he found in Miami."

"I don't see anything about Sowanake," Farzan said. He shuffled through some searches. "Nothing comes up at all under that surname." They tried a series of spelling variations, and they only hit on nineteenth-century Native American registries. "If he works undercover, they probably keep him out of the news. Or maybe Sowanake is an alias," Farzan said.

"Or maybe he's not involved," Jacks said. "He stuck his neck out to get us to safety and cover up that we're still alive. Maybe he dropped out of the agency completely. I mean, he could have had an epiphany, couldn't he? He helped me get out of trouble when he realized Gainsway never intended to let anyone out of Boca de Anjo alive."

"How would Dickerson be tracking down werecats? You think he has another werecat turncoat?"

Jacks rubbed his eyes. "I don't know. Anything is possible. Maybe he cracked open something from the Báalam-Tet." A memory rushed back to Jacks. He squirmed, disgusted by the notion. "There was a passage in the book about the psychic connection with strays. If Dickerson figures that out, he could root out werecats everywhere."

Farzan heaved a sigh. Then he turned a sharp gaze at Jacks. "You're not going back to save the world."

Jacks scoffed.

"I'm serious. I don't even think it's a good idea for you to try to get in and out of Mexico with all of this going on."

"Hon, this may be the only chance for me to try to find the guy who gave Benoit the Báalam-Tet. The longer we wait, the more time Dickerson has to uncover the codex's powers."

Farzan said nothing for a while. Eventually he exhaled heavily. "This was a great idea of mine, encouraging you to find some closure. I didn't know this was happening."

"Hon, it's more than just closure."

"Okay. More than closure. What do you think you're going to find out?"

Jacks scratched the side of his head. "I don't know. Some way to repair what I fucked up."

"You didn't fuck up anything. You think this wouldn't have happened anyway? Dickerson was already on to Tepe and the Glaring. You told me that."

So many things were spinning around his mind, he didn't know what to say.

"Jacks, promise me that whatever you find out, you're not going to go after Dickerson."

That thought had occurred, but he said nothing.

Farzan turned him by the chin and stared at him squarely. "Promise me, Jacks. You cannot go back to the United States."

"I'm not going to do anything to put you and your family in danger."

"This isn't about me and my family. It's about you and me."
Jacks expected to see anger on Farzan's face, but he found fear.

"I'm not going to spend the next month or so worrying
about what might have happened to you." Farzan turned away
from him. "I can't do that. So you need to tell me. If that's
where this is leading, we can call it quits right now."

Jacks gathered Farzan's hand in his. "I promise, I won't go
back to the U.S." He kissed Farzan on the cheek. "I'll call you
every chance I get."

Farzan leaned against his side while he held Farzan's hand
on his lap.

# FOURTEEN

MAARTEN'S TRANSPACIFIC CRUISE embarked two days later. It was pleasant all the way to Hiva Oa in the Marquesas Islands with gentle surf, plenty of sun, and a light breeze for enjoying the views from the yacht's wraparound decks. Maarten had stocked up on food and liquor in Samoa, and there was no shortage of gourmet meals.

The guys gathered on the sun deck each morning for a late breakfast of steak and fish, and they stayed out most of the day playing cards while Maarten's sound system played the latest club music. The guys taught Jacks Truco so they could play teams of three when Maarten was in the mood. When their host was grumpy and aloof, retreating into the cabin with his snuff box of Valerian and a bottle of rum, Jacks sat out to let Kwame, Som-Suea, César, and Nicolas play. Sometimes they got together for five-player games of Rummy or Bullshit.

At night, they watched movies in the home theater of the main cabin. Maarten had a prodigious collection of DVDs, and while in Samoa, he had purchased some recent releases since everyone besides Jacks had seen everything in the library multiple times. The novelty of living with werecats returned to him at times. Kwame was ninety-four years old. César and Som-Suea were in their eighties, and Nicolas was almost forty. Yet they all looked and acted like buff dudes in their twenties, and the truth was they had hundreds of years ahead of them. It reminded Jacks he had hundreds of years ahead of him as well.

At times, that hit him with an existential sadness, thinking about Farzan growing old and frail while he was impervious to the ravages of time. What would he do when he outlived Farzan? Join Maarten's group on their perpetual vacation? The guys had formed a tight companionship, and he couldn't say he ever perceived a chink of loneliness in any one of them or a longing for something more. But it had to feel monotonous, never really having anything to do.

Some nights, after the guys had tossed back a lot of rum-spiked milk punch, a certain vibe would percolate with teasing pokes and gropes and little ear bites as they hung around a card table in the main cabin. Arms would sling over shoulders, and the guys would wade into the darkness on the far side of the cabin, which had a grand, high-backed sofa where they could meld into a cuddle pile. That was his cue to make himself scarce. The guys were hot, but he didn't feel the unstoppable, sexual pull that had drawn him in when he had cruised with them in the Caribbean. He wanted to be faithful to Farzan.

Usually when things turned sexual, Jacks would go up to his bedroom to turn in for the night. One evening, feeling wide awake, he stepped out to the deck by himself to look out on the water.

The air was bracing, but he ventured to the railing, feeling restless and confined. The rumbling ocean surf surrounded him, and he was bathed in its infinite, briny breath.

He brought out his cell phone and texted Farzan. *Miss you like crazy. xo*

He had no signal to send the message. He stuffed the phone into the pocket of his shorts to try sending it later.

He heard someone and turned around. Kwame. The big guy gave his sarong a little tuck and joined him by the railing.

"What are you doing out here on your lonesome?"

"I just felt like a little air before I call it quits for the night." Jacks said it like it was no big deal, though he was grateful for the company.

Kwame took a good account of him. "I think you miss Farzan."

"I do." Christ, tears were welling up inside him. That seemed awfully dramatic. They had only been separated for a week. But Jacks couldn't control it. His eyes burned, and his face shrank up. Kwame sheltered him with one arm and rubbed his back.

He drew a deep breath. "I'm sorry. I really love hanging out with you guys. I don't mean to be a buzzkill."

"Why apologize?" Kwame kneaded his shoulder. "You are in love. Of course it hurts when you cannot be with your man."

He met Kwame's gaze. "That guy in Côte d'Ivoire you told me about. Do you still think about him sometimes?"

"Henri. Yes, I think about him every now and then. I still remember his birthday: December 21st. He would have been 112 years old this year."

"Do you ever wonder how things might have been?" Jacks fumbled a bit to clarify. "I mean, if you and Henri could have made a life together?"

Kwame gave him a strange look. "We made a life together."

"I mean, if Henri hadn't died. Do you wonder how it would have turned out?"

"I see." Kwame turned pensive for a moment. "Of course, I thought about that all the time when I was younger. But if you are asking me because you want advice about you and Farzan, you have to remember, Jacks, my life back then was very different from yours now. I was with Henri before I was reared. I did not even understand what had happened to me until a year had passed after he died. By then, I had put our relationship in the past, which is not to say I no longer loved him. But it was different. I suppose I'd seen more of the world to put things in perspective. Henri and I loved each other, but even if he had not been murdered, who knows, there could have been a dozen other reasons for us to go our separate ways. A wandering eye. Jealousy. Could be we would have simply grown apart."

"Did you ever fall in love after him?"

Kwame looked out to the shrouded ocean. "I used to fall in love all the time. I had a boyfriend in Marseille for some years. It was, as they say, complicated. He was married, and in those days, no husband left his wife to live with a man. After that ended, I moved to Paris, and I met a young journalist named Fabien. He was 'in the closet' as well, so there was no future in it."

"Things are different now," Jacks started to say. "I mean, people live their lives openly. There's gay marriage." He wrestled in his head for what he was getting at. "I guess I'm trying to understand how to live like this. Do you ever wish you had that one person to settle down with? Someone who could be there your entire life?"

"Naturally, I do. And I have him. And him and him and him." He glanced at the cabin. "Som-Suea, César, Nicolas, and even Maarten. He has just been off licking his wounds lately. We are all bonded to each other. A group of husbands. You find that strange?"

Yes, Jacks did. Though he didn't want to say it. Before Benoit and before Farzan, Jacks had been all for sexual experiences in their many variations, but he hadn't considered that to be love, and certainly not settling down.

"It's hard for me to understand. I never fell in love with two people at the same time, let alone four. I mean, you feel the same way about each one of them? You never get jealous?"

Kwame snorted out a laugh. "Things change as you get older. When I was your age, I would not have believed it was possible myself. I learned that sex and love are two very different things. So, it does not bother me when this one or that one has sex with someone else. Maarten taught me that when he brought me into his pride."

Jacks thought about Kwame's romp with Javier. "And no one cares if you fool around with someone outside of the pride?"

"To us, our bodies are one thing. Our souls are something else. This is what bonds us—giving our souls to each other." He grinned devilishly. "Though it is nice if you are going to share your body with someone outside the pride to allow the others to share him, too."

Kwame had meant to be funny, but it drove a nail into a sore spot. Maarten had bragged to Jacks about having slept with all seven guys on the boat, when there were seven, all in one night. When Maarten had seduced him into group sex, it hadn't felt like sharing. It had felt like being used so Maarten could notch up another conquest. "I don't know. It seems like more of a game to Maarten."

"Could be this is not for you." Kwame said.

"I guess I'm too conventional."

"Some werecats spend their lives with just one mate. I told you about my friend Sterling."

Jacks nodded. He wished like mad he could talk to Sterling and his husband. To figure out how they made it work. He told Kwame, "When I first discovered my feline soul, I was terrified about the future. Then things got better for a while. Now, I'm terrified again."

"This is very special that you and Farzan found each other. I see the love between you. Some people do not find that connection in ninety years. Some do not find it in four hundred."

Jacks felt the tears coming back again. "What do I do when he dies?"

Kwame looked at him firmly and kindly. "You grieve and honor him, and then you live. As it is with all of us in the world."

THE GUYS HAD warned Jacks that the long leg from the Marquesas to the Galapagos Islands was a rugged journey. There was no harbor for thousands of miles, and the Pacific rose up in angry swells, rocking the 120-foot yacht in a perpetual, queasy motion. It was too gusty and cold to spend much time on deck.

Their captain, a Dutchman named Ollie, kept close tabs on the weather conditions by radio. Winter was a dicey time to make the crossing. It was the middle of typhoon season. Luckily, their route skirted a tropical storm farther north in the Pacific, though there were days when the yacht heaved harrowingly from the rough surf, and pelting rain didn't let up from morning to night. For the worst part of the two-week sail, Jacks took Dramamine at four hour intervals and subsisted on weak tea and chicken broth. They had no cell phone or internet connection, either. Some days, he emerged from his cabin to join the guys in the home theater where they binge-watched seasons of American TV shows and played games on Xbox. Some days, he didn't venture out of his bed at all.

They finally hit a lull thirteen days into the journey, and sunshine flooded the curtains to Jacks' balcony while he lay on his stomach. Voices traveled from the deck below. He went to his bathroom to splash cold water on his face and see if there was any chance of making himself look presentable. His coppery bearded face was pale and gaunt, and his shaggy hair hung stringy and flat around his head. They were conserving water for the trip, which meant one or two showers a week. The other guys took communal baths. He was sure that had turned into some kinky fun, but he relished his next opportunity to take a long, hot private shower.

He pulled on a fresh T-shirt and shorts and went to join the guys on deck. Just as he was making his way to the stairs, Maarten came through the other side of the narrow, upper deck hallway.

Maarten had avoided him and most everyone else since they had embarked from Samoa, and Jacks had left him to his private party of Valerian and booze. He was startled by Maarten's appearance. There had always been a magnetic glow on his handsome, light-skinned face, but he was ashy and drawn and he had dark, puffy circles beneath his eyes, which had dulled to slate gray. He spared him a brief glance and stepped to his room with a bottle of liquor tucked under one arm. Jacks caught up to him midway down the hall.

"It's been quite a trip."

Maarten said nothing, nudging past Jacks on the way to his room.

"How're you holding up?" he tried. "I've barely been able to keep anything down since the Marquesas."

Maarten spoke in a faint grumble. "If you can't handle it, we should have saved ourselves the bother of picking you up."

"That's not what I meant."

Maarten kept moving, his back turned to Jacks. That pissed Jacks off. He followed after Maarten, nearly knocking into his bony frame.

"Hey, are you really going to be like this the entire time? I don't mind that you hate my guts, but you've got people who care about you. You could at least be civil toward them instead of locking yourself up all the time like a junkie."

Maarten pushed forward, arriving at his door. Jacks called after him, "I used to admire you. What happened, Maarten? The guy I knew didn't go running off pouting like a child."

Maarten faced him with a flicker of his former fire. "You don't understand anything."

Jacks drew up closer, locking eyes with Maarten searchingly. "Then tell me what's going on."

"You left us. I don't owe you any explanations."

"You wanted me gone. Don't you even remember?"

Maarten turned his head, and a shadow covered his face. "You left the pride while we went back to collect our dead."

He was speaking of recovering the bodies of Annika, Thierry, Jean-Luc, and Lars from Barbados. "I asked if I could go with you," Jacks said. "You told me to get lost at the nearest port."

Maarten swayed and righted himself, assuming an aggressive stance. The potent odor of rum seeped from his body. "You took Kwame away. You tried to break up the pride."

Jacks drew back, gathering it was the alcohol or whatever else Maarten had been ingesting. In a fight, he could easily take him in his inebriated state, but there was no need for things to come to that. There was probably no point in trying to reason with Maarten either, though Jacks couldn't stop himself.

"All I ever wanted was to be your friend. If anyone is breaking up your pride, it's you. What are you going to do? Embalm yourself in that room for the next three hundred years?"

"Stay out of my goddamn business."

"You think this is what Annika would have wanted? She would have wanted you to live, not give up on life."

"Don't talk about my sister." He glared at Jacks, though his expression was weighed down by substances, more like a drunken squint. Jacks held his ground. At least he had gotten Maarten to talk.

Maarten tightened his grip on the neck of his rum bottle. The bottle cracked and fell to the floor.

As though Jacks had been the cause of it, Maarten launched at him. He still had some feline strength in his inebriated state, but Jacks caught his arms and absorbed his momentum as his back met the wall of the corridor.

Maarten wrangled to free his hands and tried to bite his neck. Jacks pushed him back, and they stumbled together into the door of Maarten's room. Unlocked, the door gave way. Maarten tripped backward, falling out of his grip, and he landed on the floor with a thud. He laid there, groping weakly to right himself, while Jacks stood over him.

Jacks reached out his hand. "C'mon. I'll help you up."

Maarten looked around as though he had no recall of what had happened. Shakily, he took Jacks's hand, and Jacks helped him stumble over to his bed. A half dozen empty liquor bottles littered his night stand. The curtain-shrouded room stunk like a clothes hamper soaked in booze.

Maarten slumped onto the bed, and Jacks sat down next to him. "Christ, Maarten. You're scaring the hell out of me."

Maarten laid down and curled into himself.

"You have so much, and this is what you're doing with your life?"

Maarten didn't answer him. Jacks felt like shaking him or slapping him in the face to bring him back into reality. He held back those impulses. Maarten was like a vortex, engulfing everyone around him into his inner world of excess and destruction, but he was also the first werecat who had accepted

Jacks as a friend. He was selfish and bullheaded, but that little act still counted big in Jacks's heart.

"You were there for me when I needed you. When you're ready, I'll be there to return the favor."

He gave Maarten a pat on the back of his neck and left him to his privacy.


FIVE DAYS LATER, as they approached the Panama Canal, Jacks was able to pick up a Wi-Fi signal and Skype with Farzan on Captain Ollie's laptop. Seeing his face on the screen lifted his heart right out of his chest.

They talked about regular things at first. Farzan's mother was preparing a big dinner for Christmas, even though their family didn't celebrate it. Mrs. Mohammed thought of the holiday as a patriotic duty since they were Muslim-Americans. Jacks wished like mad he could be there to celebrate with them. For him, Christmas had always held the promise of being part of a family, even though his memories of home weren't exactly warm and fuzzy. With Farzan, Mrs. Mohammed, and Sammy, he knew it would really feel like a family celebration. The sound of Sammy and Mrs. Mohammed's bickering voices in the background brought a big grin to his face. He caught Farzan's attention and blurted out words he had imagined saying for days.

"Marry me."

Farzan zoned in on him cautiously. "What did you say?"

"Marry me. Make me the happiest man in the world."

"You're asking me to marry you over Skype?"

Jacks stared into his eyes. "I am."

Farzan shifted in his seat. He smiled and scowled and came back to Jacks with a look of mild terror. "What am I supposed to say?"

Jacks laughed. "Yes or no. I was kind of hoping for a yes."

Farzan glanced around the room. Sammy and his mother must have been close by in the living space, adjacent to their bedroom where he was sitting with his laptop. He spoke in a lower voice. "Jacks, you can't just...do this."

"Why not? I love you. I want us to be a family. I want to marry you, Farzan. So I'm asking: will you marry me?"

"Jacks, I think you're asking me this because we're thousands of miles apart, and you're lonely and worried we might never see each other again."

"Yep. That's true."

Farzan's voice rose. "That's not a reason to—" He caught himself and spoke in a whisper. "It's not a reason to propose to me, Jacks."

"Why?"

"Because you're not thinking clearly."

"I've never been surer of anything in my life."

Farzan stared at him. Jacks melted. It was adorable to see Farzan beside himself.

"We never even talked about this," Farzan said.

"I'm talking to you about it now."

"It's not even legal in Samoa. How do you propose we get married?"

He shrugged. "We can do the ceremony in New Zealand or Australia. Wherever. That part isn't important to me. I just want you to know you're the one man in the world for me. I was hoping you felt the same way."

Farzan's eyes got misty. "Of course, I feel the same way. So if that's what this means to you, then yes, I'll marry you."

Jacks put his hand on the screen of the laptop, and their hands touched in a virtual embrace. He had counted the moments in his life when he had felt grown up, a real man, the way adulthood was supposed to be. The first time he had sex.

Seeing his name on his first paycheck. Signing a lease for an apartment, which he paid for with his own money. This was many times bigger than any of that.

"You better make it home, Jackson Cherokee."

"Jackson Cherokee-Mohammed."

Farzan snorted out a laugh. "Farzan Mohammed-Cherokee. I'll ask Sammy to take video when my mom explains it to our imam."

THEY TRAVERSED THE Panama Canal and cruised into the gentle, aquamarine Caribbean Sea, making a stop at Grand Cayman to refuel and restock before setting a course for Cancun. Of the ports on the Yucatán peninsula, Cancun had the most suitable facilities for Maarten's yacht, and it wasn't far from Jacks's destination, Valladolid, where he was to find Benoit's mysterious Zapotec contact based on Kwame's lead about an artist's colony.

It was the middle of the Christmas holiday week, and the seaside resort town bustled with vacationers. A human tarpaulin was spread across its white sand beaches, and its shoals were an amusement park for jet skiers, banana boats, and parasailers. Tourists in flashy sports car rentals clogged the narrow arteries through town. No one thought this was good timing except Jacks. He hadn't seen masses of people enjoying their lives in a long time, and the normalcy of it took the edge off his constant fear that the world was falling apart. His companions preferred quieter and more exclusive harbors. They made a jaunt into town one night to have drinks at a gay beach bar. Otherwise, they stayed on board the yacht.

Jacks and Kwame spent some time getting caught up on recent news via Captain Ollie's laptop. They discovered troubling happenings.

Dozens of news stories from the U.S. spoke of domestic counterterrorism operations, rounding up persons of interest who were said to be linked to a South American dissident organization that they had now named the Glaring. One of them was familiar to Kwame, an American werecougar named Verner Battle, who he had met just a few seasons ago when Maarten's yacht had docked in Key West.

"Verner was no terrorist," Kwame said. "He despised the Glaring's politics. He owned a nightclub that depended on human patrons. He told us he had even been president of the Key West Chamber of Commerce in the '90s."

The story got worse as Jacks and Kwame looked closer at the articles. Secretary McCuthers claimed the Glaring was affiliated with Iranian terrorist proxies like Hezbollah and Hamas and had a single-minded agenda to kill Americans. No news outlets made mention of the hybrid nature of its members, and the focus on supposed operatives in the States didn't make sense. The Glaring had had its stronghold in Brazil. Tepe had organized attacks in the U.S. in the past, but after the U.S. blasted his base, they would hardly have the infrastructure to conduct an operation on American soil. Dickerson's new counterterrorism agency was weeding out any werecat he could locate.

Meanwhile, they discovered that incidents with domestic cats had escalated. News coverage from Wichita, Kansas claimed an unnamed viral outbreak was responsible for cats attacking their owners. The mayor had ordered residents to relinquish their animals to shelters, and neighborhood vigilantes had taken to killing domestics, proudly outfitted in T-shirts with a cat's head in a crosshair target and the slogan: "Go Fur Free." A photo of a pickup truck loaded with dead animals made Jacks's stomach turn. Animal rights groups had called for a boycott of the city, but hundreds, maybe thousands of cats had already been killed.

In Las Cruces, New Mexico, impounded cats had broken free from a no-kill shelter, murdering the staff and escaping into the desert. Some of the animals had been found electrocuted after tunneling into a power station that serviced a nearby military base and short-circuiting the wiring. The governor had called in the National Guard to patrol the vicinity.

It was a war, just like Farzan had said. But none of the reporting connected the dots between the rounding up of "Glaring operatives" and the domestic cat attacks. Two men had been taken into custody in Kansas City, Missouri. A suspect from a nearby Indian reservation was being held at Fort Leavenworth in Kansas.

"What is their plan?" Kwame said bitterly. "Withhold the truth so they can lock up all the werecats and destroy the strays without any interference?"

Jacks grimaced. "They can't keep that up for long. Not in this day and age. Even if Dickerson has the media in his pocket, there's cell phone videos, animal rights activists, and conspiracy theory bloggers. Someone is going to make a connection." A chill passed through him. "Then it's only going to get worse. There'll be hysteria and vigilantes going after werecats just like those fucking idiots in Wichita."

"I should go with you to Valladolid," Kwame said.

Jacks said nothing. It wasn't a bad idea to have the big guy with him in case Dickerson's counterterrorism project had turned up information about werecat activity in the Yucatán. For all he knew, it could have become an international effort. But Jacks had already led Kwame into one disaster. He ached remembering that.

Kwame patted him on the back. "I won't take no for an answer."

# FIFTEEN

THE NEXT DAY, Jacks and Kwame packed hiking bags with changes of clothes and some provisions and caught a comfortable, tourist-class bus from Cancun to Valladolid for twenty dollars. Once they left the coastal town, the highway route was reminiscent of their travels in South America, from the shrubby, tropical countryside to the slow-moving junctions at tin-roofed pueblos. The land was essentially flat, and being the dryer season of late December, everything looked sun-weathered beneath the brilliant sky. When the bus entered the Yucatán inland state, modest sign posts pointed out byways to villages with exotic names of Mayan heritage: Catzin, Sisbichen, and Yalcoba.

They arrived in Valladolid by late morning, disembarking in the city center, an immaculately preserved checkerboard of stone-laid plazas, Spanish Colonial buildings, and the dominating, tree-lined, sixteenth century Cathedral of San Gervasio, strung with Christmas lights for the holiday. While their fellow passengers dispersed for sightseeing and transfers to the nearby Mayan ruins, Jacks and Kwame huddled on a shaded street side to review a print-out from Captain Ollie's computer.

An internet search had turned up a lead on the artist colony. It was the Instituto Grubar, which offered workshops, tours, and residencies on a former henequen plantation five miles south of Valladolid. They spotted a line of taxis at the curb by the cathedral, and Jacks tried out talking to a middle-aged driver in Spanish. They climbed into the back seat of the shiny, yellow sedan and zipped off to the outskirts of town.

In the car, Jacks told Kwame about his interaction with Maarten. "I tried with him. Have you ever seen him this far gone? He's like a different person."

Kwame frowned. "We all tried. I spoke with the others, and we decided that after Mexico, we will take him back to South Africa no matter how much of a fuss he puts up."

"You think that will help?"

"I do. He put off saying goodbye to Annika, staying drunk and high so he doesn't have to think about it. This is the irony with grief: it weighs down harder the more you try not to release it. We have been carrying around Annika's ashes for nearly half a year. Maarten knows Annika would want to be returned to the bush, where the white lion shaman reared them."

Jacks agreed. Though he wondered where that would leave him. He was counting on Benoit's Zapotec mystic to give him some insight into how to stop the war between werecats and humans. But what if they couldn't find him? What if he was dead or had no answers?

Their driver took them to a country highway, and they left behind the quaint city and its tidy grid of streets. Once they passed a gas station outside of town, there was nothing to be seen but hearty, dry forests and overgrown pastures. Farther down the road, they came up to a weathered, stone-walled compound enclosing acres of craggy, fallow fields. The taxi drove through an arched gate whose grandeur had eroded over centuries.

The plantation's henequen plots had withered to weeds and dirt. It felt to Jacks like they were trespassing on a cemetery. The neglected grounds conveyed a collective sadness, as though the souls of a forgotten people haunted the place.

A main road led to a mansion house with a grand, arched porch, all built from limestone and blackened with age. The porch was decorated modestly with wooden chairs and potted palm trees. A painted banner said the building had been appropriated as the Instituto Grubar, and signs pointed to a Centro de Bienvenida and a Tienda for the artists' wares. Kwame paid the driver, and they grabbed their packs and climbed out of the taxi.

The taxi drove off, and the two men glanced at each other for a puzzling moment. They hadn't talked about how they were going to inquire about Benoit's mysterious guru. They didn't even know his name.

Jacks took a draw of air into his mouth. Pleasant earthy scents of pottery and paints filled his sinuses along with a smattering of human odors, but he didn't detect any werecats. He looked at Kwame. "You picking up anything?"

Kwame shook his head.

His attention turned to a dander scent. A well-fed, black and white tabby had sidled out from the mansion's open double-door, taking a sly account of their arrival. As soon as Jacks spotted her, she skittered into the interior of the mansion.

He smirked. "C'mon. I have a feeling we've come to the right place."

They followed the sign to the welcome center, which was through the mansion's high-ceilinged foyer and into the left wing of the ancient house. Terra-cotta floors and vaulted portals suggested the estate's former glory, but it was sparsely furnished and oversized for its current occupants. Open terrace doors let a welcome breeze into the house, though it still smelled like a cellar, with a trace of stale tobacco. Jacks also detected the black and white tabby. She was keeping an eye on them from some hidden place. He tried sending her a friendly message and heard her scampering away.

The Instituto's Welcome Center was a wood counter with brochures, but no one was there. He glanced at Kwame with a shrug and clapped down on a dulled, metal call bell.

He heard rustling from a back room behind the counter, and a young, braless woman presented herself in a well-worn T-shirt with a silk screen image of Frida Kahlo. Her hands, her arms, her T-shirt, and even her face were blotched with some kind of paint or stain. She spoke to them in Spanish. When Jacks replied with his clumsy command of the language, she switched easily to English.

"Our schedule of classes is on the brochure." She pointed out a trifold on the counter. "Fridays we're open to the public. There's a weaving workshop in the morning and ceramics in the afternoon." She eyed them over. They probably looked like backpackers by their clothing and scruffy faces and hair.

She knotted her long, brown hair behind her head to keep it away from her face, and, if Jacks wasn't mistaken, she stood straighter to push out her bosoms. "There's information on applying for our artist's residencies here." She brought out another brochure. "The next application period opens January 15th."

Their little black and white voyeur jumped up on the counter and strutted between the clerk and Jacks and Kwame. The young woman rubbed the back of the cat's neck.

"This is Ixchel," she told them. "Our feline resident."

"She's beautiful." Jacks reached his hand to allow Ixchel to sniff him. The cat cautiously accepted that greeting, hovering her muzzle over his open palm and twitching her whiskers. She quickly jumped down from the counter and disappeared into the backroom.

"How did you find the Instituto?" she asked. Jacks picked up a mixture of energies from her—an instinctual withholding fighting against a flirtatious attraction, like two poles of a magnet. The clerk was probably in her twenties and pretty enough to be appealing but not in an intimidating way. She looked to have some indigenous heritage with her Asiatic eyes, long, straight hair, and light complexion. Jacks liked the fact that she wore her work on her skin and her clothes unapologetically, and he was drawn to her earthy vibe. He grabbed hold of some charm and a story he had sketched out in his head.

"We're actually trying to track down an old friend. The three of us went to college together and spent some time down here in Mexico. He was a bit of a free spirit. After graduation, he went globe-trekking, and everyone lost touch with him." He glanced at Kwame. "We're in Cancun with some buddies, and we thought: what the heck, we'll check out the Instituto. Our friend had mentioned he used to visit someone here. We figured if we didn't find the guy himself, maybe someone heard about him passing through."

"What's his name?"

"Benoit Guichard."

Her eyes flashed, and her cheeks darkened warmly.

"You know him?!"

"He was one of our biggest benefactors." She gave him a puzzled look. "But he hasn't been by here in a long time. Has to be over a year."

THE SIM RU PROPHECY   197

Jacks looked to Kwame and grinned. "That's the best lead we've had so far." He fixed in on the clerk. "Benoit Guichard? A good-looking French Canadian? He lived in combat boots and distressed jeans?"

"Yeah, that's him. I didn't really know him very well." She cocked her head shyly. "Funny, you sort of remind me of him."

"How so?"

"I don't know," the clerk said, her embarrassment now palpable. "The way you came in here, self-assured. The way you held your hand out for Ixchel."

Jacks let her squirm a bit. He figured there was no harm in playing with her attraction, especially if it would help them find Benoit's contact.

"We had a cat in the apartment we all shared back in college," he told her. "She was crazy about Benoit. I bet Ixchel liked him, too."

The clerk nodded.

Jacks leaned back. "Hey, my name's Jacks, and this is Kwame."

"I'm Magdala."

"Nice to meet you, Magdala." Jacks offered his hand and shook hers.

"Likewise."

"Would it be too much to ask if we could look around the place a little? I mean, we can come back later if it's not a good time. It would just be really cool for us to see where our buddy used to hang out. We were like the Three Musketeers. Maybe there's someone who knows where he was off to after he left."

"Zyanya," Magdala said.

Jacks raised his eyebrows.

"She's our year-round artist-in-residence. She's the only person Benoit ever talked to."

"Really?"

"Yeah. Benoit was very private. He didn't interact with any of the artists besides Zyanya. Most people didn't even know he was a patron. He wasn't flashy about his money or curious about our work. Do you guys know if he had family down here?"

Jacks shrugged. "I don't think so. Why?"

"Just a theory some of us had." Magdala lowered her voice. "Zyanya has to be eighty, maybe ninety years old. We thought maybe she was a relative of his, like a great-grandmother."

Benoit was the son of a Frenchman and a Colombian woman, both of whom died in the early nineteenth century. Could Benoit have tracked down a relative on his mother's side? At eighty or ninety years old, they'd have to be a great-great niece or cousin. Jacks said nothing.

"I'll show you around," Magdala said. "You're the only visitors we've had all day. I think Ixchel can keep an eye on things on her own."

Magdala led Jacks and Kwame through a terrace door to the mansion's grounds. It was a weedy property with a brick courtyard, a colonial-era hacienda workhouse, and, more recently, constructed bungalows in the distance. Here and there, artists sat beneath shaded eaves. A middle-aged man chiseled at a barbaric stela. A pair of younger women worked at wood carvings, and in another spot, a young man was painting a giant mural, stretched on canvas against one face of the hacienda, incorporating Mayan glyphs in a dizzying, psychedelic design.

"The original plantation was built in 1786," Magdala said. "Our founder, Manuel Grubar, purchased it from the local governor in 1991. Most everything in the mansion house and the workhouse is original construction. The factory was in operation through the 1980s until it was no longer profitable. That's when henequen production moved to more modern facilities here in the Yucatán and abroad. Some of our residents still use the sisal fiber for canvases and hand-made crafts. It doesn't take much to cultivate henequen. We have fields on the southern end of the property that have been through fires and the years when the owner raised cattle back there. It's a stubborn plant."

Jacks took it all in with admiration. The plantation had first struck him as dismal and haunted, but there was a pleasant, peaceful quality to its operation. The artists had created a vegetable garden with vine tomatoes and watermelons, and their bungalows were painted in bright pastels and decorated with wind chimes and feathers.

"Is Manuel Grubar still alive?" he asked.

"No. He died in 2001. A group of his friends formed a board of trustees to keep the Instituto going. Manuel's vision was to create something beautiful from a place of exploitation and misery. You know the history of the henequen plantation?"

He had inferred it wasn't a pretty history, but he was curious to hear about it.

"The Spanish used the Mayan people as slaves. At one time, two hundred slaves were living in barracks on this plantation, and this isn't even the biggest one in the region. In the early twentieth century, Korean immigrants were lured to Mexico with the promise of jobs and forced to work the factories for no wages. Henequen is a blood crop, just like cotton and tobacco in North America."

Jacks shook his head woefully.

"Manuel was a popular local artist, and he was also mestizo, with Mayan ancestry, like myself," Magdala went on. "While many of these old plantations were turned into resorts for wealthy tourists, he wanted the property to be used for something to benefit the local community. It hasn't been easy. As you can see, we've struggled to fund the upkeep of the buildings. A good portion of the mansion is uninhabitable due to structural damage. But we take it one season at a time, relying on donations and the sales of our wares. Many of the artists-in-residence receive scholarships. Manuel strove to make the Instituto a place where every artist is welcome."

They rounded the main workhouse to a dirt road that traversed one wing of the artists' bungalows. The path was shaded by rows of silk-cotton kapok trees. A long, wooden building that looked like a stable house stood off at the far end of the road.

"How did you end up here?" Jacks asked Magdala.

"I did a residency three years ago and never left. I'm more a handcrafter than an artist. I work with jicara husks. It's an ancient Mayan trade. You dry the husks, and they can be carved and lacquered to make bowls and jugs." She brandished her hands. "That's why I'm permanently covered with varnish."

She blushed again, and Jacks grinned at her.

Magdala gazed ahead. "The stable house has been repurposed as an artist's studio. It belongs to Zyanya. It's also where she lives."

Jacks caught a chill, realizing he was retracing Benoit's steps to visit the artist, who had to be the Zapotec mystic he had spoken of. He had assumed the mysterious spiritual guide was a man, though Benoit had never said he or she.

"I should warn you," Magdala started to say. "She's a little... eccentric. She's incredibly talented, but she almost never leaves her studio. She has a well around the back and an old-fashioned coal-burning stove. Francisco, our groundskeeper, brings her groceries each week, and she basically takes care of herself. I wouldn't trouble her to bring you around, but she and Benoit were very close. I'm sure she'll want to talk to you if Benoit's

gone missing, and there's any way she could help find him."
Magdala added. "Also, she's blind."

Jacks suddenly felt rotten about his lie. He realized it could
get worse if Magdala hung around. "Can I ask you a favor?"

"Sure."

"There are some sensitive things concerning Benoit. After
you introduce us, do you think we could have some privacy?"

"I have things to do around the mansion anyway," Magdala
said. "Take all the time you need. Or all the time Zyanya will
give you, I should say."

She walked them to the sliding, stable door, knocked vigor-
ously, and called out Zyanya's name.

Jacks stood back with Kwame, itching with suspense.
Magdala slid open the stable door and called out to the woman
in Spanish. "Zyanya. Hay visitantes para usted." She waved to
them to join her.

The interior of the house was dark but for the sunlight
trailing from the doorway. Any other natural light was filtered
nearly to extinction by high, paneled windows that looked like
they hadn't been washed for decades. Noisome scents assaulted
Jacks. Strangely familiar from his childhood, an acrid stench of
pulped paper dominated the house, with undercurrents of glue
and paint along with human urine and feminine odors.

Magdala found an oil lamp by the door and lit the wick
with a match. That revealed a better part of the abode and
made it no less startling. It was a forest of man-sized Catrinas,
skull-faced women in bright, feathered bonnets and skeletal
men in fancy suits and stovetop hats. The concrete floor was
littered with strips of paper and trays of paints and brushes.
Flies buzzed around a rubbish bin and discarded plates with
half-eaten meals. Jacks swallowed hard to hold down his stomach. It was the lair of a madwoman.

Magdala stepped around the disarray, calling out in Spanish. "She speaks English as well," she told Jacks. "But her hearing has gotten bad."

An ancient woman emerged from an unseen hollow of the home, as terrifying as her morbid models. She wore an apron spattered in many colors as though she had just come from butchering and reanimating one of her creations. She waved her fragile arms for balance as she shuffled into the light on bare feet with overgrown, curled toenails. Her thinning gray hair was coiled up on her head in a bun, which seemed to be the only thing about her suggesting a former nobility.

Magdala took her side to gently offer her assistance, but the old woman shooed her away. Jacks felt uncannily that she sensed their presence. Magdala spoke to her in Spanish, explaining the reason for the visit.

"I know why these two came here," Zyanya croaked at her irascibly. "Ixchel told me. Tell Francisco to bring cold beer. We'll be out in the yard in the back."


AFTER MAGDALA LEFT, Zyanya waved for Jacks and Kwame to follow her through the stable house and out to daylight again through a rear door. After seeing the old woman's response to Magdala, he decided not to help her. Her steps were slow and deliberate, but she must have retained some sight. Either that, or she had a preternatural sense of her surroundings. She navigated her helter-skelter Catrinas without bumping into anything and found the fire door to the backyard entirely independently.

A bench and a single wooden chair awaited them. The backyard overlooked a rolling, abandoned pasture that extended to the distant stone walls of the plantation. Chickens roamed, scrabbling in the crabgrass. Jacks and Kwame took seats on the bench while the ancient woman lowered herself into the chair. The daylight revealed more clearly her Amerindian features. A rounded face, aged with leathery jowls. A strong, angular nose. Her lips seemed to be molded in a perpetual frown, though the impression of it was not precisely misanthropic. More like an attitude that quartered no artistry nor mischief.

Zyanya sniffed and broke the silence. "How did Benoit die?"

He looked at Kwame. Was it a guess based on the unlikeliness of visitors showing up for another reason? Benoit had told Kwame's friend she was a psychic. He didn't know what to say. It would be unkind to lie to the old woman, but how could he tell her that he killed Benoit? "There was a fight. In New York City."

The bottom jaw of her toothless mouth slid back and forth, but she let that answer go unembellished.

"I'm sorry," he said. "This must be strange for us to show up out of the blue—"

"Benoit was your maker. You reek of him. That's a nice memory for an old woman. I never met one of his lovers in the flesh."

His face went beet red. Though she said it quite matter-of-factly, the expression "lovers" had always felt to him simultaneously old fashioned and overly sexual. Besides, smelling Benoit on him was embarrassing and weird. No werecat had noticed that before, and Zyanya wasn't even a werecat based on the scents he was picking up. He smiled nervously. "We were only together for a few months. Last spring."

She turned her head to Kwame and pointed a bony, overgrown, yellow-nailed finger in his direction. "Don't think I can't smell you too, Werelion."

"Pleased to meet you," Kwame said.

She gave him a sharp nod.

"Zyanya," Jacks started to say. "How is it that you can—"

"Smell you? You never met my kind before, have you? That's understandable. Precious few of us are left." She fixed in on Jacks with her clouded, cataract eyes. "I am a Soul Seer, Werecougar. Though I see less lately in the light of day than I can smell or hold in my mind's eye. Since I was a little girl, I could see and talk to the spirits from the other realms. It is a gift passed down from my Zapotec ancestors." She stared grimly away from him. "The souls from the afterworld visit me as well. That is why I know you are withholding what you know about Benoit's death."

Jacks shivered. It seemed impossible to believe, but—

"You knew that Benoit died because he visited you?"

Zyanya nodded.

"W-when? What did he say?"

"He is at peace now, awaiting Sim Ru's return."

He had no idea what to make of that. Sim Ru? The prophecy?

Zyanya leaned toward him. "Poor dear. Didn't you know the dead watch over all of us? Benoit has been watching you since you left New York."

"Is he here?" He couldn't help himself from glancing around, stupidly. "Can you tell him that I'm sorry...that I didn't mean to—" He couldn't bring out the words. He wondered if he had crossed over to insanity. He was suddenly freezing cold on a ninety degree day, and he felt surrounded by the souls of the dead.

"Benoit is never far from me," the old woman said. "You have no reason to fear. He wouldn't have forgiven himself if it was you who had died in the fight."

Jacks looked up at her brown, wrinkled face, and he winced back tears. How could he doubt what she said was true? After everything he had seen and experienced since he had become a

werecat, the old woman's psychic ability was merely another
layer of the supernatural. He hadn't realized how much he
needed to believe Benoit's death hadn't been his fault. He had
been defending himself. He had been defending Farzan. Jacks
felt Kwame's hand on his shoulder, comforting him.

The groundskeeper Francisco came around the house with
bottles of beer in an ice bucket. He set the bucket down on the
patio floor and left without a word. Kwame retrieved two beers,
twisted off the caps, and handed one to Zyanya and one to
Jacks. Jacks took a long draw on the bottle, finishing half of it.

Kwame grabbed a beer and retook his seat on the bench. "A
Soul Seer," he mused. "It is said the Ashanti witchdoctors see
and speak to human and animal souls."

"So they may," Zyanya said. "It is a gift once known by
many as I have heard. Though I've only met two others—the
seer from my village and an old fool who used to dig up graves
in the Yucatán until the dead chased him away. My people's
seers were rooted out by the Spanish or converted to Christianity." Her thin lip curled. "Possessed by demons, the Spanish
said."

"Did your people know of the rearing?" Kwame said.

"We knew of it from the Olmec and later the Aztec people.
The Zapotec have lived upon the earth since the beginning of
time. We are the Cloud People. Some call us the Watchers."

"Do you have wereshamans?" Kwame asked.

Zyanya took a drink of her beer. "The wereshamans serve
the feline god. He is not our father."

Jacks honed in on the conversation. "You gave Benoit the
Báalam-Tet."

"I did," the old woman admitted. "It was handed down to
me by the Soul Seer from my village before he died. But it was
no use to me."

Jacks thought about his theory that Dickerson was using

secrets from the ancient codex to enlist strays to find werecats. He explained the situation to Zyanya.

The old woman frowned. "No magic can be summoned from the book unless it is the will of the feline god. If this man is hunting down werecats, he must be doing it through some other capacity or witchcraft."

"Or maybe he's using another Soul Seer like you," Jacks said.

She grew quiet. He hoped he hadn't offended her. He studied the pensive expression on her aged face.

"I have seen corruption and betrayal," Zyanya spoke, in a somewhat equivocating tone. "That shadow finds men of all kinds and natures."

Kwame broke into the conversation. "If it is a Soul Seer they're using, we could find him and stop him." He turned to Zyanya. "Could you help us?"

Zyanya snorted. "Help you find a Soul Seer in the United States? No. I do not wish to, Werelion. This is my home. I do not leave here. Besides, this is not the reason why you have come to see me."

Both Jacks and Kwame stared at her blankly.

"You have come to awaken Sim Ru and ask for his assistance."

Another shiver pierced through Jacks' bones. He glanced at Kwame. "I don't even know what that means. The Sim Ru prophecy? I came to see you to find out if there's a way to bring a peaceful end to the fight between humans and werecats."

"You have read the Báalam-Tet," Zyanya said.

"Ye-ah. Well, we tried. There's a lot we don't understand—"

Zyanya cut him off again. "So shall he awaken on the night of nights when the eye of the god of death is in union with Sim Ru's six sons."

Jacks looked at her helplessly.

"The full moon and the signs of the feline sky gods," Zyanya said with a touch of weariness. "It is in two days' time. The first day of the new year."

He fell silent.

"You will need to know the rites," the old woman said. She set down her beer. "But now I will return to my studio. I must work. They say it is good for my health."

WHILE ZYANYA WENT into her studio, Jacks and Kwame stayed out on the patio in a spell-struck phase and polished off the rest of the beer.

After a while, Jacks asked Kwame, "What are you thinking?"

"She's a powerful psychic. I think if she can talk to the dead, I would like to ask her some questions."

The possibility was tantalizing to Jacks as well. Could she contact Annika and bring Maarten a message that would help him overcome his grief? For himself, Jacks wondered if she could help him contact Benoit, though no sooner than he had thought it, he felt a sting of self-reproach. How would Farzan feel about that?

"You think we can impose on her like that? We just met her."

Kwame took a long swallow of his beer. "We hardly know her, and she wants you to awaken Sim Ru."

Jacks grew shifty. What would that entail?

"Imagine it," Kwame said. "He is a powerful god. What if he could bring back souls from the afterlife?"

Jacks stood up to work off the eerie feeling crawling through him.

Kwame went on. "What if that is what the book meant?

Unleashing an army to raze the earth. If Sim Ru could return to the earth every werecat who has passed—"

"Do you want to be responsible for that? It would be chaos."

"More chaos than the world we live in now?"

Jacks hadn't realized how much Kwame had veered toward werecats dominating humankind, avenging the U.S. military's round-up of their brethren, not to mention centuries of extermination. Part of Jacks was enticed by that as well. But once that door was opened, there was no closing it. He couldn't do that to Farzan and his family.

"Think about it, Jacks," Kwame said. "To bring back Annika, Jean-Luc, Thierry, Lars—"

"So werecats can claim the world?"

Kwame said nothing.

"There ought to be a way that we can coexist."

"Do you think any humans are asking their gods about that?" Kwame said.

Jacks paced. "I don't know. Maybe. We don't know." He looked at Kwame sharply. "Is that what you want? To obliterate humankind?"

Kwame bowed his head. "I do not know anymore. After what I have seen in the past few months, I cannot answer."

"Don't you care about Farzan? Didn't you love Henri? And your parents?"

Kwame looked up at him with bloodshot eyes. "I did. But maybe this is the way it is supposed to end. After so many years of suffering."

"No," Jacks said. "I don't believe that."

Kwame looked away, grimmer and colder than he had ever seen his friend before.

"How can you believe that?"

"How long have you lived this way? Eight months? Nine? You cannot understand."

"What can't I understand?"

"You think you can change the way of the world. You think the past few months have taught you everything. You have not lived long enough as a monster to understand how hard the world can be."

That raised Jacks's hackles. "I had to kill the first man who ever loved me. I was fucking hunted down with nets and tranquilizer darts and set up as a patsy so the military could take out dozens of werecats."

"And you think the world owes you justice for that? You think you will find a way to change the hearts of men and our dual soul brethren so that we can forgive and live happily ever after?"

"I thought you believed there was a way. Isn't that why you came here with me?" Jacks raked his hand through his hair. "What's the alternative?"

"You have two choices. Awaken Sim Ru and accept his judgment or walk away and leave our fate in the hands of humankind."

"That's insanity. Why does it have to be one extreme or the other? Why are you acting like it's all up to me?"

"Because it is, Jacks. It started with Benoit, and then the choice passed down to you. Can't you see? Every decision you made has led you closer to fulfilling the Sim Ru prophecy. This is something you cannot barter with." He looked down at his feet. "Though you can pretend it is not so, and we will all reap the consequences." Kwame stood and walked away.

"Kwame," Jacks called after him. "Where are you going?"

Kwame disappeared around the side of the house, not looking back.

FOR A LONG while, Jacks sat on the patio, knowing Kwame needed some space and not having any idea what he would say to him anyway. On one hand, he respected that Kwame was older and had been living as a werecat much longer than him. Plus, the possibility of bringing Annika, Jean-Claude, Thierry and Lars back from the dead meant everything to Kwame. If Jacks could do that, it would take away Kwame's grief, and Maarten's and all the guys in his pride.

But at what cost? The end of humankind? Did it have to be one extreme or the other? Why did Jacks have to be saddled with that impossible choice?

He wondered if Kwame had ditched him and headed back to Cancun. That didn't seem like Kwame, but at least an hour had to have passed while he sat there alone. The sun had descended overhead toward afternoon. Jacks stood up from his bench and wandered into Zyanya's house.

The darkness of the interior was disorienting until his feline vision sharpened, helping Jacks to navigate the rows of Catrinas. He was amazed the old woman had created so many giant models, each one rendered with fine details, from the maddened expressions on their skeletal faces to the ruffles and garish patterns on the ladies' dresses and the oversized buttons and the quilting of the men's suits. Magdala had said Zyanya was eighty or possibly ninety years old. Could she be even older, imbued with the gift of longevity like werecats? Wandering through her weird creations, like totems to some underworld deity, he could imagine the house as a welcoming place for the souls of the dead.

He found her in a far corner of the house, kneeling on a mattress on the floor, her bed apparently. She did not stir. She appeared to be preoccupied with some sort of meditation. Jacks found the oil lamp Magdala had used, and he foraged for a box of wooden matches from the floor. Neither he nor Zyanya needed the light, but it provided some semblance of normalcy with which to ground himself.

As he brought the oil lamp toward her, she broke from her meditation and spoke to him in her croaking voice. "You do not know how to leave an old lady to her privacy, do you, Werecougar?"

He set down the lamp and rooted out a spot to sit on the floor a few paces from her bed. "You can call me Jacks. I'm sorry I disturbed you. My friend and I had a fight." He heaved a breath. "I didn't know where else to go."

She shifted around to face him. "I was not getting much work done anyway. Just visiting an old friend." She settled into a seated position with her legs curled beneath and her aged shoulders slumped forward. "The years pass quickly," Zyanya said. "I do not have the endurance I once had. My advice to you is to never grow old if you can help it."

Jacks smirked. He looked at the shelf above the head of her bed, overfilled with barbaric vessels and busts and figurines. One was a spouted jug whose chamber was a crouching cat looking over his shoulder. The animal's exaggerated mouth, bearing his sharpened teeth in a human-like grin, reminded Jacks of the glyph for the werejaguar king in the Báalam-Tet. "I like your collection," he told Zyanya. "They look ancient."

"My idols? Many of them are ancient indeed. Passed down through generations. Take a closer look if you care to. I can no longer admire them myself. But each one is a relic of magic from the past, and I like to be amid their energy."

He stood up and stepped lightly around her to inspect the feline jug. It was situated among fetishes of many types and sizes, some which looked like tribal chieftains and some like animals of religious importance. The cartoonish cat had been etched with spots, a work of pre-Colombian pottery, he figured. He wondered about the significance of the cat's pose.

"The jaguar of the backward glance," Zyanya said.

"What?"

"That is the idol that has drawn your eye. It is Benoit's favorite as well. A relic of the Chavín people and an artifact of your history. That is a wereshaman of the fifth century B.C."

He stood back from the relic as though it was the ancient wereshaman himself.

"The Chavín were not so fanciful in their artwork as the Mayans and the Aztecs, but they knew well some jaguars of the forest are not merely jaguars. The cat that looks over its shoulder is a weremaster."

He studied the rendering. That simple, turning back of the head conveyed so much more—a mark of powerful magic. He wandered back to the foot of her bed and seated himself facing her, which he figured was more polite. "How did you meet Benoit?"

She smacked her dry lips. "Your kind has a way of finding me. Before Benoit, I had a werejaguar companion for many years. He was three hundred years old, but he still called me abuela." Her mouth pursed wryly. "Lost souls. They all call me abuela. Someone to talk to when everyone else in the living world has turned them away. It was Rodrigo who told Benoit about me. That's how he turned up at my door. Forty years ago, it must have been."

Zyanya's aged face glimmered. "He was a handsome werejaguar, wasn't he? In all my years, I never met a man or creature more beautiful."

He silently agreed. Though there was a lot more to Benoit than good looks. "I loved him. But it was complicated. He wasn't such a nice guy in the end."

She nodded. "Passionate types, born on the name day of the water-bearer god, are vulnerable to obsession. Benoit wanted to understand his place in the world, but he could not accept losing you. He has come to terms with that now, and he is proud of you. You are his legacy."

Jacks was humbled, but it didn't entirely make sense. "He didn't tell me about Sim Ru or anything he learned from the Báalam-Tet. He barely mentioned you."

"He tore you away from the life you had known. What do you think would have happened if he had told you about Soul Seers and ancient prophecies?"

He considered that. "It would have been too much for me to handle at the time." Emotions welled up inside him. It was strange, but he felt like he could tell the old woman anything. She seemed to know him inside and out even though they had only just met.

"Sometimes I feel like I need him. Like a part of me is missing, and I've broken to pieces, and they'll never be put back into place." His sinuses watered with tears, and he wiped his nose. "I don't know what that is. I'm in love with someone else, and I wouldn't change that, even if Benoit came back. But I miss him."

"He's your maker," Zyanya said. "You'll always have that link. But every child must grow and discover his own path."

Jacks recalled something else. "Benoit had the Báalam-Tet. Did he want to summon Sim Ru? If he did, why did he keep the book locked up in a safety deposit box?"

"Benoit wrestled with the decision of awakening the god. He was afraid. As you are, Werecougar."

He fidgeted with the pocket button of his cargo shorts. He had asked the question, plunging into the topic, but he wasn't sure he was prepared to hear the answers. "What will happen?"

"You have read the prophecy."

"I did. But does it have to be that way? I want to ask Sim Ru for guidance, not a reign of terror."

Zyanya was quiet for a spell. "He is a fearsome god. There are forever new histories to be written, but I cannot say if he will countenance any request besides destruction."

Jacks fidgeted some more. "I don't know if I can do it. I'm afraid of what will happen to the people I love." He shivered and a blush bloomed on his face. "This is all so strange to me. I keep falling in and out of believing that it's real. I never believed in any god. All through Sunday school and confirmation and being dragged to church by my mother until I had the guts to tell her that it wasn't for me. It just never rang true for me, y'know?"

Zyanya's blank eyes passed over him. "But you have felt that Sim Ru is real."

"I saw him. In my dreams." He wouldn't have told anyone else that, besides Kwame, fearing they would think he had lost his mind. "Does that mean he's waiting for me?"

"I thought it would be Benoit who would stand at Sim Ru's throne on his Night of Nights. By banishing Benoit from the earthly realm, you have taken that duty for yourself."

"Does it have to be me? I mean, any werecat who knows about the prophecy could claim it."

"That is true," Zyanya said. "But only one will. I think that Sim Ru has chosen wisely."

"What do I say to him?"

A frown stretched across Zyanya's wrinkled face. "That is for you to choose."

"You mean, I can ask him anything?"

"If you have earned a place at his throne, you may. But that does not mean he will grant your request."

His knee bounced while he sat cross-legged. He drew a breath and controlled that tick. "What do I have to do? The book said something about making a sacrifice at his temple."

"On the night of the moon aligned with the six sons, I will

take you there. It is no longer much of a temple, but it is sacred ground. To stand before the god's altar, you must make the ultimate sacrifice. You must relinquish the part of you that belongs to the earthly realm. Only that offering will grant you passage to the spirit world. If it pleases Sim Ru, he will allow you to return."

# SIXTEEN

LATER THAT DAY, Magdala returned to check on Jacks. She
said Kwame had come up to the mansion house to wait for him,
so Jacks went back with her and left Zyanya to her meditations.
A late afternoon torpor had fallen over the artist's colony.
People had retreated to their bungalows, and the only sound
was the pastoral tide of katydids.

"Did you find out anything about your friend?" Magdala
asked him.

"Ye-ah. I'm actually thinking about staying in town for a
couple of days. Any place you'd recommend? I'm on kind of a
tight budget."

"You could rent a bungalow right here. We generally
reserve them for artists in residence, but we've got a couple free.
It's $40 a night, if you don't mind being so far from town." She
gestured around the sleepy grounds. "This is just about as
exciting as it gets here. Sometimes people get together for cards
or dominoes after dinner, if you can handle that much
excitement."

"It sounds perfect."

Magdala brightened. "It will be nice to have someone here around my age. Will it be just you or will your friend be staying as well?"

Jacks hoped Kwame would want to stay, but he couldn't say for sure. Magdala went on without an answer.

"I can help you guys get settled in after I close up the visitor's center and the gift shop. I've got a radio at my place if you want to come over after dinner and have some beers and listen to some local music. You like bachata and merengue?"

He caught where that was leading. She was a really nice person, and he couldn't keep playing into her flirtation. "You have Wi-Fi here? I should check in with my boyfriend later."

"Oh! Sure. I can give you the password to our network. It only works in the mansion house, though."

She stared straight ahead, and they walked along in silence. "Hey Magdala," Jacks said. "I really appreciate you showing us around and introducing us to Zyanya."

"Don't mention it. So, um, how long have you and your boyfriend been together?"

"Eight months now. I proposed to him a week ago. Guess I should start calling him my fiancé."

"Wow. Well, congratulations. Are you going to get married back in the states?"

"We haven't decided." The conversation was veering back to shaky territory. He couldn't explain how he had ended up in Samoa. As unlikely as it was for that information to get back to Dickerson via Magdala, he wasn't going to risk anything going wrong on his trip. "What about you? Seeing anyone?"

Magdala chuckled mildly. "The artists around here generally aren't boyfriend material. At least the ones who have been interested in me. I'm starting to get worried about my game. All the good-looking guys go straight for Zyanya."

Jacks shared another grin with her, then something

occurred to him. "You mean, there have been other good-looking guys looking for Zyanya?"

"Just a couple weeks ago actually. I really need to find out what her secret is."

"This is probably going to sound totally weird. But was that guy who just came looking for her a really clean-cut type? Blond hair? Aviator sunglasses? Sort of a dickish, law enforcement personality?"

Magdala shook her head. "Couldn't have been more different. Tall, dark, and Latin. He had that Che Guevara look. With the hat and the military dungarees." Her face lit up. "The face of a telenovela heartthrob and the earnestness of a revolutionary. He had me at 'ola.'"

Jacks blanched. He hadn't thought about Tepe seeking out Zyanya. Why hadn't she told him?


HE FOUND KWAME nodding off in a wooden chair on the porch of the mansion house. He approached him a bit heavy-footed to get his attention. Kwame's eyes popped open, and they appraised each other. Jacks felt like he needed to apologize, but he wasn't sure what for.

He eyed the doorway to the house. Magdala was inside taking care of some business, and it was otherwise deserted. He spoke quietly to Kwame, "Are we still friends?"

"I flew off the handle. I shouldn't have taken it out on you."

Jacks waved his hand. "No big deal." He pushed one of the porch chairs closer to Kwame's and took a seat.

"You know I would never wish any harm to Farzan and his family," Kwame said. "With everything that has happened on the news, my nerves have been raw. My anger, too. And the possibility of bringing back the people I loved overwhelmed me."

In the midst of what Jacks had learned, their argument seemed really minor.

"You have a huge responsibility on your shoulders," Kwame went on. "It was not right to tell you what to do or to suggest you have not been through enough to decide."

"It's cool, Kwame. You've always had my back. You have a right to be pissed after everything that's gone down."

Kwame looked around them. "This place is haunted. I do not have Zyanya's gift, but can't you feel it?"

Jacks remembered the eerie feelings that had clutched him earlier in the day. "Yep."

"It's like a mecca for lost souls. Or a prison for them. I have not felt so close to the threshold of the spirit realm since I stepped into that shop in Marseilles where I met that Ashanti witch doctor who could see my feline soul." He bowed his head. "I think that is also what overcame me. I feel the dead all around that woman. So much injustice. I felt like I could hear their cries for vengeance."

Jacks wiped his clammy palms on his shorts. "Believe me, I was on the verge of losing it, too."

"What you want to do is right, Jacks. We should find a way to coexist." Kwame looked Jacks squarely in the face. "Rousing Sim Ru's reign of terror is not the answer."

Jacks leaned forward in his chair, closer to his friend. "That may be exactly what we need to stop." He proceeded to tell Kwame about his visit with Zyanya and what he had learned from Magdala.

Kwame drew air through his wide nostrils. "If it was Tepe, he did not linger. Are you sure Magdala was describing the same man?"

"She had to be. It's too big of a coincidence. Some scruffy guy who looks like a freedom fighter popping in on Zyanya right before the night of the prophecy? That's Tepe, and we know exactly what he's after."

They were both quiet for a while, pondering over the matter, while the wind sighed through the ancient Royal Palm trees that lined the drive to the mansion house.

"Why wouldn't she tell you about Tepe?" Kwame said.

"I don't know. But we need to find out. In the meantime, I think it's a good idea for us to stay put. If Tepe comes back, we might have a chance to surprise him."

MAGDALA SHOWED THEM to a bungalow beyond the hacienda workhouse. Their lodging wasn't much more than an aluminum hut with twin cots. No plumbing. One light fixture above the door and one inside. Magdala warned them the electricity was unreliable. It only took a rainstorm or sometimes just a gusty night to knock out power in the countryside, but it came back when the storm passed. The shower house was a short walk in the opposite direction of the hacienda.

Jacks had never been particularly interested in camping or roughing it, but through his travels in Brazil, he had discovered he was a lot more adaptable than he had thought. He didn't need more than a roof over his head and a place to lie down for the night. The coil spring mattress on his cot seemed comfortable enough.

Later, he went up to the mansion to use the Wi-Fi. With the time difference, Farzan was twenty hours ahead of him, which made it midafternoon in Samoa. Jacks used the Facetime app on his cell phone to call him and found Farzan was with Sammy running errands in town.

They had a short and choppy video call during which Jacks told him in a coded way that they had made contact with Benoit's friend and were staying at the artists' colony to get more information. Jacks couldn't bring himself to give Farzan all the details. He wasn't sure how well he could explain his meeting with Zyanya anyway based on the strength of their Wi-Fi connection and with Sammy clowning around to cut into their conversation. He told Farzan they were learning things about the Sim Ru prophecy, but he left out that it was two nights away and would involve relinquishing his physical body, basically a ritual suicide. He felt awful about hiding that. But he didn't need to make Farzan hysterical, thousands of miles away.

Farzan looked at him with warm, chestnut eyes. "I miss you."

"I miss you too."

"What are the chances you'll be back next week?"

A lot of things would have to come together quickly for that to happen. A plane ticket? That had been a thought since he wasn't sure Maarten would be willing to ferry him across the Pacific again. But Jacks wasn't sure if it was safe to test his passport. Things had changed since Sowanake assured him he could use it anywhere in the world besides the U.S. He could be detained and deported by customs.

Farzan filled in the silence. "I know that's probably not realistic. It would just be nice if you could make it back before my mom and Sammy leave."

"I'll try, baby," Jacks said.

He went down to the hacienda where they served dinner to the artists at picnic tables in a concrete courtyard. It all looked very festive with Christmas lights strung from trees and folksy guitar and vocal melodies playing on a PA system from another era. Kwame and Magdala had claimed a table and were already eating. About a dozen artists had turned up for dinner.

Smoky, charred odors came from a cooking station where a middle-aged Mayan woman was grilling marinated steaks, tortillas, and corn. She'd set up big, aluminum pans with rice, beans, and a salad with tomatoes. When Jacks came over, she heaped his paper plate with steak, a tortilla, and an ear of corn. Jacks slyly pushed the last two off to the side. He grabbed a beer from a cooler and joined Kwame and Magdala.

They were having an animated conversation in Spanish, laughing at something he couldn't follow. Magdala introduced Jacks and Kwame to the various residents of the Instituto— Claudio, a man with a weathered face who gave them a gap-toothed smile; Mirna, a pretty, thirty-something Colombian woman with twin hair braids, and the muralist they had seen earlier, a reclusive young Spaniard named Raul. Kwame must've told her he was gay. Magdala tried to pull Raul into conversation with him, but Raul was helplessly shy and awkward. Many other names and faces whirred past Jacks as Magdala rattled off introductions. They all seemed like nice people, but it was too much to take in all at once.

When dinner was finished, a group of older men planted themselves at a table for dominoes, filling their tumblers with some local, homebrewed liquor and puffing up cigars. Magdala quietly told Jacks and Kwame they were 'los perrons,' the big dogs. The rest of the company dispersed in cliques. Jacks and Kwame filled a bucket with cold beers and followed Magdala back to her bungalow to take her up on her offer of exposing them to the flavors of Yucatán radio.

Her bungalow was decked with chili pepper and palm tree light bulbs for the holidays, and she brought out velas to decorate her little, outdoor table. They served themselves beers and sat down on her plastic chairs. Magdala reemerged from her house with her bread box-sized AM/FM radio and turned up the volume to a lively cumbia station.

Jacks hooted and cheered while Kwame grinded and spun Magdala around her little front plot. Kwame was amazing. He seemed to know every language around the globe, and he picked up local customs with ease. They dragged Jacks from his chair to dance with them, and they all laughed and hollered while Jacks fumbled through the movements, trying to lead Magdala then whirling around in Kwame's sturdy grip. They fell out from dancing, all a bit breathless and sweaty, and plopped down on the lawn furniture to drink their beers.

"I guess I'm the belle of the ball," Magdala said, cozying up in her chair with her knees tented in front of her beneath her oversized, cotton shirt. "Two men all to myself for the night."

Jacks chuckled. "Where did you learn to speak English so well?"

"I spent two years at University of Southern California until I lost my scholarship, and my parents couldn't afford it. I'm the oldest of three girls, and I was my family's great hope. They wanted me to become an American doctor or a lawyer. Instead, I ended up making roadside knickknacks for room and board."

He glanced at her windowsill where she had displayed some of her jicara husks. Some had been crafted into snowmen. Another one looked like a squat version of the Virgin Mary. "I love your artwork," he told her. "You're really talented. Your parents should be proud of you."

Magdala took a long draw on her beer. She wiped her mouth with her forearm, showing a touch of clumsiness from the alcohol. "They're waiting for me to grow out of it. I guess I will someday. I'm only twenty-four. Still time to make something of myself after dropping out of college, right?"

"I'm a college drop-out, too. Worse than you. I left college in my last semester, senior year."

Her eyes grew big, and she clinked bottles with Jacks. "To college dropouts." She looked to Kwame. "What about you? Are you part of the club?"

"I never finished college."

Magdala's grin curled up on one side. She looked like she was putting some things together. "You guys lied to me. You said you graduated college with Benoit."

Jacks tried to clean things up. "We twisted the truth a bit. We all met in college, but none of us graduated."

"I wasn't buying it anyway," Magdala said. "Benoit didn't seem like the kind of guy who had a bunch of bros from an American college. So what are you? Two dudes backpacking around the world to find yourselves?"

He glanced at Kwame. Magdala was a little drunk, but he couldn't try to pass off some half-assed story to her. "Something like that."

"So much mystery with you two," Magdala complained loudly. She glugged down the rest of her beer. For a slight, young woman, she was a fast drinker. Jacks wasn't sure if it was her third or fourth. "I don't think you even came here looking for Benoit. Maybe he was your friend, but that's not the reason you showed up."

Jacks didn't dare say anything.

"I think Benoit told you about Zyanya, and you wanted to meet her yourselves."

He gave her a noncommittal shrug. It seemed like a fairly innocuous accusation. Maybe something he could work with.

"So, what did the old lady tell you?" Magdala's eyes lit up with a spark of mischief. "Did she read your aura? Bring you a message from a dead friend?"

He said nothing. Kwame shifted a bit in his seat.

"What's the big deal? I know Zyanya's doing some kind of business on the side. Why else would she have strangers from out of the country popping in to see her? Every one of you with some shifty, hush-hush story? What is she? A Zapotec witch?"

Her tone was getting heated. "I'm really sorry," Jacks said. "We shouldn't have lied to you."

She reached down to the bucket and grabbed another beer. Jacks studied her. He wished he could tell her the truth. But what would happen then?

"Tell me something real," she groaned. "What the hell is there to hide? You barely know me. You'll probably be gone in the morning and never see me again."

Kwame started caving in. "It's a complicated story."

"Everything's complicated," Magdala said wearily. "You think I planned my life this way? Living in the middle of nowhere? So desperate for affection my only prospect is hoping I'll get lucky turning a pair of jotas?"

Jacks wasn't sure if she was headed to a meltdown or being funny. Looking over their fearful faces, she cackled drunkenly. He coughed out a nervous laugh.

"Don't take offense at me calling you jotas," Magdala said. "I know a lot of gay artists, and none of them mind when I call them that."

The two men grinned at each other. "We're not offended," Jacks said. "You're a good-looking girl. Maybe if you got out of this place more often—"

"What? You think I'd meet my Prince Charming? Let me explain my options in Valladolid. You have the barachos who haven't got the self-esteem to have a relationship with an educated woman, and you have the rico suaves who work in tourism, looking for a rich, white woman to take care of them."

That was an advice situation beyond Jacks's expertise. Though he had an instinct about the bigger picture, thinking about everything Magdala had told him.

"Maybe your problem is you fall for the wrong guys."

Magdala looked at him like he had three heads.

"Benoit. That Che Guevara Brazilian. Me. Some people

have a tendency to attach themselves to people they can't have."

She buried her head in her hands. "Ai Maria, you're psychoanalyzing me now?"

"This is true," Kwame said. "Could be you are afraid to try a relationship with a man who is available to you."

Jacks leaned in toward her with a mischievous smirk. "Admit it, you've got it bad for the gays, so you can tell the straight guys they're not good enough."

"Oh my god, you guys are so annoying. Is this what you do? Backpack through the countryside bringing brilliant wisdom to the lonely and the downtrodden?"

Jacks passed a smile to Kwame. "At least we're getting laid."

"Hijole," Magdala swore. "I think the two of you have cured me of chasing after gay men."

"Maybe you should consider becoming a lesbian," Kwame said.

They laughed and clinked beer bottles over that. The music cut out for some news bulletin. The announcer's dialect was too foreign and he spoke too fast for Jacks to make out much of it. But he noticed Kwame listening keenly. That went on for a troubling span of time. When it finished, Magdala's face twisted up in a frown.

"Can you believe this bullshit? They're using that feline virus as an excuse to kill people crossing the border."

"What happened?" Jacks said.

"Ten migrants were shot by U.S. border control in Texas," Kwame told him. "They were pulled over by authorities, traveling in a truck. When they tried to escape into the desert, the officers opened fire. Three children. Four women."

"The Mexican media isn't exactly a paragon of objectivity," Magdala said. "They like to stir up outrage over U.S. foreign policy. But this is almost too bizarre not to be true. They have an outbreak of some kind of virus that makes cats aggressive, and the U.S. wants to blame it on Mexicans?"

Jacks couldn't stop himself. "The virus is bogus." That comment squelched Magdala's rant.

Kwame told Jacks, "They also said that campaign in Wichita spread across the country. Officials are mandating cat owners turn over their pets. They reported on a crematory where hundreds of animals were destroyed."

Jacks felt sick to his stomach. And quickly about to blow a gasket.

"What do you mean, the virus is bogus?" Magdala asked them.

"The cats are fighting back," Jacks spat out. "They're fighting back, and they haven't got a fucking chance."

Magdala looked at him like he was joking. "Fighting back?"

Jacks cracked his knuckles, trying to loosen the tension in his body. Kwame answered her. "Some months back, the U.S. started rounding up domestic terrorists. This is a sham. They are not telling people who they are really detaining."

Magdala went for the dial on her radio to turn down the volume on an accordion ballad. She stood, glancing at them with a mix of absurdity and nervousness. "It might be the beer, but you guys are freaking me out. What is all this domestic terrorist stuff and cats rising up against their owners?"

Jacks took a long swig to collect his thoughts. It was all about to come out, whether from him or from Kwame, and as cool as Magdala was, he was pretty sure this would introduce more weirdness than she could handle. Weirdness that she would feel obligated to share with other people.

The tension in his body coiled up in his stomach like a cramp. His palms sweated, and a sudden restlessness pushed him up from his seat. He felt as though his heart would burst out of his chest if he didn't work off some kind of venom coursing through his veins.

Buzzed from the beer, Jacks couldn't place the cause of his sudden affliction. Until he saw that Kwame had also shot up from his chair, surveying the shrouded grounds, stiff and wary, with his nostrils flared. Kwame had picked it up first. The familiar swampy pheromones.

Tepe was near.


JACKS ORIENTED HIMSELF to the direction of Tepe's scent. It was a still and sultry night, thick with sweet and earthy odors.

He was only getting traces of the werejaguar from a considerable distance away. Kwame, who was one step ahead of him, looked toward the far end of the row of bungalows, a murky expanse that stretched toward the borders of the old plantation. That was the way to the stable house where Zyanya lived. The two men exchanged a quick glance, and then they sprinted down the trail, leaving Magdala behind.

They gained up quickly, Tepe's scent getting stronger as they drew closer. Jacks bore down on his diaphragm and burst into his cougar self, sprouting forelegs and hocks that would propel him faster. Kwame shifted into lion form. The plantation grounds were dark enough for them to be unseen, and everyone was in their bungalows or back at the hacienda as far as Jacks knew.

They came up on the darkened stable house, and Kwame, whose longer, muscled legs gave him an advantage with sprints, reached the door first.

From inside, they heard the wild, scurrying of claws scrambling on the floor. Jacks and Kwame quickly telepathized a plan. Jacks would go in through the front entrance, and Kwame would come around the door in the back.

He pawed open the sliding, stable house door and looked inside. The place was a pitch black void, and while his night vision adjusted, familiar gluey and paper odors attacked his sinuses. He detected Zyanya's scent, a mix of sweet sage and funky female odors, and the dangerous, peaty pheromones of Tepe. But he couldn't spot either of them in the house.

He felt in his gut that he had entered the scene of a crime. He could swear the temperature had plunged, though it was a hot night, and the stable house had no air conditioning. He sensed icy wraiths in the shadowed corners of the ceiling. The old woman was a magnet for the souls of the dead, and they were watching.

Then he noticed the stench of iron.

From the back of the house, a creaky door flew open. A flurry of movement disappeared into the night. Jacks was ready to chase that noise, but he needed to check on Zyanya and hope Kwame would catch what had to be Tepe taking flight.

He wove through the Catrinas and arrived at the corner of the house where the old woman kept her bed. Zyanya lay pale and open-mouthed, gurgling on her own blood with her throat gouged from the werejaguar's jaws. Blood pooled on the mattress around her neck. In a blink, Zyanya stilled, lifeless and at peace.

Jacks heard someone at the front of the house and shifted back into his human self. Despite the shock of discovering Zyanya's dead body, the danger of the situation jolted him. It would be tricky enough explaining what he was doing in the helter-skelter house of a dead woman, let alone if someone came upon him as a cougar.

"Zyanya? Jacks? Kwame?"

Magdala stood at the open front door. He listened to her

rooting around, grasping the oil lantern from the floor with a clang, and striking a match.

Light pierced through the disheveled house. Magdala shifted around, trembling. Jacks called out to her. She staggered through the Catrinas with her lantern. The light shone onto Jacks, crouched beside the dead woman. Magdala stifled a cry.

He approached her cautiously. "She's gone. It was a jaguar attack."

That was pretty close to the truth, and her wounds had to show the cause was a wild animal. Still, Magdala stared at him.

Kwame broke through the back door, back to his human form with his chest heaving for breaths. He took in the scene wild-eyed and lurched over to Jacks.

*I tried to catch him, but he made it to the road and took off in a Jeep.*

Jacks gazed at his friend helplessly. Zyanya was dead, and Tepe had made off in the night.


MAGDALA RAN BACK to her bungalow to use her cell phone to call the police and an ambulance. Residents from the Instituto emerged from the night-shrouded plantation grounds wearing expressions of shock and grief. The cook from the hacienda fell down on her knees and howled, ripping at her hair. Los perrons, as Magdala had called them, went into the stable house, and they came out muttering to each other, which Jacks could follow in his alert state.

They had heard that jaguars lived in the woods beyond the plantation. Attacks on humans were rare, but not unknown. The wildcats were more apt to be drawn to cattle ranches, and one of the perrons mentioned a story about a jaguar dragging off a rancher's eight-year-old son in a village not far away. Though this was all stories and possibly folklore, another of the perrons pointed out. What would make a wild animal wander into an old lady's home and rip out her throat, when there were goats and hens for easier pickings on the property?

Jacks and Kwame stood off on the periphery of the stable house grounds, not speaking to anyone, and afraid of drawing attention by talking to each other out loud. From time to time, the residents glanced at them, no doubt wondering why two strangers had been looking to pay a visit to the old woman so late at night. It had to be obvious to anyone who had looked inside the house that Zyanya had been the victim of a big cat attack, but a cloud of suspicion hung over the two men. They had arrived at the Instituto just that day.

*Why would Tepe kill her?* Jacks asked Kwame.

Kwame frowned. *Could be to stop her from helping you fulfill the Sim Ru prophecy.*

Jacks shook his head helplessly. Without Zyanya, the ancient rite was lost to him. He had questions he had needed to ask her. He didn't even know the location of the sacred ground she had spoken of.

*How did he find out about Zyanya?* Jacks asked his friend. *Did Benoit mention Tepe? Could they have crossed paths?*

*I cannot say. Benoit did not speak of Tepe while he was with us, but as you know, he was very private. There is another possibility—the domestics.*

Jacks shivered. Of course, scouting out information from domestic cats was always an option. He remembered the nosy, tuxedo cat they had met when they first arrived at the Instituto's Welcome Center.

*Ixchel?*

Kwame gave him a quiet nod. *A likely suspect. We should see what she knows. If she has not already run away with Tepe.*

A police car and an ambulette drove onto the property, parting the little crowd and pulling up to the stable house. Two police officers and a medic team went inside. Jacks and Kwame waited, on edge.

The medics brought Zyanya out on a covered gurney and lifted her into their van. The ambulette rolled away, no sirens, no flourish, just doing its job. Meanwhile, the pair of officers in caps and navy-blue uniforms went over to speak to Magdala. It looked like a routine exchange, and only once did she gesture to Jacks and Kwame, provoking a glance of mild interest from the men. Then, the officers climbed back into their car and drove off into the night. The business with the authorities was over, an anticlimax.

The residents wandered back to their homes. Jacks cued Kwame, and they meandered over to talk to Magdala. She stood wooden, clutching herself with her arms, and though it wasn't a welcoming vibe, a conversation needed to be had.

"I'm sorry about Zyanya," Jacks said.

Magdala looked him over sharply. She was clearly shocked sober. "Why did you run off to her house?"

He hesitated. Everyone had dispersed, but he didn't want to spark a heated conversation. He told her quietly, "We were trying to protect her."

"How could you know she needed protection? There was no cry for help, no sign of a struggle. The stable house was clear across the property. We were talking one minute, and the next you two go running to her house."

Tears sprouted from her eyes, melting his heart. He stepped closer to her, and she backed away. "How could you *know*?"

"Magdala, there are things we need to explain." Would she bolt and call out for help? He didn't think so. She could have tried to point suspicion at him and Kwame when she had spoken to the police. "First and foremost, you have to believe me. We had nothing to do with Zyanya's death. But we haven't been completely honest with you."

Magdala's face was suspended with fearful curiosity.

He tried to start gently. "You were right. We didn't come here looking for Benoit." He glanced at Kwame, grasping for some way to explain what would surely seem unimaginable to Magdala. "A long time ago, Zyanya gave Benoit a book. It had... instructions. That Brazilian man who came to see Zyanya a few weeks back, that's who killed her. He needed information from her. Information he didn't want anyone else to have. He's a mass murderer, Magdala. His name is Tepe."

"I don't understand. You said Zyanya was killed by a jaguar."

"He was." Jacks stopped there. He couldn't bring the words out he needed to say.

"What information could Zyanya have had for a mass murderer?"

He raked a hand through his hair. "It's about a ritual. It has to take place on New Year's Day."

Kwame broke in. "You knew Zyanya had psychic powers. She was connected to the spirit world."

"That's why all the strangers you mentioned came to see her," Jacks said.

Magdala shifted her glance from Jacks to Kwame and back again. "You're not making sense. Why can't you just tell me what you're trying to say?"

Jacks and Kwame exchanged a look. Kwame nodded, and he answered her. "The man who killed Zyanya was a were-jaguar. A shifter. Man and feline."

Magdala's face contorted in an ugly scowl. Then she snorted a bitter laugh like they were playing a game with her. Jacks gazed at her, pleading that there was some inkling inside her that could be reached.

"Magdala, you had to have known there was a connection between Benoit, Tepe, and me. We're different. You felt it. And the reason we ran off to the stable house is because we can sense our own kind."

Magdala backed away from him like he was deranged. "I should have told the police you two had some fucked-up story for coming here."

"Please, let us explain—"

She looked at Jacks viciously. "I want you out by the morning. If you're still here, I'm calling the police."

She staggered away from them, disappearing into the night.

# SEVENTEEN

JACKS AND KWAME turned in for the night in hopes of having clearer heads in the morning. But later, while he slept in his cot in their little cabin, Jacks saw Benoit.

He had fallen into an exquisite slumber. It was warm and luscious, and he was vaguely aware he was sleeping on a bed with soft, luxurious sheets and a down comforter. Benoit brushed the side of Jacks's head adoringly, a comforting sensation that grew into something wanting and sensual. Without opening his eyes, Jacks reached for Benoit, entangling their bodies. He raked his hands through Benoit's thick, shaggy hair and brushed their lips together.

He was making love to the man who had dragged him down a rabbit hole, but nothing else mattered when Benoit held him with his claiming, devouring force. They were disastrous partners in life, but in bed, they fit together like lost souls reunited.

Jacks opened his eyes and beheld Benoit with his dazzling emerald eyes, strong European nose, overgrown jet-black hair, and five day's growth of beard. In the strange manner of dreams, he felt neither wonder nor fear from the circumstance of being in bed with his ex-boyfriend who he had fought to the death. Then he reached for Benoit again, and he grasped thin air and found that he was laying on the bed alone, tangled in the comforter and sheet.

Some instinct called him to look above the bed, and he saw Benoit hovering in the night. His surroundings were all at once indistinct, but he could see the crisp light of stars and Benoit looking down upon him, haloed in a pale celestial glow. Jacks stretched his arm to grasp Benoit's hand, and he was weightless, rising in the air, lifted by an ethereal force, but always just out of reach of Benoit. They floated high, leaving the ground many fathoms beneath them. He realized, ludicrously, that he was naked, rising high up in the sky. But he could not stop himself from floating upward and did not want to give up trying to reach Benoit.

They rose into the clouds, and drifting banks of fog revealed a desolate and mountainous place. He understood where he was going and looked to Benoit for some message from the spirit world to guide him. Benoit gave him a tiny smile of assurance. Then he disappeared as a shadow dissolves in dawning light.

Jacks arrived at the tall, gray platform of rock. The giant, mottled beast, Sim Ru, shrugged his head toward him. He could not look away from the monster's amber eyes. He tried to remember the questions he needed to ask. They had completely fallen out of his head.

The beast growled into his head, *Only one shall know.*


IN THE MORNING, Jacks told Kwame about his dream while they were in their cots. He would have normally judged the things he had done and seen as unconscious fantasies, but this was now his third vision of Sim Ru. Zyanya knew Jacks had been visited by the sabretooth god. He had to face the fact it was a message.

Kwame agreed. "This is your path, Jacks. Our father god is waiting for you."

He leaned back at the head of his bed, propped up against the wall of the bungalow. A lot had been contained in that short dream. Not only was Sim Ru waiting for him, but Benoit had come to show him the path he must take. Maybe Zyanya had told Tepe Jacks would be the one to unlock the prophecy, and Tepe had killed her in a rage.

The Soul Seer was gone now and unable to guide him. Had the dead souls that surrounded her forewarned her of her fate? Had she hidden her previous visit from Tepe to protect Jacks because she knew he would be killed if he tried to thwart him? Jacks could only guess.

"We should try again with Magdala," Kwame said. "She knows these parts. She might know sacred places that could be the location for the ritual."

That seemed to be their only bet. Time was running out. The next day was New Year's Eve.

"It would be a lot easier if she didn't think we were con artists or lunatics," Jacks said.

Kwame climbed out of bed and went to his backpack to rustle out some clean clothes. "Let's get washed up. Try to make a good impression." He winked at Jacks.

He stayed back in his cot for a moment. "Hey," he called to Kwame. "Benoit brought me to Sim Ru last night. It was like he wanted me to take over where he had failed. Kind of like you said. Like Zyanya said. Maybe he's not a bad guy after all. He just...lost his way."

"I never thought he was a bad guy. He was not the first and he will not be the last to lose his way."

They took showers in the bathhouse, dressed, and went to look for Magdala. She wasn't at her bungalow, so they headed to the mansion house, hoping they would find her working there. In the late morning sun, the Instituto had quietly come back to life. Artists were out and about working on their arts and crafts in shaded stations around the grounds. It didn't seem right at first for everything to be going on like Zyanya's death had never happened, though Jacks supposed the familiar routine helped their community cope. He glanced back at the stable house and saw someone had installed a whitewashed wooden cross in the yard, and people had piled pink and purple flowers around it. As they passed by groups of artists, the residents nodded to them and quietly said good morning.

At the mansion house, a sign announced the gift shop and the welcome center were closed for the day, but the guys decided to check out Magdala's office behind the front desk all the same. Along the way, Jacks tried to locate Ixchel, but he couldn't pick up her scent. At the welcome center, he heard movement and a phone conversation in Spanish coming from the back room.

They stepped quietly around the counter, waiting for Magdala to finish on the phone. Then Jacks stood in the open doorway, and Kwame drew up behind him.

Magdala startled when she saw the guys, and then she double-looped the scrunchy on her ponytail and turned away from them to busy herself with some papers at a faded, hardwood secretary. "The bungalow was only available for one night. Check out time is eleven."

"Magdala, could you give us a chance to explain?"

She faced him angrily, though her hand was trembling at her side. "I told you before, you need to leave. I'll call Francisco to throw you out."

Jacks stayed put. "We're not monsters. But that man who

killed Zyanya, he is a monster. You and everyone here could be in danger."

She went back to her papers, gathering them into piles. Her hand jerked, sending a manila folder off the table with its contents fanning out on the floor. She stooped down to pick up the mess, and Jacks hurried to help her. When he came an arm's reach from her, she glared at him. "I don't want your help. Get out of here."

"We're not going to let you push us away."

Magdala flopped down the folder on the desk. "Why?"

"Because you know there's something going on here. Something that's bigger than any of us."

"I don't know anything." She swept back a loose strand of her hair and qualified that statement. "I know Zyanya was killed right after the two of you showed up with your loco stories."

"Do you understand what we are?"

She drifted a step away from him and told him forcefully, "Ai Maria, I thought maybe the two of you were on drugs last night with all that shifter bullshit. But you're just as insane in the light of day."

"Zyanya believed. She didn't just believe. She knew. It's always been this way. Especially here in Mexico. This is where it began, Magdala. The Olmec. The werejaguar priests. The tradition passed down to the Mayans and the Aztecs. It's in your roots as well. Your ancestors knew about the jaguar god."

"We're not living in the Middle Ages. Some folk beliefs are preserved in our art, but I assure you, my people do not believe in men transforming into cats." She busied herself straightening out papers. "You think I'm some impressionable, young mestiza you can trick? I'm not stupid."

"Do you want us to show you?"

She glanced up at him for a moment. Jacks looked at

Kwame. His friend nodded. The mansion house was still. There was no trace of people anywhere inside or on the nearby grounds.

Kwame stepped farther into the room where he had some space. Then, after a quick, tense grimace on his face, his body morphed into a majestic, dark-maned lion, standing on all fours, the height of Jacks's hip.

Magdala shrieked and scrambled to the far side of the secretary to put a barrier between her and the giant cat. It brought a smile to Jacks' face for a moment. He petted Kwame's tufted mane, and Kwame brushed his snout against his leg. All the while, Magdala stared in terror and wonder.

He gently guided her to the three-hundred-pound lion that had materialized in front of her eyes. Her chest heaved and her hand shook, but she allowed him to place it on the side of Kwame's giant muzzle. Gradually, she roamed over his magnificent mane and hide, tearing up, smiling, and glancing at Jacks as though it was a miracle.

"I would have shifted myself, but we figured you'd find Kwame more impressive," he said.

His friend looked up at him with feline hauteur.

"On balls alone, this guy puts me to shame," Jacks added. "You can come around and see for yourself."

Kwame bucked his head against Jacks's leg, sending him swaying for balance.

Magdala clasped her mouth. "I'm dreaming. I passed out, and this is all a dream."

"It's real. It blew my mind too when I first discovered it. But do you understand now?"

While Magdala backed away in a daze, Kwame morphed back into his six-foot-five West African self. Magdala's hand leapt to her chest, and the color drained from her face. "I don't feel so good."

Magdala swooned, and Jacks caught her in his arms before she hit the floor.


THEY CARRIED MAGDALA to a sofa in the welcome center and got her some water from the cooler. The hollow groan of Jacks's stomach led him to investigate the mini-fridge in the backroom office. By luck, he found a leftover plate of grilled chicken. He and Kwame were famished, and they expected a long morning, explaining things to Magdala. When Magdala awoke groggily, they sat around the welcome center lobby eating and drinking while Magdala asked them many questions.

He exerted as much patience as he could. She was understandably shaken and running the emotional gamut from mania to disbelief. He and Kwame took turns filling her in about the history of feline weremagic while picking through the greasy chicken parts and gnawing them down to the bone.

"You sure were right about me getting stuck on the wrong sort of guys," Magdala told Jacks. "Not only have they been gay, they've been a different species."

He smirked.

"Are you like vampires?" she asked. "Do you use some kind of glamor to seduce people?"

Jacks pointed his elbow at Kwame while he nibbled the last bit of meat off a chicken leg. "That's Kwame's angle. He gets lucky wherever he goes."

Kwame came back at him with a scowl. "We are not vampires." He passed Jacks a wise look. "Though some of us are more irresistible than others."

Magdala stared at Jacks in fascination. It was getting a bit unnerving. They had serious business to work out, and the clock was ticking. He wiped his mouth and fingers with a paper towel, wadded it up, and tried to explain the Sim Ru prophecy. "Tomorrow night, we have to get to the site of his temple and hope that Tepe hasn't found it first. If he awakens Sim Ru, there's going to be bloodshed. The prophecy says it could be the end of humankind."

Magdala let out a vacant laugh like a psychiatric patient. She stood and stepped around, clutching herself. "This is a lot for me to take in."

"I know. It was a lot for all of us."

"If you know it was this guy Tepe who killed Zyanya, we should go to the police. They can lock him up before he unleashes this doomsday you're talking about."

"No," he told her. It came out more forcefully than he had anticipated, and he stood, trying to calmly reason with her. "Magdala, we don't have time for that. For one thing, the police would never find him. For another, we can't be trying to explain this to a bunch of cops. They'd think we're high or crazy. Like you did. They might want to lock us up."

"So, why are you telling me about it?" Magdala said.

"Because we need your help. Zyanya told us the ritual must take place on sacred ground. She said it's not far from here, but she never told us exactly where it is."

"You think *I* know what she was talking about? This is my first time hearing any of this."

"Maybe it's a ruin, or a burial site. Think Magdala. Is there any place like that nearby?"

"There are Mayan ruins all over the Yucatán. Chichen Itza and Coba are both about an hour away."

He shook his head. "It wouldn't be Mayan. Something older."

"There's like twenty maybe thirty archeological sites in the Yucatán. I think I have a brochure in the office."

He stood in her path to the backroom and held out his

hands. "We don't have time to run around to random archeological sites."

"What do you want from me? You don't need me. You need an archeologist."

"You live here. It's got to mean something to you."

"I don't know," she moaned.

Kwame put his hand on Jacks's shoulder.

"I don't know," Magdala shouted at Jacks. "Why are you harassing me?"

"I'm sorry. I didn't mean to scare you." He needed so badly for her to have a clue to the location of the ritual. "Zyanya was going to take us there. That had to mean it's within walking distance. Is there anywhere unusual she used to go? Does it make you think of anything?"

Magdala shook her head. And blinked. Jacks caught that little glimmer of recollection.

"Francisco took her for walks sometimes. Along the train tracks." She retook her seat on the sofa with her knees drawn up in front of her. "There's an abandoned railway through the countryside. Where they used to transport henequen from the hacienda. A few years back, a couple of the artists found an arrowhead back there that looked like it was pre-Columbian."

Jacks looked at Kwame encouragingly.

"But you have to understand, this is Yucatán," Magdala said. "Everything is built on ruins. People turn up ancient artifacts in their backyards practically every day."

"It's the best lead we've got," Jacks said. "Thank you. How 'bout you take us there to have a look around?"

"Jacks," Kwame muttered.

He drew a breath. He understood Magdala had been through a lot already, but he was itching to get down to the train tracks. He turned to Kwame to suggest that they check it out on their own.

"What are you going to do if you find that guy Tepe?" Magdala asked.

Jacks didn't answer right away. If he told her they would probably have to fight Tepe to the death, he had no idea how she would react. As it was, he worried about what Magdala was going to do when they left her. Confide in one of the residents about what she had seen and heard? The hysteria would spread like wildfire. Or was she so freaked out she would go to the police?

*She should come with us*, he telepathized to Kwame. Kwame eyed him crookedly.

"I'm not going to go to the police," she said, "But if there's some shapeshifting psychopath lurking around the property, don't you think I deserve to know how you're going to handle it? I should clear out the residents. They're my responsibility."

"If Tepe's out there, you can be sure we will put an end to him," Kwame told her. "He had no problem killing an eighty-year-old woman, but you can believe he will not get past the two of us. We will keep you safe."

"Why don't you come along?" Jacks told Magdala. He ignored another stern glance from Kwame.

Magdala stood and smoothed out her T-shirt dress. "I can't believe I'm saying this, but all right, I'll take you down there. Just give me some time to finish a few things in the office."

Jacks and Kwame waited in the lobby while Magdala did what she needed to do in the backroom. Jacks was too restless to sit for more than a minute or so. He kept his ears attuned to Magdala's movements and the possibility of her making a call from her phone.

He could tell Kwame was stewing. After watching Jacks pacing around for a few minutes, he came out with it.

"I thought the idea was to get information from her, not to put her in danger."

"Yeah. Well, the whole goddamn world's going to be in danger tomorrow night if Tepe gets to Sim Ru before us."

"That doesn't make it right."

"She'll be fine. If we run into Tepe, we'll be there to protect her."

Kwame glanced at him, dubiously. Jacks came over to speak more quietly. "Y'know, I never realized how annoying it can be having to explain ourselves to humans."

"Cut her a break. This is the first she's hearing about our kind."

"And that's our fault? People are ignorant. Why's it always our responsibility to help them understand?"

"How else will they understand?" Kwame rubbed his stubbly chin. "Didn't you need someone to explain it to you when you first found out?"

"That's my point. I was desperate to understand because everything about werecats is hidden and suppressed. I *had to* figure it out to survive. For her, and the rest of humankind, we're just freaks of nature. And we have to be all understanding and patient, hoping they can find it in their hearts to accept us?"

Kwame crossed his arms behind his neck and leaned back in his seat. "There are many burdens in life."

Jacks sat down next to him on the sofa. "I'll apologize to her. But doesn't it piss you off sometimes?"

"I think you saw that yesterday. The way I reacted after Zyanya confirmed the powers that the ritual can unlock."

Jacks eyed the door to Magdala's office. "She could go to the authorities and have us run out of town. We could all be eliminated, and for 99.9 percent of humankind, that would be totally fine. It would be like the world returning to 'normal.'"

"These are strong feelings to have the night before you have to face Sim Ru and ask him for a way werecats and humans can live peacefully together. Are you having second thoughts?"

"I'm not having second thoughts." Jacks struggled with his words. "It's just...I can say things and not really mean them entirely, can't I? Just to you, because we're friends, right?" Kwame nodded. Jacks told him, "Just yesterday, you were saying that the only answer was for Sim Ru to come alive and even things with humans. That wouldn't be the worst outcome, would it? If I could ask him to save certain people. Like Farzan and his family."

"I said that out of anger. That is not the right state of mind in which to make a decision."

Jacks paced some more to work off his unsettled energy. "I know. I wouldn't ask for that. Not like Tepe. He told me back in Boca de Anjo, traitors need to be made an example of. If he gets control of Sim Ru's power, he won't just punish humans. He'll go after us and any other werecat who tried to stop him."

When Magdala finished her work in the office, they headed out from the mansion house with a backpack filled with bottled water. It was the height of the day's heat, mid-afternoon, and the grounds of the Instituto had cleared out for the daily siesta.

Jacks and Kwame didn't mind the Yucatán torpor. Their feline physiology made them adaptable to extreme climates, and they barely sweated. For Magdala's sake, they took things slowly as they made their way down the road to the hacienda. Her face was quickly shiny with sweat beneath her wide-brimmed hat, and she finished her water bottle by the time they reached the terminus of the old, corroded iron and wood plank railway line.

From a crumbling, concrete platform at the back of the hacienda workhouse, the tracks stretched through spiny, untended fields of henequen and onward to scrubby wood-lands. It was hard for Jacks to imagine the plantation in its heyday. The railway beams and planks had sunk into the crusty earth and worn away in places, overtaken by crabgrass. The fields themselves were like a desert landscape, a decade or two away perhaps from overtaking the train tracks completely. Ash-gray iguanas and quick-footed geckos had made a haven of the forgotten pastures. Along the way, Jacks spotted a coppery-brown pit viper coiled up ahead on the tracks, and they waited out its gradual retreat into the brush.

"Back in the 1800s, they built many of these railway lines on ancient Mayan roadways," Magdala told them. "This one dates back from the time they used mules to pull the henequen trams. It goes all the way to Valladolid and onward to Merida on the west coast."

Jacks studied the railway. Whatever mounded earth had once existed to signify a road must have crumbled and settled through the centuries. "Is this one built on a Mayan roadway?"

"I have no idea. Francisco might know. He's been the groundskeeper here since before the Instituto got its start. I heard that some years before Manuel Grubar bought the plantation, they tried to use it as a tourist site. We still have some of the trams they used for old-fashioned mule pulls through the countryside."

She had relaxed a bit. If she had managed to make a surreptitious call to the authorities or to rifle off an S.O.S. email, she was playing it off very well. Though Jacks doubted Magdala had been that sneaky.

"I'm sorry I came at you so hard back at the mansion house." he told her.

"De nada, pendejo." She smiled to herself from that little putdown.

"I was just stressed. Not that I'm making excuses."

"Believe me, I get it. You two have gotten me stressed too."

They followed the tattered railway into the woodlands.

Thicker, weedy patches hemmed in the tracks, and gnarled, tiny-leafed trees provided some gracious shade from the ferocious sun. Venturing into the thick vegetation amped up Jacks's vigilance. The wild, desolate trail provided many vantages for an ambush. He exchanged a wary glance with Kwame. The air was thick with foliage, and he smelled scat from a small mammal like a coati, but no scent of wild cats.

Until they approached a tunnel of tree cover that obscured the way ahead.

Jacks halted his companions, and they stepped behind the brush on the side of the tracks. Kwame's nostrils flared. He smelled it, too. They silently conferred. The scent was familiar, but it wasn't Tepe. A diminutive domestic with a distinctive dander and ammonium odor. If Jacks wasn't mistaken, it smelled like Ixchel.

Magdala looked from one man to the other, whispering in a panic, "What is it?"

Jacks put a finger to his lips. They could surprise the meddling domestic if they were stealthy about it. He looked to Kwame, and they telepathized a plan. He told Magdala, "It's Ixchel. Probably keeping an eye on things for Tepe." That didn't ease her agitation much, and when he tensed up his gut and stretched and contorted into a two-hundred-pound cougar, Magdala nearly tripped over her own legs.

Kwame caught her. "Stay here." He pointed her into the brush where she squatted down and made herself small. Jacks prayed her rustling hadn't alerted their duplicitous quarry.

He slunk over to the other side of the woods with supremely light and soundless steps. The plan was to surprise Ixchel from opposite directions, hemming her in. He immediately dialed in, excited to be back in his stealthy, feline body, his blood rushing in anticipation of the capture. He could step through the brush without the faintest disturbance of his surroundings, winding around the bushy trees, stopping here and there to peer through a gap in the leaves. He couldn't make visual contact, but he smelled that he was closing in.

The woods were still except for some tiny, orange-faced shrikes, chattering overhead and nibbling on ants on the branches. Deep within the forest cover on the other side of the tracks, he spotted Kwame, camouflaged in the leaves and thistle, a stalking lion.

The scent trail led him deeper into the woods, and then for a confounding moment, it seemed to disappear completely. He dropped his jaw, breathing in the air through the sensitive passageways on the roof of his mouth. He picked up nothing.

How could the tabby have vanished so quickly? Jacks scanned low across the ground in the direction of his original pursuit. Ixchel had many places to hide if sensed that they were coming. But he wouldn't have lost his lock on Ixchel's scent, and she couldn't have scurried off through the dry brush that quickly without making a sound. He skulked ahead.

A querulous chirrup piped up from above. A colony of shrikes scattered from a bushy dogwood just a few yards away from Jacks. He peered up at one trembling limb and followed it inward. Ixchel had scrambled up the tree, a higher vantage to throw her pursuers off her scent and keep an eye out for their movements. A smart idea, but the birds gave it away.

He took the tree trunk at a full gallop, scaling it quickly with his clawed fours, and he grappled up to the limb where Ixchel was perched. The smaller cat hissed and puffed out her fur. She sidled backward on the tapering limb, which drooped beneath her weight. With a sudden lunge, Jacks caught her neck in his jaws and braced himself on the swaying branch. He waited out the tabby's vicious struggle, taking a stinging swipe at his ruff with her rear paw. As he bore down his fangs on the delicate scruff of her neck and telepathized to her, she quieted like a kitten in the jaws of her mother.

Jacks clambered down from the tree a bit less elegantly than he had come up, hitting the ground with his forepaws and with Ixchel safely stowed in his jaws. Kwame had meandered over to the tree, watching him with feline approval. He pushed in close and gave Ixchel a lap of his tongue across her muzzle.

Magdala gained up on them, drawn out from her cover by the commotion. At the sight of Ixchel in Jacks's mouth, she exclaimed, "Don't kill her!"

Kwame morphed back to human shape. "He's not hurting Ixchel. We need to hold her captive until we find the site that Zyanya spoke about. We can use her as a lure for Tepe."

Magdala looked from Ixchel to Jacks to Kwame and around again. There was a lot she didn't understand about Ixchel's connection to Tepe, but in the end she acquiesced.

"All right. I think I may have found the place you're looking for."

She drew them over to a hollow in the woods back in the direction from which she had come. It didn't look like much of anything at first—a bald nook among the weedy trees, not more than six yards in circumference. It might have been left bare by natural circumstances.

Magdala stood in the middle and stomped her sandaled foot on the ground, making a blunt sound. Beneath scattered leaves, Jacks perceived a slab of stone, and then he made out a patchwork of gray and mottled slabs. The mortared grooves had decayed and filled in with dirt and weeds. An excavation might reveal the roof of a greater structure or perhaps it was all that was left of an ancient building's stone floor. Glancing around, he noticed a lightly trampled trail that led back to the railroad tracks, which were just a few yards away.

"I'm not an expert, but this looks pretty ancient to me."

Magdala brushed aside some leaves with her sneaker to reveal a greater portion of the blackened, limestone surface. "This is incredible. There are archeological sites just a few miles away, but I guess they never discovered this one. These woods are still part of the Instituto's land and before that, the plantation owner's. It doesn't look like anyone has touched this structure."

It was hard for Jacks to investigate very closely while minding the furry hostage clenched in his jaws. Meanwhile, Kwame squatted down and retrieved a string of jade beads from the floor. Nearby, he found chicken bones, immaculately cleaned of their meat and white as sun-blanched shells against his palm.

"Someone knew of this place," he said. "She was leaving offerings."

Jacks imagined old, blind Zyanya making secret treks out to the site, carrying a strangled hen from her yard to leave on the stone floor in oblation to a god that had to be Sim Ru. She had said the cat was not the "father" of her people, but maybe she did it for the werecat friends she was so fond of.

He lowered his muzzle to the ground while Ixchel squirmed a bit. It wasn't easy to draw in a scent while carrying the kitty in his mouth, but faint traces of jaguar spray seeped into his sinuses. Tepe had been to the site and marked it. He sent that message to Kwame, who stooped at one spot on the patchwork stone floor, noticing something. Kwame cleaned off a greater portion of one of the plates and stepped around, looking at it from different angles.

Jacks trotted over to take a look. Kwame had revealed a toppled, stone-carved head, which had once stood guard on the ancient platform. Its form and detail was familiar from the glyphs in the Báalam-Tet—a man's head with a jaguar snout and growling jaws, wearing a many-draped headdress.

The werejaguar king.

Magdala covered her gaping mouth. They were standing on the stone bricks where centuries ago people had made sacrifice to an all-powerful feline deity, the sacred ground where in one day's time Jacks was to relinquish his physical body to stand at the throne of the great sabretooth god.

"That's Olmec," she said. "But how and why, I have no idea. I've never heard of any of their temples here in the Yucatán. Their ruins are hundreds of miles away in Veracruz."

"Could be they traveled farther," Kwame said. "Or it's an imitation by a later civilization."

Ixchel mewed pitifully, trying to gain Magdala's attention. Jacks gave the cat a shake in his jaws and telepathized to her.

*Don't bother trying to gain her sympathy. And don't get any bright ideas about sending a message to your master. I'll break your neck like a twig. Consider me your master now.*

THEY STOWED IXCHEL in Magdala's backpack, Jacks shifted to human form, and they hiked back to the bungalows to rest and plan. Tepe must have forged a bond with Ixchel when he had visited the Instituto a few weeks back. Telepathically, Jacks forced out of her that she had alerted Tepe to their arrival and tipped him off to attack Zyanya when she was alone last night. She was a despicable accomplice, but in the hierarchy of cats, a domestic would always bow down to a werecat. Now that she was in the hands of a werecougar and a werelion, Ixchel would cede to their authority and help them catch Tepe in a trap.

At dinner time, they took a table on the periphery of the Instituto's residents, drawing a few curious glances from los perrons, but generally blending in. Magdala was part of their secret confederacy now. It had happened in an unspoken way.

Jacks gathered that she understood the supernatural dealings at the Instituto, and she had taken on their mission so she could better understand. He wasn't sure if she fully appreciated what was at stake. How could she, having seen nothing of Tepe's terrorism or the U.S. government's handling of werecats? Still, he warmed up to Magdala again. He respected her being willing to help them and making good on her promise to keep things quiet.

After dinner, she joined the men at their bungalow where they had locked up Ixchel. They stayed up late into the night in case Tepe was plotting another visit. While darkness blanketed the grounds, they played Crazy Eights and drank coffee con leche to stay alert. Around midnight, just after dinner in Samoa, Jacks left Kwame and Magdala to call Farzan.

Naturally, Farzan had just finished a big, home-cooked meal. "Maman thinks I'm going into hibernation," he complained. "She's determined to fatten me up for the next six months."

"You look great to me." Jacks stared into Farzan's deep brown eyes. "God, I miss you so much."

Soon into their conversation, Farzan's expression turned grave. "Did you hear what's going on in the U.S.?"

Jacks mentioned the news brief on the radio last night, but that was all he knew.

Farzan glanced around, looking like he was worried about being in earshot of his mother or brother. He leaned in closer to the video screen. "The president held a televised briefing this morning. He brought in the surgeon general to issue a report. They're saying this supposed feline virus has spread to humans. Wichita went under quarantine three days ago, and they just quarantined Kansas City, Missouri. That's where they detained two men who were suspected of plotting bioterrorism.

The family of one of those men organized a community protest to say the whole operation was bogus. Now the U.S. government came out with the claim the 'terrorists' were infected with a virus they caught from a domestic cat."

The conspiracy blew up in Jacks's head, leaving him speechless.

Farzan read from a BBC news article he had pulled up on his laptop. "A special team of veterinarians hired by the U.S. Centers for Disease Control has isolated the cause of an outbreak of attacks by domestic cats in five U.S. cities. Studying cadavers, the medical team determined the animals were infected with a viral mutation that they have named FVR3, related to feline herpes. The CDC reports that unlike the common feline herpes virus, FVR3 is highly virulent in humans and communicable by casual contact with infected cats. The virus appears to target the central nervous system resulting in disorientation, panic, and aggressive behavior similar to its feline victims. The federal agency reports thirteen people have been infected with FVR3, and they have mobilized a national screening effort in collaboration with the National Guard."

He looked up to his video cam. "Jacks, this is ten times worse than the SARS scare a few years back. There's no international travel in or out of the U.S. They're quarantining visitors from the U.S. in China, Japan, and parts of Europe. And the hysteria over domestic cats is around the globe. We're keeping Bella inside the apartment."

Jacks felt like screaming. How many innocent cats had been killed? Everything he feared was happening. In fact, it was worse than he imagined. He couldn't help himself from jumping to the conclusion that the "feline viral screening" was a front for eliminating werecats across the country. Would it spread around the world?

"When are you coming home?"

He refocused on Farzan's face. By his exasperated expression, he'd been repeating the question while Jacks had been lost in his thoughts.

"I don't know."

"What do you mean you don't know? You've been gone for three weeks. I supported this idea for you to find out about your ancestry, but things have changed. What if you have trouble traveling now? There'll be an inspection of Maarten's boat in Panama. This FVR3 scare could catch on in Mexico, and you could get stuck there. It's not safe, and the sooner you make it back the better. I'm sorry, Jacks, but you can always go back there when things calm down."

"I can't." He told Farzan about Tepe killing Zyanya. That led into explaining everything about the Sim Ru prophecy, except one major detail he still couldn't bring himself to share.

Farzan's face darkened, and he shook his head. "No. You get out of there now. This is no time for you to be getting involved with Tepe again."

"I have to stop him," Jacks said steadily.

Farzan's voice rose up. "You don't *have* to do anything. You *want* to do this. But a week ago, you proposed to me, Jacks. That means it's no longer only your decision."

"I'm doing this for us. If Tepe gets to Sim Ru, we'll never be safe. Your family won't be safe. You heard what was in the Báalam-Tet. Zyanya confirmed it. Tepe will raise an army of werecats to murder humankind to extinction. I can't sit back and let that happen."

Farzan shifted and pushed back his hair. "What am I supposed to say? Go try to kill Tepe and hope that he doesn't kill you? I can't, Jacks. It's not that I don't believe in you, but I can't."

Jacks placed his finger on the screen of his phone, wishing

he could reach inside and hold Farzan. "I can't just hope that tomorrow night you could be taken away from me." He swallowed hard. He had to tell Farzan everything. "If I stop Tepe, there's a way for me to try to set the world right." His voice cracked. "I so need you to believe in me. Because I'm pretty terrified myself."

He told Farzan about the sacrifice at the werejaguar king's altar. Farzan was starkly still.

"If Sim Ru wishes it, I'll return to my physical body. I'll come back to you."

Farzan regained his fire. "No. I'm booking the next flight there. I'm dragging you back with my bare hands."

"Honey—"

"You can't fucking do this to me." Farzan's voice broke, and he covered his face with his hand and choked back tears. Jacks listened to a commotion around him. Mrs. Mohammed had swept into the room, demanding questions from her son in Persian. She came around and gripped his shoulder with her brown hand and stared at Jacks from the corner of the screen, desperate to understand what had transpired between him and her son.

For a moment, it felt to Jacks like it might have been worse than actually dying.

Farzan spoke quietly to his mother, gradually coaxing her to leave him to his privacy.

That was when Jacks started sniffling himself. "I'm sorry. If there was any other way—"

"Don't."

"I promise, I'll be strong and fearless. I don't want to die." He shielded his tearing eyes with his hand. "But you have to tell me, you won't hate me if I do. 'Cause none of this is worth it if you're going to hate me for the rest of your life."

"Don't promise me anything."

"Farzan, don't give up on me."

A tight, quivering smile. Then Farzan told him that he needed to be alone, and they said good night.

# EIGHTEEN

JACKS LAID AWAKE in his cot for most of the night, and after perhaps an hour or two of real sleep, his dread and anticipation jolted him alert. Sunlight shone through the slats of the bungalow's shuttered window. It was New Year's Eve. That night, he would either die and be reborn or simply die.

He, Kwame, and Magdala had barely sketched out a plan for dealing with Tepe. If Jacks failed, Farzan and everyone he loved would be killed when Tepe commanded an army to tear apart the world. Alternatively, he had to kill himself at Sim Ru's altar, hoping he was following the ritual perfectly to gain an audience with his father god. Tension in his jaw sawed into his ears, and his stomach cramped and burned. He had to succeed despite the fact his whole body was rebelling against it.

Magdala had invited them to her bungalow for breakfast, and she made fried eggs and ham on her little gas burner. After they ate on her outdoor table, Magdala went into her house and brought out a cardboard box and dropped it on the table.

"I went to Zyanya's house early this morning. I thought she might have had something we could use."

Jacks raised his eyebrows. That was ballsy considering they had heard Zyanya had a nephew and a niece driving up from Oaxaca to claim her things. Magdala picked through her strange box of loot. Feathered headdresses. Jade and obsidian beads. Little, wood-carved statues—voodoo dolls? A string of what looked like human teeth. A dulled and rusted iron dagger.

He had no idea how any of the items would help, but he smiled at Magdala, appreciating her effort. The dagger drew his eye. He did need some way to kill himself on the altar, though the weapon was a brutal method. He veered away from that terrifying dilemma and noticed his companions were staring at the stable house beyond the artists' bungalows. A pickup truck was parked on the plot, and Francisco was loading the bed with Zyanya's macabre Catrinas.

"Guess I'm not the only mercenary," Magdala said. "Those models go for two thousand, sometimes three thousand dollars. Probably more now she's dead."

"I thought she had family," Jacks said.

"None keeping inventory. Francisco must have orders from the director. Zyanya didn't have a will or any documents bequesting her work that I ever saw, but he'll claim she left everything to the Instituto. A lot of the artists do. Zyanya would have wanted it anyway. She never mentioned having a niece or nephew from Mexico City. They never visited. I never even got any mail or phone calls from her family coming through the office."

Kwame stood, glancing at Magdala. "Suppose we took some of the Catrinas?"

Magdala laughed. "Ai Maria. They don't exactly travel well. What do you want to do—strap them on your backs and walk out of here hoping no one notices?"

"Not to steal or to sell. We need a strategy to surprise Tepe. Do you think some of those models are big enough for us?"

Jacks got it. He watched Francisco rolling one of the Catrinas out of the house with a handcart. The groundskeeper was not a small man, and the model of a buxom, skull-faced lady in a flowery bonnet was bigger than him. Big enough for Kwame to stow inside if he squatted down. And the stinking paper, glue and paint would camouflage their scent from Tepe.

They explained the plan to Magdala. She looked from one to the other. "You're serious?"

"We'll need your help," he told her. "We'll have to cut them open to get inside. Can you do some touch-up work afterward so they look intact?"

The humor drained from Magdala's face. "You're serious. I guess, if you think it will trick this guy Tepe." She looked to the stable house where Francisco's truck was filled with some dozen Catrinas. "We've got our work cut out for us. As soon as Francisco leaves with his first load, we need to get into that house. We'll have to grab some of the Catrinas and bring them back here to cut seams into the models and do the paint and patch up work. Never mind figuring out how we're going to get them out to the woods without anyone seeing."

THEY SPENT THE rest of the day working on their Trojan horse Catrinas, and by nightfall, they were ready to haul two massive models out to the woods. Kwame had the inspired idea of borrowing some of the flowers and candles people had left in front of Zyanya's house. They would make the temple in the woods look like a memorial site for the Soul Seer to confuse Tepe. Jacks telepathized to Ixchel her part in the scheme. When Tepe arrived, she had to tell him people from the Instituto had found out the place was special to Zyanya and decorated it with her artwork and the flowers.

For New Year's Eve, the residents were holding a party on

the grounds of the hacienda. They had strung lanterns in red, green, and white and filled the picnic tables with candles. Some of the artists had brought guitars and drums, and later there would be fireworks. Magdala told them she'd come down with a migraine and would try to join them later. When the musicians started playing and rowdy voices hailed from the yard, Jacks and Kwame hauled their Catrinas and the flowers through the dusky grounds and met up with Magdala and Ixchel behind the hacienda. Inside, they found an old tram car to put on the tracks. They loaded the colossal models into it and pushed it through the plantation into the woods.

Carrying an outdoor lantern, Magdala led them to the werejaguar king temple, and they dressed it up. Magdala wore a wristwatch and checked the hour frequently as minutes ticked toward midnight. When they were done, it was nearly time for Jacks and Kwame to hide themselves.

In the fleeting moments of conversation, Kwame caught Jacks's eye. "You are certain you want to do this?"

"It's why we're all here, isn't it?"

Kwame stared at him harder. Jacks's palms were sweating, and he couldn't keep still. He felt the weight of Zyanya's iron blade, which he had stowed in the big pocket of his cargo shorts. "If anything happens to me, you'll look out for Farzan, won't you?"

Kwame nodded somberly. "You told him?"

"Yeah." Jacks grinned wryly. "I think the wedding may be off."

"You are a brave man. And if anything happens to me, you'll tell Som-Suea, César, Nicolas, and Maarten?"

"Of course."

Magdala watched them fearfully. "You've fought Tepe before, haven't you?"

"No," Jacks said. "But we've fought werejaguars before."

Magdala dug into a deep pocket in her peasant skirt. She brought out a silver revolver, dulled with age. Jacks stood back from the sight of it.

"I found it in Zyanya's things," she said. "I figured it couldn't hurt."

"Have you ever used one of those?" Kwame said.

Magdala shook her head. Jacks stared at the wide-barreled gun in her slender hand. The silver was tarnished and rusted in places. It probably hadn't been used in decades. "Magdala, maybe that's not such a good idea."

"I might have to defend myself, right?" she said.

He looked at her steadily. "You're staying down the tracks, well away from here, no matter what you hear."

Magdala returned the gun to her pocket. "Just trying to be helpful."

"You've been helpful," Kwame told her. "But a big cat fight is no place for you."

Magdala nodded tensely, and she checked her wristwatch. "You guys should probably get into the Catrinas."

They had found a big, bustle-skirted model for Kwame and a tall gaucho with a dapper scarf, vest, and sombrero for Jacks. Kwame's Catrina also had an enormous, bell-shaped hat decorated with pink feathers, which made Jacks grin. They had placed the models on opposite sides of the altar like giant, showy pillars. The two men tucked themselves inside their respective disguises, and Magdala sewed up the seams and did some final touches so they looked intact.

It was cramped and stuffy inside the Catrina. They had poked eye holes just below the knot of the gaucho's scarf, which also provided Jacks with precious air.

The wait was hot and uncomfortable. They had gotten into the Catrinas a half hour before midnight in case Tepe showed up early, and that was a long time to be stuffed inside the paper-mâché shell, unable to even raise his hand to wipe his perspiration from his eyes. He focused on listening keenly. That sense was dampened by his paper-layered cocoon. He could hear the primordial sounds of the dusky forest but nothing beyond that background noise. As time ticked by, he hoped Tepe wouldn't show up, and they wouldn't have to fight him after all.

Ixchel mewled to someone. Jacks could see her sitting on her hind legs and perching her head at the edge of the temple floor, deciphering something in the black night. Her wee, raspy voice entered his head.

*They come.*

He stared into the space beyond Ixchel. He could see the opening to the trail to the railroad tracks but not much beyond that. A rustling through the brush drew his attention. He tried to zone in on that area as best as he could. Three figures emerged from the trail.

Jacks drew a breath to battle his dread back. He recognized the murderer Tepe in his olive fatigues, snap cap, and dark goatee.

Tepe looked around the altar warily, and his companions drew up beside him, muttering oaths in Portuguese. It stood to reason Tepe would bring backup, though Jacks had hoped he wouldn't. Most of his militia had to have been wiped out in Boca de Anjo, and Dickerson had also engineered that follow up operation in Boa Vista. Jacks didn't know these guys. One was darker skinned with short wiry hair, and the other was closer to Tepe's complexion with a less appealing face: bumpy skin, a ratty beard, and a scar running through his lips.

Tepe and his men stepped around the altar. They looked at the Catrinas a bit fearfully. It must have been a shocking find— the towering models with skeleton heads set up in the middle of nowhere. The ruse was working perfectly. They just needed to wait for the moment Tepe came nearer to ambush him.

Tepe crouched beside Ixchel, engaged in some telepathic exchange with her. Meanwhile, the dark-skinned man got bolder and approached Kwame's matronly Catrina. Jacks lost him in his limited eyehole vision, but he heard him call back to his companions in Portuguese and chuckle. Then Jacks heard him shove the Catrina. He tightened like a spring. If the man pushed it over, he would discover Kwame.

*I have to do this now.* Kwame said in Jacks's head.

Jacks clenched his diaphragm, and in the heartbeat before his transformation, he heard Kwame bursting through his papier-mâché shell with a lion's roar. Jacks shredded himself free and charged at Tepe. He had to make the kill fast. If they didn't complete this stage of the operation quickly, they would miss the deadline for the ritual.

He pounced on his startled target, toppling him onto his back. As he lunged for Tepe's throat, his quarry burst into jaguar form, eluding his jaws and sending the two of them into a tumble.

He broke out of that melee, snarling and puffing out his fur. He had gouged Tepe's shoulder, but that was barely a hindrance now. He had needed to finish him off while he was in human form. Now he faced an adversary who was twice his size and had thick, muscled limbs and a jaw span that could clamp down on his entire head.

He stood his ground and telepathized to Tepe. *You're not going through with the ritual.*

Tepe's jaguar self was bigger than any of his henchmen—a jungle cat killing machine with fist-sized rosettes mottled on his brawny neck and barrow. His snarl vibrated through Jacks's bones. Then Tepe eased up for a moment, taking in the voice and scent of his attacker.

*Jackson Dowd*, he purred into Jacks's mind. *This is my lucky night. Now, on top of unleashing Sim Ru's reign, I get to kill you.*

They had tumbled away from the temple. Beyond Tepe, Jacks glimpsed Kwame lording over the man he had surprised, while motes of fur and debris from the Catrinas still hung in the air. Kwame's muzzle and beard were darkened with blood. The other henchman, now shifted into a spotted jaguar, had crept into an attack position, gauging a strike. Kwame could take him and then help Jacks subdue Tepe. If he could bide some time.

*You'll have to kill me before midnight*, Jacks told Tepe. *Even if you do, you'll have to get through Kwame. I don't like your chances with that.*

Quick as a cobra, Tepe leapt at Jacks and buried him beneath his heft. Jacks twisted his body to free himself. He could barely squirm beneath the jaguar's powerful limb-span, and then he yelped in agony as fangs pulverized his shoulder. His limbs flailed out in a panic to claw the jaguar off him. He had precious moments to get away before his strength would be drained by Tepe's deep bite. Tepe was clamped solidly to his shoulder and sealed so tightly around him that Jacks could feel Tepe's thudding heart against his chest, delighting in the thrill of capture.

*Let go, Jackson. Die now, and you won't have to see the carnage I unleash when I come back with Sim Ru. You won't have to witness me ripping out your boyfriend's throat.*

Jacks scored Tepe's haunches with his hind claw, but it barely bothered him. His heartbeat fluttered, and the world began to spin. He bucked his shoulder against Tepe's jaws in a final effort to free himself.

A gunshot pierced the night.

By the mercy of the gods, Tepe sprang away from that blast,

leaving Jacks to clumsily right himself. Magdala stood at the mouth of the trail to the railroad tracks, Zyanya's revolver hiked up to the sky in her hand, smoke pluming from its barrel. She had no doubt saved his life with that warning gunshot, and she was now ridiculously vulnerable. She could fire off a bullet into the sky, but she didn't look capable of hitting a moving target.

Tepe had already zeroed in on her with his tail lashing behind him. Yards away at the altar, Kwame had the other jaguar's throat in his mouth, and its body hung limply. But he was too far away to protect Magdala.

Tepe charged at her. Summoning every ounce of strength he had left, Jacks leapt after him. His claws connected with Tepe's haunches, and he clamped down on Tepe's hind leg.

Jacks merely hampered his momentum. But after hanging on for a while, Tepe swung around to get him off of his leg. Tepe ripped off the tip of Jacks's ear with a snap of his jaws, and Jacks lost his grip on Tepe's leg. His wounded limb collapsed.

Tepe sidled around him, judging a final strike. *Now you die*, Tepe hissed into his mind. *I'll kill the girl afterward.*

The gun erupted again.

Jacks watched transfixed as Tepe's yellow eyes widened in shock. His head seemed to hang on invisible strings for a moment, and then he saw the scatter of dander and smoke spreading out from the back of his skull.

Tepe foundered, lifeless. Magdala stood behind him with the revolver shaking in her hand. Bitter saltpeter smudged the air. Jacks stared at Magdala in admiration. Even at close range, it took nerves of steel for her to fire off that shot.

Shifted back to his human self, Kwame jogged over to her. Magdala did not budge from her spot nor loosen her grip on the gun.

"Is he dead?" she asked.

Kwame carefully put his arm around her. He looked down at Tepe's curled body. "Yes."

Jacks drew in ragged breaths. The pain from his shoulder was nearly paralyzing, and he had lost a lot of blood.

Magdala shrieked and cowered into Kwame's arms. Tepe's death had returned him to his naked, original self: a young Brazilian man, belly down, with a bleeding bullet hole in the back of his head.

"Oh my god, it's..." Magdala's voice trailed off.

Kwame nodded. "Tepe."

"I killed him."

"In self-defense," Kwame told her.

Magdala shielded her eyes and doubled over. "I'm going to be sick."

"Take deep breaths," Kwame said.

She looked at the gun as though discovering it for the first time, and it fell out of her hand. "I need to sit down."

Kwame helped her shuffle slowly toward the altar. He looked over his shoulder to Jacks. *Are you okay?*

Jacks couldn't move, and now he realized he couldn't even muster the strength to communicate. He tasted iron in the back of his throat. His vision dimmed, and he fought against the shadows pushing in from the corners of his mind.

"Jacks?"

He heard a distant cheering cry and a celebratory pop and crackle. In his fragile state, he imagined at first it was the welcoming fanfare of his entry to the afterlife. Then he remembered the party back at the hacienda. New Year's Eve.

"Jacks, it is time."

Kwame carefully lifted him from the ground and carried him in his arms. Jacks was vaguely aware he had been laid down on a stone surface. Kwame's tense face fluttered in and out of his vision. He was freezing cold and dying of thirst. Kwame was trying to reach him.

"Jacks, can you hear me? It's midnight. It's the hour to enter the portal."

"He's dying," Magdala shouted. "We can't go through with this. We need to get him to a hospital."

"It has to be done," Kwame barked at her.

Delicate scraps of memory drifted through Jacks's head. The Sim Ru prophecy. Finding a way to stop the world from persecuting werecats. Farzan, who was counting on him to survive.

*Jacks, if you can hear me, I need you to tell me what to do. If you die here, you will not be able to enter the portal. The book said it must be done by your own hand.*

Jacks tried to answer him, but just grasping for his inner voice made him wretch and swoon.

*Jacks, answer me. If you do not wish to go through with it, we can get you help.*

He strained to send his reply. *No.* Then willing his wracked body to respond, Jacks bore down on his diaphragm to shift. It felt like his body was being turned inside out, and he was left a bloodied, skinless mass of nerves and flesh. Kwame gripped his hand as he shuddered from the pain. That little act of comfort gave him the strength and clarity to reach inside the pocket of his shorts and grip the dagger in his hands.

Kwame guided him to point the tip of the dagger into the cleft of his sternum. Jacks didn't know if he had the strength to do it, but he didn't fear the pain. Strangely, it seemed like the only antidote to his agony.

He looked at Kwame. They hadn't fought three were-jaguars that night for him to give up on their chance to summon help from the feline god. Kwame's frightened eyes welled with tears.

"Come back to us, Jacks."

Magdala shrieked overhead. "This has gone far enough. It's fucking insanity. Back away from him, or I swear I'll shoot."

With Kwame's hands clasped over his, Jacks bore down on the blade. Kwame's strength helped send it true, carving through cartilage, between bones and splitting open his beating heart. His vision blew up in technicolor from the brutal, exquisite pain.

A woman's scream and a thundering blast echoed in his ears. Then the world fell away.

# NINETEEN

JACKS RAN WITH the wind across a vast, endless plain. He felt like he could run for eternity and never tire. His bare legs were super powered like an Olympic athlete, and his bare feet were made for racing across the terrain. Still, he could not outpace the wind, whose tail whipped and whistled him onward to a sightless distance. If he could beat it to its destination, he could claim it. He knew its name: U-no-le, in an ancient language from a time when the gods gave life to all things on earth.

He climbed the air with weightless steps, up to the purple twilight sky. He could not outrun the wind on land, but he might reach her vertical extremity and ride her, like bridling a giant eagle. U-no-le was massive and powerful. As Jacks climbed higher, she swirled and shrieked at him, spinning and weaving. He tried to catch her in his arms, but she sent him tumbling away. He launched himself upward like ascending invisible stairs. He tasted ozone in his sinuses, and he drank in the air like ice cold water from a mountain spring.

He arrived at great, gray cliffs of stone that towered even

higher into the clouded heavens, with many valleys grooved in between like giant fingers. Suddenly, he stood in one such valley, shielding his face from a squall of sand. His feet sank into a sandy floor cap. He fought for traction, pushing through the storm, traveling across some barren zone.

He saw a man who was also wandering. Grasping the stranger's arm, he asked which way to the sky where he had danced with U-no-le and tried to climb atop her. The man faced Jacks, and his mouth was worn away as though it had been scoured to nothing by the sandstorm. So were his eyes, his nostrils, and his ears. Jacks followed the speechless, faceless man through the pelting gales, hoping the man might lead him out of the awful place. Along the way, he came across other men and women, also featureless. A few had paired up in silent huddles on the shifting dunes of sand, perhaps drawing comfort from the simple contact. Most wandered by themselves.

U-no-le had played a trick, luring Jacks to this land. He shouted for her and stomped his feet like a child. His anger burned and throbbed, and the sand seemed to melt beneath his feet. It was up to his shins and rising. He strained to lift his legs, but he was sinking fast and could find no leverage. Grains of sand slipped through his clawing fingers.

The desert swallowed him. Rather than being buried and suffocated, he found himself dropped into a meadow of fuzzy wildflowers, bordered by ice-capped mountains. He had traveled into another finger valley. This was a much more pleasant place with a bright sun overhead and a breeze as fresh and bracing as springtime in an Alaskan meadow. Jacks rambled through it, enjoying the sensation of damp grass against his feet and the kiss of the sun on his bare shoulders.

He saw a small huddle of people and headed toward them. It looked to be a tribal gathering of some sort. When he reached the group, he discovered it was not people at all. Sitting in a circle was a fly, a shrew, a fox, a wolf, and a big brown bear.

They took no account of his presence, or each other's for that matter. Then, the shrew suddenly ate the fly. The fox pounced on the shrew and gobbled it up. The wolf snapped up the fox in its jaws, chewed it to bits, and swallowed it down. The bear swatted the wolf across the head with its big claw, scooped the stunned animal up in its paws, and proceeded to eat the wolf whole.

The bear glanced at Jacks. The animal seemed satiated and even slightly embarrassed by his behavior. Then, with a sneeze and a mighty wretch, the bear regurgitated his companions onto the grass in a jumble. They were each thoroughly intact, and they retook their places in the circle. After a few moments, the shrew ate the fly, the fox attacked the shrew, the wolf killed the fox, and so on in a cycle Jacks guessed would repeat into infinity.

He rushed onward to the mountains to climb the great shelf of rock whose summit disappeared into the mist. He had never scaled such a vertical slope before, but he sorted out grips and footholds, using a preternatural upper body strength to hoist himself up the face of the cliff. A man-sized, black and white peregrine falcon circled above him. Jacks knew it was U-no-le watching him, and she would swoop down and catch him in her talons if he should fall. He didn't need her help, though he was glad for her company. He grappled his way to a height where the rock was damp with condensation and clouds clung to the cliff. Then he raised himself to the summit, scraping and bruising his thighs and his knees as he scuttled over the edge.

Here was Sim Ru's throne: a raised bank of rock in the center of the tallest, flat-topped cliff that rose above the clouds. Jacks had seen it in his dreams, and he staggered toward the throne with his head bowed. As before, the majestic, spotted beast was turned away from him on his massive fours with his stocky tail curled behind him. The god's head was lowered and shifting to and fro. The surface of his throne and the lower legs of the beast himself were occluded by a thick mist. Jacks reached the foot of the stoop and waited. He could not stop his hands from quivering nor bring air into his lungs.

Sim Ru turned his muzzle toward him, and the hedge of fog around his mount scattered in a breeze. His jowls and ruff were stained dark crimson. Between his giant forelegs was a mangled carcass Jacks recognized as the mottled jaguar Kwame had killed at the temple ruin. Nearby, a man's corpse had been ripped apart to bone and sinew—Tepe's first henchman, the other victim of that fateful night. The monster swathed his muzzle with his big tongue, and he scoured his whiskered cheeks with his giant paw, savoring his feast.

Jacks's throat closed up. As in his dream, words eluded him. What was he to say to a god?

A voice dug into his head, thunderous and terrible. *What tribute, cougar?*

He was empty-handed, not to mention naked as the day he had been born. He reasoned it was best not to dance around the question, nor did he endeavor to penetrate the god's mind.

"I have nothing. But I bring news of great suffering on earth. Such that only you can appease." These words—some formality conjured from his subconscious or a reenactment from a past life.

The god arched his brawny back. He was practically more bear-like in proportions than feline. He stretched his jaws open in a ferocious yawn, and then he narrowed his gaze at Jacks. *What tribute is news? Can it be eaten? Can it be fucked?*

Jacks swallowed a dry gulp. He gestured to the mount. "I laid two kills at your altar in respect to your might."

The beast pitted his forelegs in front of him, staring down

at Jacks, a giant showing off his crushing stature. A mocking chuckle rattled through Jacks's head. Then the god's voice rose up. *You bring me no kills. These were slain by your lion friend. You bring me lies and stories. You haven't even much meat on your gangly primate limbs.*

"No. I killed myself to seek your guidance. As it is written in the Báalam-Tet." He did not dare to look at the god directly. "Our kind is in danger. We need your help."

*Our kind has always been in danger. Why should I help?*

"You are our god."

Sim Ru raised himself on all fours and stepped along his throne. *A god abandoned. Who comes to bring tribute to my shill? A cougar, barely experienced in the ways of the world.*

"I am young, but I have seen much."

*You have been but a blink in time.*

"But I have given myself to you. Show me what I need to know. I want to learn."

Sim Ru settled down to a sphinxlike position, appraising Jacks. His amber eyes now glowed, irises flecked with gold, like the fiery surface of the sun. *You speak of suffering. What have you seen?*

A flurry of violent sounds and images invaded Jacks's head. He saw prehistoric hunters stabbing at a felled sabretooth cat and hacking its proud fangs. He saw lions netted and caged and then prodded out in a Roman arena and baited and battered by men with bronze shields and nailed clubs. He saw poachers with muskets in a jungle blasting apart the skull of a tiger and binding its legs to a wooden rod to carry the animal away as a trophy. So many gory scenes of predation flashed in Jacks's mind's eye, his legs wavered, and he kneeled on the stony ground, stricken.

"Please, no more."

The god's bitter laughter dispersed the sights and sounds.

*What do you know of suffering, cougar? A mere whelp, afraid to stray from the protection of his mother.*

"I'm not afraid. I sacrificed my life to see you."

Sim Ru looked at him with big, amber eyes. *What are you? You do not look like a fighter to me. More like a fool.*

A bleak thought occurred to Jacks. "Maybe I was a fool to seek you out."

*What did you say?* the god growled.

Jacks said it louder, though his whole body trembled. "Maybe I was a fool if I killed myself to come here just so you could insult me."

The god raised himself on his forepaws again, and his voice shook through Jacks's bones. *I am Sim Ru, the Eternal. The Maker of War and Destruction. You shall quiver at my feet and beg for mercy.*

Jacks was already quivering, but he would not beg for mercy. He would rather be eaten alive than allow his journey to end pleading for his life to a cruel god who did not make good on his promises. He had been through death once already.

"You're supposed to help me. On the night of the eye of death aligned with the six sons. You're supposed to help me."

He heard the great cat settling down on his haunches above him. *So it was sworn long ago*, he grumbled. *But a cat minds his own counsel when it comes to granting favors.*

"If every cat on earth died, you'd have no one to rule over," Jacks said. "Is that what you want?"

*Cats make difficult subjects*, Sim Ru said. *It is their nature to despise their master.*

"We despise being killed by humans even more."

*What is it you want then? Vengeance?*

Jacks chose his words carefully. "Some of us want vengeance. But not me. I want justice, but not at the expense of innocent lives. I want peace. As it was in the olden days."

*What does a cougar know of olden days?*

"I know what was told to me. And what I read in the Báalam-Tet. The era of the werejaguar kings, and the golden ages of the Zulu, Ashanti, Waghia, Suea-Saming, and Cherokee. The days when the wereshamans were revered by their tribe." Boldness grew inside him, and he said more. "Your sons gave them the gift of dual souls, and they lived peacefully with men."

*A cat cedes nothing to man. And a man seeks only domination. So it has been from the dawn of humanity. Say what you have come to ask of me, and we shall rule again. You cannot bargain with nature.*

He seemed to pry inside Jacks's head for that bloodthirsty desire he thought he had shaken free some nights ago. The glory of cats rising against their captors. A savage reprisal that would make Dickerson and General Gainsway's attacks on werecats pale in comparison. But that was a base temptation. It was not who Jacks was.

"Help me free the werecats who have been taken prisoner and help me save the domestics. That's all I want."

*The world has changed. There are no wereshaman to protect your kind. Your feline gods are forgotten. Man has created new gods. What you want can only be accomplished when I reclaim what was mine. When the king of kings returns to earth, he shall show no mercy.*

Sim Ru's quickening heartbeat thrummed through Jacks, a monstrous cat delighting in the vision of the carnage he would unleash. Once it started, it could not be undone. "The world *has* changed," Jacks said. "Some of us live with men as brothers." He hesitated, unsure of the god's attitude on certain other matters. "Some of us live with men as lovers," he said. Sim Ru cocked his head, looking at Jacks as a lion might consider a rabbit that had popped out of its hole in a coat and top hat. Before eating it. "We don't want them to be killed," Jacks said.

*You waste my time,* Sim Ru grumbled. *I waited two millennia for the one who would spill his blood at my altar, and that is a long time for even me.*

"Give *me* time," Jacks said. "Give me something." He pushed back his hair. "You say you waited two millennia. Why? All that time, you watched your descendants getting trapped and slaughtered. You could have done something centuries ago."

Sim Ru chewed at the big black pad of his foot. *I gave you life. I gave you tools for survival. But even a god has enemies who seek to destroy what I created. They shall know my glorious retribution and perish with the men who worship them.*

Was he speaking of a human god or gods? Christianity had certainly done its part to wipe out feline mysticism, and Jacks supposed Islam had similarly banished the old traditions in other parts of the world. He had always thought of cultural imperialism as man-made rather than guided by a divine hand. What more was at stake by unleashing Sim Ru? The annihilation of the "new gods" themselves? That was quite a bit more than he could comprehend. The proportions of his dilemma seemed staggering now. He didn't want to be responsible for the destruction of men or gods.

"I'm living proof there's another way," he said. "I am two souls—feline and man, and I don't want to destroy either."

Sim Ru puckered his muzzle.

"And there are others like me. And humans too. That's why it has to be possible for us to coexist without war."

*You are a fluke. A flaw. A pestering mutation in felinekind. Or perhaps you have not lived long enough to understand your nature.*

"I earned the right to ask for your help. Whatever power that entails."

Sim Ru stretched his jaws open and snapped them shut in another yawn. Despite that blasé gesture, Jacks sensed he was getting somewhere. He remembered something from his dream and his purpose was suddenly crystal clear.

"Time. You can give me time."

Sim Ru licked his chops disinterestedly.

"Let me return to Earth and set the imprisoned werecats free and stop people from killing the domestics. You can suspend time."

The feline god stood up on his fours, arching his back and stretching his forelegs with a scrape of his claws against stone. He looked at Jacks again, devouring and stern. *This is what you want, cougar? A trick of magic? It will not change anything.*

"It is what I want." Jacks remembered another important stipulation. "And to return to my physical body on Earth." He was asking a lot, and his hopes hung on a wobbly peg, expecting honor from a god of destruction.

*What shall I receive in return?*

What did Sim Ru want? Jacks could not begin to imagine. Only the most dreadful possibility occurred to him: tribute that could be eaten or fucked as the god had said.

Sim Ru chuckled inside his head again. *You would not make much of a meal, nor a plaything to satisfy my loins.*

Cold sweat rolled down from his temples. "Then name what you want."

*If I release you, you will be the werecougar king. It will be your duty to unite the tribes under my dominion. They must know that all werecats on Earth bow to me. This is my decree, and you must swear it will be so. Once it is sworn, it cannot be undone.*

"That is...generous," Jacks said. "How will I do it?"

*You have fulfilled the ancient prophecy. If I return you to the earthly world with the power to do what you desire, it will be your trial to keep your covenant with me. Do not think me a fool. What has been given can be taken away. Will you swear it?*

Sim Ru watched Jacks, still and alert, as a lion bullying his lessers. Jacks had many questions, but the god was hardly disposed to discuss a game plan for achieving what he had asked of Jacks. It was a far better bargain than being eaten in any case. "Yes, I will."

The sabertooth held him in a deep, fiery gaze. *Then free your army.*

Jacks felt like he was shrinking. Everything was fading, and then the world spun like a celestial eddy. Gradually, he was aware he had been transported to another place that was dark and airy. The god and his throne were no more.

AS IT HAPPENED, Jacks would say that every one of his actions was lucid and deliberate, though to describe it later would sound impossible. His mind was a whirring machine with infinite stores of information. It had pieced together modes of quantum physics and probably other sciences that he had never heard of by name. These abilities had been given to him by Sim Ru. All he had to do was dig inside the dimensions of time and space and create a wormhole that burrowed through those dimensional fibers, and he was off at the speed of an electrical current.

He focused on a location, and there he was, disgorged from his spectral tunnel, without a sound and requiring only a moment to regain his equilibrium and bearings. He was inside a military detention center, a high security facility within a government campus in Atlanta, Georgia. Jacks recognized it vividly, an atom from the universe of knowledge he had gained from Sim Ru on a temporary basis.

It was nighttime, and the building was fully lighted for 24/7 operation, though there was a dampened aspect to it, like the last hours of summer daylight at an extreme northern latitude. A peculiar sense of low gravity startled him for a moment, until he reasoned that this was what the world was like in the interstices of time. His own body was a sort of projection of himself, like a satellite image being broadcast from millions of miles away. He drifted through tidy, institutional hallways where uniformed soldiers were as stiff as mannequins at their checkpoint desks, one in mid-chew while his half-gnawed banana was raised at his side in an absurd salute. A two-handed clock posted above a corridor did not move beyond the hour of midnight.

The detention center's walls and doors were no barriers. Jacks passed through them as easily as light passing through a paper filter. The detainees were locked in a ground floor wing called Unit H-1. He was certain of that and how to get there, as though he had previously studied the layout of the facility and every aspect of its operations. He had never met any of the men, but when his intuition guided him to penetrate into a cell marked 105, he recognized the first werecats Dickerson had captured, Manuel Ponce and Ivan Syarrudin.

Their bodies were wasted in their hospital gowns, and they had grown raggedy beards like abandoned derelicts. They were each on metal cots, their arms riddled with needle punctures from some cruel study of their metabolism and chemical experimentation.

Jacks summoned mass into his body, capturing the atoms that surrounded him, vacuum-like, and filling himself until he had achieved a workable density. His feline senses returned to him at once. He smelled their werecat musk and the sterile, medicinal odors of a facility. They had been drugged.

He laid a hand on Manuel's shoulder, transmitting a rejuvenating energy. Manuel coughed and gasped like he was surfacing for air from the depths of the ocean. His eyes popped open, and he shrunk up on his cot and stared at Jacks while Jacks woke his cellmate Ivan in a similar manner.

With a steady look, he told them what to do. They followed him into a wormhole that slingshot them from one cell to another to free every one of the detainees: Kwame's friend Verner Battle, the two men from Kansas City he had heard about from Farzan, a fellow Cherokee from Oklahoma, a woman from Texas, and four men and a woman who had been rounded up from Colorado Springs.

In cell 119, Jacks found Agent Sowanake, now a prisoner in a hospital gown, betrayed by the country he had been so proud to serve. Like all the prisoners, he had been drugged after being broken down physically. Whatever sick treatments the government had subjected them to must have suppressed their natural healing abilities.

Sowanake looked at Jacks in wonder, and then he glanced timidly away, overwhelmed by shame. Jacks guided him and all the others into the spectral tunnel, thirteen survivors in total. His wormhole sped them in the space of a breath to a wooded location in the Canadian Rocky Mountains, several thousand miles away from where they had been jailed and tortured.

Beneath a frozen night sky, he pointed the prisoners to their freedom. They had acres of pinewoods in which to hide. They could mend their physical wounds, and in time begin again with their lives. Most of them were so disoriented and skittish that they shifted and raced away to the shelter of the woods without a moment of sentimentality. Sowanake lingered, without words, though his humbled expression conveyed his gratitude. Then he reared and clambered after the others into the snow-dusted forest, a mountain lion in flight.

Now Jacks needed to save whatever domestics he could and command them to stop fighting for their werecat masters. He lightning-tunneled to the shelter he had heard about in Little Rock, Arkansas. It was a warehouse building where hundreds of cats had been caged, awaiting transfer to a vault where they would be suffocated with carbon dioxide.

He hurried through opening the cage doors and used his telepathy to guide the cats into his spectral, traveling void. He was a werecat Pied Piper, leading the frightened kitties to safety. He chose Los Padres National Forest in California where the coastal Pacific climate was more temperate than the wintry Canadian Rockies.

He zipped to Kansas City, Lubbox, Texas, and five other veterinary facilities across the country where cats were being destroyed. After he transported the last batch to the Californian refuge, he realized that even with time suspended, collecting every captured domestic was a mission too vast to accomplish. Though the world was frozen, time was ticking in Sim Ru's heavenly realm. He had no idea how long the god would grant him his magical powers. Not to mention that populating the Californian forest with thousands of domestic cats would put the freed kitties in danger as well as the local wildlife population. He needed a solution that would work its way out after his intervention that night. It came together rapidly in his head, and he delayed one of the rescued cats with a telepathic message.

*Tepe is dead. The war's over. Spread the word.*

The ginger tom gave him a respectful glance, and Jacks heard him chattering to his brethren.

He surged into another wormhole, plowing through the frozen world to the headquarters for the Central Security Service's Bioterrorism Research Agency in Fort Meade, Maryland. The six-storey glass and steel office building was populated by just a skeleton crew of security guards and maintenance workers in paralyzed poses. Jacks had arrived on the sixth floor, offices for the agency's senior management.

He faced a door with a grand, military insignia and a detestable name plate in cast bronze, Cpt. Andrew Dickerson, Director of the B.R.A. Jacks passed through the paneled door and drifted through an anteroom with twin work stations for staffers. He diffused through a second door to Dickerson's private office. The grandeur of the fucker's recently appointed workspace disgusted him. His office had couches and a worktable that could seat a dozen. Floor-to-ceiling tinted windows provided a panoramic view of the high-tech compound's towers, satellite dishes, and silos. The molded walls displayed commendations and framed photographs with military generals and even the President.

Jacks pushed on to Dickerson's L-shaped executive desk and sat down at his high-backed, oxblood leather chair. He rolled out the keyboard to his computer and tapped awake the flat-screen monitor on the desk.

He needed a user name and a password and to sort through drive directories. Jacks sped through that with the ease of a computer hacker. He had two objectives: to find evidence that the feline virus was a hoax and to destroy the government's records of suspected werecat "terrorists." He discovered the first in a folder of memoranda between the B.R.A., the C.D.C., and a list of government officials.

Calling up names and email addresses from his encyclopedic brain, Jacks wrote a confessional note from Dickerson, and attached a docket of confidential memos and photographs of the killing chambers for domestic cats. He fired off the email to Secretary McCuthers, and copied it to a score of national and foreign media outlets as well as animal rights organizations. To further dismantle Dickerson's campaign, he hacked into two other government accounts and sent an email from the Surgeon General and the Secretary of Agriculture to the heads of every state department of health with a directive to cease and desist with the campaign to trap and kill domestic cats.

Jacks then turned to Dickerson's terrorist conspiracy. That was trickier since he couldn't go to the media. If the public knew the government had been hiding an operation to round up feline shifters, it would create a whole new shitstorm of hysteria. He went through military and law enforcement databases, bookmarking every record on the detainees and persons-of-interest. He accumulated a shocking number: 103. Keying in administrative passwords, he deleted all of them.

Those were only the records in central databases. It might hamper investigations for a while, but incident reports and investigative documents were no doubt stored in government PCs and local police networks and even old-fashioned file cabinets. Or people's memories. Once again, Jacks worried how much he could accomplish before his teleporting ability was taken away from him. He decided the best he could do was to dismantle the organization that steered the campaign.

He cleaned out the B.R.A. drive as well as Dickerson's and General Gainsway's personal drives, and just in case they tried to restore the data, he hacked into one of Fort Meade's missile silos. There was a warehouse on the base for the National Security Agency's mainframe. Jacks programmed the coordinates and an automatic missile launch at 12:01 in the morning. The implications of the deed halted him for just a moment. He could clear out the few personnel in the building so there would be no casualties, but it would cripple N.S.A. operations well beyond the B.R.A.

What else could he do? He needed to throw Dickerson off the trail. It was far less savage than killing the man and everyone else who knew about the conspiracy, and the act of self-sabotage would ruin Dickerson's career and be the end of the B.R.A. Jacks pressed the enter key to confirm the release of the missile. The strike would happen sixty seconds after time was restored, and an investigation would quickly turn up that the launch had been programmed from Dickerson's computer.

He had one last item to delete. Dickerson had to have a method beyond informants and wiretaps to track down the detainees. He'd thought it was Sowanake, but it wasn't. That left one possibility, which he had come upon through his brief encounter with Zyanya. Another Soul Seer.

Zyanya had spoken of a Soul Seer who worked on archeological projects in the Yucatán until he was chased away by the spirits of the dead. Sowanake had also mentioned an archeologist—Dr. Philip Reyes, who the military brought in to study the Báalam-Tet. Jacks dove into a wormhole leading to a Tudor-style McMansion on a quiet, suburban cul-de-sac outside of Scottsdale, Arizona.

When he emerged in the professor's immaculately appointed, oversized house, he felt the familiar icy shadows of hovering phantoms. It was the same eerie energy that had surrounded Zyanya. Souls unhinged from the earthly world were impervious to the halting of time.

The house was dark and still, and a clock on the microwave oven in the kitchen was frozen at midnight. Jacks made his way through the first floor living room, which was decorated with Zapotec tapestries and mounted wooden masks, and he found Dr. Reyes's study.

The dreadful, haunting feel of the home proved Dr. Reyes

was a Soul Seer, but Jacks needed to confirm he was helping Dickerson find werecats. The Báalam-Tet was open on a mahogany table next to a yellow legal pad where the professor had transcribed the codex's glyphs. Jacks went to the study's antique colonial desk where there were more notes, none of which mentioned the detainees.

He opened the bureau's top drawer. Loose piles of papers, pens, staples, and paper clips cluttered the space. He fished through the documents. They looked to be a random assortment of invoices and receipts, but then Jacks spotted a credit card receipt from a diner in Kansas City. A baggage claim stub from Little Rock. A scrap of hotel stationery with a name and an address scrawled by a ballpoint pen: Manuel Ponce, 44 Savona Ave., Coral Gables.

Jacks fixed on that evidence with venom. It was exactly what he had been looking for, though part of him had hoped he wouldn't find it. Reyes was using his psychic ability to help the government root out werecats.

He pushed the drawer closed and glanced at the ceiling. Dr. Reyes was up there. Jacks could smell his human stink. He had to be stopped. Of everything he accomplished that night, it was the most critical objective. He could do it brutally and vengefully, though drawing a breath to cool himself down, Jacks thought through the implications. He had already created a very strange narrative for people to follow. A wild cat attack on a professor of Mesoamerican archeology linked to the B.R.A. would arouse deeper investigation, bringing up questions about the nature of Dickerson's detainees and the connection to the government's plot to destroy domestic cats. Jacks needed to keep the narrative consistent. Maybe create an intrigue that suggested Dr. Reyes's involvement in that night's sabotage of General Gainsway's B.R.A.

He floated up to the second floor and a scent trail led him

down a darkened, wood-floored hallway to the professor's bedroom. He lived alone in his capacious house. Besides having ugly things to hide, he must have sworn off bringing people into his personal life since it was haunted by unhappy souls looking for a connection to the world they had once inhabited, just like Zyanya's had been.

The professor was asleep in a four-poster, antique baroque bed. His extra income from the government appeared to be keeping him well-stocked with extravagant furnishings. He was a slender man with thinning hair. Fiftyish or in his early sixties. Wire-frame eyeglasses and an idle electronic tablet sat on his bedside table.

Jacks didn't know what he had anticipated, but the peaceful ordinariness of the man had him hesitating for a moment. It would have been easier if Reyes had the face of the devil. Reyes was just a mild-mannered, unimposing academic. Somebody's favorite professor maybe. A colleague's occasional coffee companion. A timid man of a certain age who was easily overlooked when people passed by him in the campus quad.

Jacks pushed that aside. Reyes was also responsible for the arrest and torture of thirteen innocent people. He was a Heinrich Himmler to werecats.

In the bedroom closet, he found a small travel suitcase. He filled it with clothes from the professor's armoire. He grabbed the eyeglasses and a leather wallet from the nightstand and stowed them in the valise. Then he spotted by the curtained doors to the bedroom balcony a cast iron doorstop shaped like an antique laundry iron.

Jacks picked it up and crept up to the sleeping professor. He raised it, and, wavering for just a half-dozen shallow breaths, he struck Reyes on the side of the skull like hammering a lamb for slaughter. He swore he heard an otherworldly gasp, and he looked above him. The shadows of the wraiths were swirling around the ceiling. Then they were sucked away, disappearing as though devoured by an ethereal drain. The room went still. The souls were gone. The witnesses to Jacks's cold-blooded crime could only report it to another Soul Seer, if they chose to do so.

He carried the diminutive professor, his suitcase, the Báalam-Tet, and his notes into another wormhole.

A destination from his imagination came to mind, and he quickly found himself on a sightless ledge, above the remote reaches of the Arctic Sea. Frozen in time, its waves of seawater were peaked in an eternal landscape of frozen spurs. Its cold, briny spray was suspended in the air, as thick as a snow squall.

He threw off Dr. Reyes's ragdoll body and his suitcase, and they broke through the surface of the static ocean and disappeared. They would sink many leagues, never to be found. Then Jacks looked at the Báalam-Tet. It felt like sacrilege to plunge the codex into the ice cold, briny water, where it would gradually disintegrate, the words of an ancient werejaguar king lost forever.

Yet it had to be done. Jacks couldn't spend the rest of his days hiding the codex and worrying about its discovery. So, he kissed it, like he would kiss goodbye a loved one in a casket, and he let the book go, along with all of Dr. Reyes's notes.

Jacks hung over that spot, breathless from all he had done that night. A glimmer in the night sky caught his eye. It was a star, flickering in the multitudinous celestial lights above him, and from that point, he traced a pattern that stood out crisply as a giant cat's head. Sim Ru. The god was watching him. A Cheshire cat as big as a harvest moon. The god's eyes glowed like embers. Jacks remembered that in exchange for returning him to the earthly world, he was now indebted to the god to unite his kind.

The ocean churned with rolling waves, and a gust of wintry

wind shrieked overhead. Time had returned. Jacks looked to the face of Sim Ru in the sky, but he was gone, and his own body was disappearing rapidly.

JACKS SHOOK AND GRASPED out to break away from the awful sensation of vanishing to nothing. He clasped his throat and his face to confirm he had a body. He could feel his hands, move his legs, and hear his own frightened breaths. He was spooked to discover he had been laid out on a stone surface like a corpse at a funeral, but mercifully, he was alive.

"Jacks."

Kwame crouched beside him, his face glazed with sweat and contorted like a madman.

It brought Jacks back to the world as he had left it. His shirt was gashed open and soaked through with blood, though there was no other evidence of his self-inflicted wound. Votive candles weakly illuminated the shrine. It was littered with dunes of shredded paper, the remains of the grotesque Catrinas. Though it felt as though many hours must have passed, everything seemed uncannily the same as when he had left it. Fireworks still screamed and crackled in the distance from the New Year's Eve party at the hacienda.

Kwame held Zyanya's revolver that Magdala had used to kill Tepe. He must have wrestled it away from her when she was pointing it at him to stop Jacks from carrying out the sacrifice.

Jacks heard Magdala whimper, and he turned to her. She looked nearly as destroyed as the Catrinas, hair tossed, her peasant skirt twisted, trembling as she righted herself where Kwame had thrown her.

Kwame pulled Jacks into his thick arms and clutched him tight to his chest. "Jacks. Thank God you're alive."

Jacks gently pushed away from him. He was happy to see Kwame as well, but he was crushing his ribs. He looked at Kwame, wanting to tell him everything but not knowing how to begin.

There would be time to explain. Beautiful, abundant time. For now, he told Kwame, "I saw Sim Ru. Everything is going to be okay."

# EPILOGUE

JACKS SAT ON on a wooden chair on the back porch of his apartment in Apia. It was a Saturday morning, and in their typical routine, he and Farzan had brought out coffee and breakfast from the bakery down the street to eat together while enjoying the South Pacific panorama. Jacks had a sausage roll and a coffee heavily diluted with warm milk. A bag with Farzan's sticky bun and coffee rested on the vacant chair beside him. Bella was out, lying in a sunny patch where shade from the roof's awning had not yet overtaken the porch.

He nibbled a bit at his roll. He didn't want to spoil the quality time with Farzan, but his stomach growled. Between Farzan's medical school schedule and his work at the casino resort, they only had a few mornings and nights a week to spend together. Bella's ears perked up, and she swiveled her head at the sound of a door shutting and a heavy-footed gait.

Farzan pushed open the screen door and came out to the porch in the tank top he had slept in, his pajama bottoms, and his flip-flops. He had a magazine tucked under his arm and a look of vindication on his face.

"I knew he had it. It's been sitting in their pile of mail since Thursday. I practically had to push my way in to get his wife to look for it."

He was referring to their landlord who lived downstairs and sometimes got their mail by mistake. Farzan still hadn't adapted to the laidback attitude of the locals, even though they had been living in Samoa for six months.

He brandished the magazine cover for Jacks to see—a blown-up photo of Andrew Dickerson's beleaguered face with the headline: *Pussycat Enemy #1: The Strange Case of Navy Captain Andrew Dickerson.*

It was *Mother Jones* magazine. Excerpts and sound bites from the article had made the rounds on news outlets on the internet, and Farzan had waited three weeks to get his own copy. He had been calling the magazine's 800 number all week to reconfirm the delivery date. Now, he held his glossy copy with reverence, as though it was a feature story on Jacks himself.

Farzan set aside his bag of breakfast and flopped down in his chair. Jacks leaned over while Farzan read the article aloud from start to finish. Most of the story they had heard about already. The government's retraction of the feline virus hoax. The exposure of a military scandal, which had led to a congressional hearing on Secretary McCuther's Bioterrorism Research Agency. General Gainsway had resigned, along with a quartet of other government agency heads, Dickerson had been fired, and the B.R.A. had been dissolved. The thirteen supposed terrorist detainees had disappeared without a trace, just before a missile malfunction, engineered by Dickerson, destroyed the intelligence community's entire computer system in Fort Meade, Maryland.

Farzan read from the article triumphantly. "Even within the 'don't rat' boys' club culture of the military, Andrew

Dickerson stands out as a quixotic paragon of staying on message. On the campaigns in Brazil that killed thirty-four civilians, which even the CIA director admits were based on 'bad intelligence,' Dickerson maintains with the defiance of a young Oliver North that he was acting as an 'agent of freedom.' Perhaps he is better characterized as a boy-next-door serial killer. Unrepentant. Delusional. Constantly turning the tables to paint himself as the victim. When asked by Congresswoman Shirley Fitzpatrick what he has to say to the children of the families whose pets were taken away for destruction under his direction, Dickerson responded: 'This is the cost of freedom. I acted on an urgent prerogative. The military's duty to protect the citizenry must not become politicized, and that's exactly what's happening. I'm the fall guy.'"

"What an asshole," Jacks commented.

"You got him good," Farzan said. "He sounds like a total lunatic. Listen to this: 'The Surgeon General, upon handing in his resignation, turned over documents his office had received from the

B.R.A. asserting an eminent threat from the FVR3 virus. The B.R.A.'s report cited studies from three prominent veterinarians at a leading center for the study of feline immunology at Cornell University, but all three experts disavowed the reports as 'fabricated' evidence that 'wildly mischaracterized' their research. At the congressional hearings, Dickerson retorted with the claim of a widespread conspiracy to suppress the work of his office. On the connection between the FVR3 and the men and women who the B.R.A. detained as terrorists, which the director of the Centers of Disease Control called 'an edict presented to us by the B.R.A. with the threat of pulling funding if we didn't sign off on media alerts,' Dickerson insists that his office obtained confirmatory lab reports that were subsequently expunged by the CDC. While refusing to comment on the disposition of the detainees, he warns that all eleven men and the two women remain a threat to public health and safety. Secretary McCuthers disagrees. Says McCuthers: 'Dickerson is a sociopath who refuses to take responsibility for the elaborate smokescreen he created to deceive not only the public but his closest colleagues.'"

Jacks chortled. Maybe Dickerson believed that what he was doing was right. He probably thought that his covert operation against werecats would make him a hero. He was a bigot who had betrayed his loyal protégé Sowanake. In the end, he got what he deserved.

Farzan finished the article. "Released from the Central Security Service, Dickerson now prepares for a military trial that could end in court martial. What awaits the former Navy Seal in his civilian life? His wife has filed for divorce and relocated to North Carolina with their three-year-old daughter. Dickerson declined to comment for this article, but his last words of testimony at the hearing may provide some hints on his next move. Responding to Massachusetts Senator Alvin Grimley at the hearings, he stated he intends to continue serving his country by using the knowledge he has gained to thwart the terrorist group 'the Glaring,' whose existence has been denied by the CIA, the FBI, and the Brazilian Consulate. This is Dickerson's white whale. Or perhaps, more fittingly, his white cat."

Farzan snickered. "He'll probably get a job as a correspondent on Fox News."

"Eat your breakfast before it gets cold." Jacks took the magazine from him, set it down on a fold-out beverage stand, and handed him his breakfast. Farzan picked at his sticky bun. Jacks could see his mind was still racing from the article.

"You couldn't have set it up more perfectly," Farzan said. "Anti-terrorist operations will be under scrutiny for years. The hearings made the military's top-secret campaign against werecats look like a joke."

Jacks was amazed himself by how well things had worked out, though he knew it was only a temporary setback. Military and government officials knew werecats were real. Sooner or later, another Dickerson would step forward to engineer a new campaign.

Meanwhile, he had promised to keep his end of the bargain with Sim Ru. It had been too much to think about since he had returned to Samoa three months back to repair what needed to be repaired with Farzan and settle back into living together.

Farzan had been cold at first, but after Jacks had explained what he had done on that miraculous New Year's Eve, Farzan had come around. He had come around even more after he saw news coverage about the B.R.A.'s conspiracy falling apart. Jacks suspected talking to his mother had helped. Mrs. Mohammed had seen how much they loved each other and already treated him like a son-in-law. Before she and Sammy had returned to New York City, she had left their freezer filled with his favorite beef and lamb stew in Tupperware tubs marked "Jacks," and she told her son on the phone that he was not to touch those.

Jacks figured he had time to work out a way to bring together werecats as Sim Ru's Werecougar King. He had earned a vacation from running around the world on urgent missions.

"So, what's it going to be for the honeymoon?" Jacks asked. "New Zealand or Hawaii?"

Farzan's glance slid away. "You know we can't afford either. Besides, with everyone coming into town for the wedding in May, I'll barely have time to get away before summer session starts."

They had decided to have a civil ceremony and reception in Samoa since it would be their home at least through Farzan's three more years of medical school. To make it legal, they had scheduled a remote appointment with New York City's Office of the Clerk. "We have a week to entertain the guests and a week for us," Jacks said. "You know we can afford it. It's Maarten's gift."

"You know how I feel about taking money from him."

Maarten's offer to pay for their honeymoon had come as a surprise, but a whole lot had changed in the past three months. Killing Tepe, who had been responsible for Annika's death, had helped with Maarten's attitude toward Jacks, and returning to South Africa for closure had made him a new man, as Kwame had hoped. Jacks had Skyped with Maarten from Cape Town, and Maarten had given him an apology and told him about his non-negotiable gift for his and Farzan's wedding.

"Hon, you're going to have to get over your feelings about him," Jacks told Farzan. "He's a different guy. And he's coming to the wedding."

Farzan clasped Jacks's hand and brought it to his chest. "Well, he's not coming to the honeymoon."

"No one's coming to the honeymoon except the two of us."

"Don't be so sure. Sammy's trying to push his way in."

Jacks snorted out a laugh.

"Can't we skip the wedding and go straight to the honeymoon?" Farzan said. "You realize what a pain this is going to be? We'll have my mom, my dad, Sammy, Rahim, his girlfriend, and his three kids all staying here plus Kwame, Maarten, and their entourage in town."

"And Magdala," Jacks pointed out. She was headed over in Maarten's yacht with the guys. Jacks was happy she had accepted the invitation. She fit in perfectly with the crew.

Farzan let out a weary sigh. It wasn't that he minded the company. He just got stressed out by the details. Jacks came around the back of his chair and embraced him from behind.

"It's going to be perfect."

Farzan leaned back against him. The morning was clear and bright. The town's enclave of multi-colored homes and buildings was gradually stirring with neighborly chatter and the groan and rattle of cars and trucks venturing out onto the roads. On the distant harbor, a red-hulled commercial barge made lazy progress on a course to disappear in the horizon.

It made Jacks think about how the world's motion repeated on an endless cycle. Waking, going off to work, sneaking in a private moment of staying put while everything circulated around you, then jumping back inevitably onto the gerbil wheel of time. Perhaps it was predictable and mundane, but it brought comfort to him in that moment. For as many days as they had together, he and Farzan would live that hectic, rat race, beautiful world together. Making a home. Saving up money for vacations and washers and dryers and birthday gifts and anniversaries. Laughing, loving, and helping each over with problems big and small. They fit together perfectly: a werecat and a man.

# ABOUT THE AUTHOR

Author Andrew J. Peters is the third most famous Andrew J. Peters on the internet after the disgraced former mayor of Boston and a very honorable concert organist. He's an award-winning author, an educator, and a cat lover. His passion is writing fantasy inspired from ancient world mythologies, and he also loves retelling classic stories from a queer point of view. Andrew lives in New York City with his husband and their cat Hugo. For more about him and his writing:

Website: https://andrewjpeterswrites.com

Facebook: https://www.facebook.com/andrewjpeterswrites

Goodreads: https://www.goodreads.com/author/show/6908025.Andrew_J_Peters

Bluesky: @ajpeterswrites.bsky.social